ODYSSEUS
ON THE RHINE

.

ODYSSEUS
ON THE RHINE

EDWARD S. LOUIS

Five Star • Waterville, Maine

First Edition
First Printing: April 2005

Published in 2005 in conjunction with
Tekno Books and Ed Gorman.

Set in 11 pt. Plantin.

Printed in the United States on permanent paper.

Library of Congress Cataloging-in-Publication Data

Louis, Edward S.
    Odysseus on the Rhine / by Edward S. Louis.—1st ed.
        p. cm.
    ISBN 1-59414-281-5 (hc : alk. paper)
        1. Odysseus (Greek mythology)—Fiction. 2. Greeks—
Europe—Fiction. 3. Rhine River—Fiction. I. Title.
PS3612.O79O34 2005
    813'.6—dc22   2004029571

ACKNOWLEDGMENTS

Thanks with great appreciation to:

Bill Hyland, for the idea

Lillian Steward Carl, for editorial suggestions

The early studies lunch group, for feedback and support

Nick Patton, for help with the map

Nikos Kazantzakis, for another Odysseus

Kristy, for continuing encouragement

"*Ulysses, so some of the ancients say, pursued his wanderings beyond the ocean into Germania. At Ascibergium on the Rhine he built an altar in the name of his father, Laertes. The barrows of the folk he left there, incised with Greek epitaphs, remain to this day.*"

—Tacitus, *Germania*

"*Of that man, Muse, tell me, he of many turns, driven far afield after he sacked the sacred fastness of Troy.*"

—Homer, *The Odyssey*

"*. . . Made weak by time and fate, but strong in will To strive, to seek, to find, and not to yield.*"

—Tennyson, "Ulysses"

INTRODUCTION

Odysseus haunts the Western imagination. Of all the heroes of the ancient world, he undergoes the greatest number and variety of adventures and metamorphoses. From Homer's epic of the eighth century B.C. to the twentieth century and beyond, the "wily," "resourceful," "never-at-a-loss" trickster, whether authors love him or hate him, like a strange attractor in a Chaotic system he bends any story to his will, makes any story his story. Tacitus in his first-century history of the Germanic folk (who scourged the edges of the Roman empire before finally bringing it to its knees in the fifth century) alluded to a legend that *Ulysses,* as the Romans called him, traveled along the Rhine—an interesting idea, particularly since Snorri Sturluson, in his thirteenth-century *Prose Edda,* asserts that the *Æsir,* the gods of the medieval Norse folk, were actually heroes who had come from Asia Minor after the fall of Troy. At least, so Tacitus tells us, someone built on the banks of the Rhine a shrine to "Odysseus' father," and since Snorri makes the Norse gods the euhemerized surviving allies of that greatest city of its age, he provides a likely explanation for why Odysseus would have undertaken such a journey, though he leaves the reason for the shrine unstated. We may guess that Odysseus, inured to the hardships of travel and addicted to the lures of adventure, sought that last of his enemies, aiming, after a tortuous journey home, to fulfill a new quest and finish a job he once started only with the greatest reluctance. In honor of his quest, he honored his father, whether in this case *father* implies a human or divine figure.

The story of Odysseus' last journey traveled with a Greek poet who went into the north in a later age. Having heard tales from travelers come south in search of plunder and adventure, he went back with a troop of them to share the traditions of the south, of the Mediterranean gods and heroes. With his harp tuned and his mead-cup full, he wove the sort of story that in the course of time either brings people together or drives them apart—so much power have the great narratives of old.

1

DEPARTURE FROM ITHAKA

Odysseus, sad to say, could never quiet his loins.

The man who above all men loved adventure had remained faithful to Penelope, after his fashion, through nearly endless travels. Circe, Kalypso, others: who could fail to forgive a man divine dalliance, as if he had had a choice?

Having seen with his own eyes shining Aphrodite, even at a distance and on the battlefield, and having spoken rather more than once, face to face, with golden-eyed, warm-tongued Athena, a mere mortal man must have earned the forgiveness even of the immortal gods if his hand occasionally dropped to his crotch as he floated, lonely, fantasizing, doomed by Poseidon to long exile, self-bound to a bobbing timber to keep his nose above water, blown slowly home by gentle Zephyrus across the middle of the earth, over the wine-dark sea.

Hermes teased him about that, even warned him, but with a mocking remonstrance free of anger, and Odysseus laughed with him grudgingly, but free of contrition—a notion of an age yet long to come and which to Odysseus, could he have understood it, would have lacked sinews.

Shame did not exist in the mind of the Greek hero.

And Odysseus never worried much about blasphemy, either. He knew his fate, lived his life, accepted his end, suffered his sorrows, and enjoyed his triumphs for as long as they dared to last.

Having returned to Ithaka and cleansed his doorstep of the swine who had dared to court his wife and fantasize about filling his bed, Odysseus sorted out his affairs as would any practical man who had watched the world burn to embers then rise anew out of the tumbling sea.

He loved the calm receptiveness of Penelope's body, the face-cleansing brilliance of his florid gardens, the hero-worship in his son's devoted eyes.

But later, at the marriage of his son, Telemachos, to Nausikaa, princess of the Phaecians and once his savior, Odysseus allowed his eye to drift to the thick, wavy hair and sleek, enticing, sinuous crescents of the daughter-in-law nearly young enough to be his granddaughter, yet whom he might have claimed for his own bride. The thought crossed his mind briefly: if only he had stayed and accepted the brave girl who found him naked and destitute on the beach, who unblushingly bathed and clothed him and took him before her father for the respite he needed, the man whose offer of his daughter Odysseus reluctantly declined.

That trait marked Odysseus, among the men of his age: he could want something desperately and yet deny himself. He could see something in other men and know whether or not he felt it, too. As he could turn his words to tune the minds of others, so he could tune his mind to turn his own desires aside.

The Phaecian king, Alkinoös, father of Nausikaa, had heard Odysseus' long, astonishing story of journeys, battles, deaths, and glories, had allowed him rest, food, safety. He would have seen the alliance with such a son as both militarily prudent and dangerously enticing, but he had returned him, lost in sleep, to his own shores on distant Ithaka. The resourceful one, having escaped traps, jaws, and guiles, had yet longed for his faithful wife, partly, perversely, to test her fidelity, but partly out of a trembling sense of the perfect unity of their flesh, as though he knew in the debt he owed to her one to pay to himself as well.

Letting his eyes caress their way down the girl's breasts and around her hips, easing the scent of her clean skin into his nostrils and throat, teasing himself with her possibilities, he turned his gaze to his son, and Odysseus felt nearly the same glory for Telemachos as if he were soon to deflower the maid himself.

No doubt Nausikaa had her charms. As the wedding ceremony droned on, he felt despite the discipline of his will the blood in him rising for her. But Odysseus, always aware of the tug of the heart and the flesh, could subdue it, if he so willed, to the wisdom of his head. So he had done in making this perfect match for his grown, sturdy son, and so he could continue to do—as long as he could keep himself from looking too closely and dreaming too fervently.

That trait, too, marked Odysseus: the practical man who could create a world of his own in his mind, the shaper of tools and tamer of horses who could also allow himself to dream.

And what a son he and Penelope had made. Strong and resolute, yet sometimes tender as a maid, Telemachos beamed and shone, barely able to keep his eye from his bride, his body swaying gently like that of a stallion nearly unable to endure the bit. Odysseus felt himself flushed with pride as a different but equally powerful current of love filled his veins.

As he stood for the wedding ceremony, his hand moved instinctively for Penelope's bare shoulder. She sat beside him as he stood, felt his touch, and grasped his hand meekly. When he had returned, Penelope had looked almost too young to be the woman he'd loved so muscularly so long ago and so longingly for so long. She bore him another son a year after his miraculous reappearance, after fallow years and so near the end of her fertility. As she watched her son's wedding and felt the power of her husband's presence, the strain grew visible in her drawn face, old about the eyes, and in the thews of her joints, so that sea-blue veins shown dully through stretched skin. Even sitting for long seemed a breathless labor.

Allowing his eyes to feel the stretched contours of her cheek, Odysseus restrained the urge to place his head in her lap and cry. He forced his eyes to beam love and strength into her eyes, hoping to sustain her by the power of his will.

His concentration drifted as, from the corner of his eye, he spotted Nausikaa bowing to receive a laurel wreath upon her brow, the outline of her rump round as a gourd.

Returning his attention fully to Penelope's weary eyes, as she gazed up at him with fear and love, Odysseus had to choke back a wince, and the danger of his sex embarrassing him passed, at least until the feast and the dance that followed.

Odysseus had loved Penelope since the first time he'd seen her, had loved her unceasingly, and yet his spirit allowed his eye to adventure and his blood, if not his heart of hearts, to stray. He petted her cheek, drawing from the lips a tired but loving smile, knowing that she shared his pride in the beauty of the children, guessing in his most hidden thoughts that she knew more about him than either of them would ever say.

At the feast Penelope ate little: nibbling at some cheese, lingering over a few ripe olives, allowing herself a few shallow sips of Ithaka's dry, leathery red wine. Odysseus, regaining also with the comfortable sense of his own home the other urges of his youth, downed great quantities of lamb and greens and pots full of wine and of water. He joined the dancing couples, the bride and groom, too nervous with anticipation to eat, the youths and maids hoping to find in another's eyes the gleam of their own pleasures, and he sang and danced and yelled and, to cool himself, shook free great waves of cold water that he poured over his face and beard.

Penelope smiled in delight as Odysseus danced rings around them all, twirling the maids, forming the boys and old men into long queues to snap their fingers as they spun and clapped and kicked to the music of pipe and drum and lyre. For Penelope's sake, and Telemachos', he kept his eye clear of Nausikaa, except when he felt certain no one could observe him. Then something deep inside him spoke of longing and envy, something bound to the memory of the open, loving, faithful sixteen-year-old eyes of Penelope, to the full, red, petulant lips of Helen, to the flawless, shimmering, gaping fascination of Kalypso, to the sweet, downy, musky sex of Circe, to the powerful curves and blazing elegance of Athena: all that he'd had and all he could never have. He wanted to feel his strength mastering a young body, controlling its rhythms and molding them to his; he wanted the sweet, grainy smell of fresh, young skin and hair to soothe the crags of his old memory; he wanted to bathe in olive oil until he glinted under the moon and the young princess thought a god had descended from Olympos for the sole reason of the perfect, gnawing sadness of her mortal beauty.

At the same time he wanted nothing more than the cool comfort of the ready embrace of the only woman who could feel and smell and taste like home and transport his wandering, tireless mind from whatever corners of the world his imagination sought to a present moment in which he could live forever.

Finding another barrel of cold water, Odysseus jerked it above his head and doused himself with it, felt it cool him all the way from his forehead to his loins to his feet, and laughing like a Fury, threw himself again to the hilarity of all into the twists and leaps of the rollicking dance.

Oh, that is the curse of old men: either to feel the youth's maddening lure of sex or no longer to feel it.

Seeing Odysseus dance, King Alkinoös and his queen—no trifling beauty for her age, Odysseus noticed—having traveled the broad sea from Phaecia to give their daughter in marriage, howled with glee at the youthful vigor of their new brother, the man they'd once thought they might call "son," and their hearts felt glad at the growing love they saw in the young couple, red-faced, eager, immune to the joys of the feast, lost in the joys of discovering each other, protected, they felt sure, by the wisest hero the world had known.

They danced with equal if more restrained pleasure. In those days who, even a crowned king, could fail to dance?

Later, under the moonlight, Odysseus lay beside his wife as the moon poured in their bedroom window. As they listened to the chucks and coos of the infant sleeping lightly nearby and of the few odd creatures buzzing in the night air, he stroked stray hairs from Penelope's face, and he felt amazed at the depths of peace and horror he could still find in her eyes, eyes longing for life, but already knowing the slowly enshrouding, creeping fingers of illness that could lead only to Death.

When a cloud covered the moon, before Odysseus could stop it, a tear fell from his eye onto Penelope's breast. She shook her head, gulped back a sob, and drew him tightly to her.

They clung together, talked quietly of the beauties of the wedding and the young couple, of how much they resembled them, of all they had ahead, and for as long as it lasted they allowed the moonlight to wash away the weight of a few more of the lonely years they'd spent apart. Legs, hands, fingers, intertwined like vines, but Penelope felt too weak to make love.

In the morning she left a few drops of blood behind when she rose from bed.

In a month she lay again under the moon with her husband's hands in hers. She looked deeply into her Odysseus' eyes, searching every corner of them for memories she could carry with her to Elysium. The old soldier gazed back, feeling for the first time in his life at a loss, but giving her all of himself that she could take with her, willing his strength into her—of courage she had plenty of her own.

Their children sat with them until the moon reached its height, then they shuffled off to the altar to pray and finally to their own room to find the comfort that strong, youthful bodies draw from each other when, whatever the course of the wider world, they flow together like wine and jug.

Sometime before morning, when the morning star is crawling to sleep, unnoticeably, with her eyes still wide open, Penelope stopped breathing. Odysseus looked into those beloved eyes long after breath had stilled, unable to free himself from their peace. He would have called, screamed, cursed, rubbed the limbs red trying to force life back into them, but after all his adventures, he knew Death when he saw it, and not even he, who had challenged Poseidon on the open sea, most resourceful of men, could keep Lord Hades from his unwilling prize.

Washing the body with the tears of the old and the young, each with its separate substance, three days later all of Ithaka cremated the body of patient Penelope under a misshapen moon, watching the wispy smoke-feathers fly away like birds.

Some tales tell that Odysseus, having returned home after the Trojan War, left his living wife to seek a fresh bride in the north; in time he left indeed, never to return, but only after her body and soul had found safe harborage in the earth.

Truly he sought new countries after, but storytellers speak unfaithfully unless they say that, among the war veterans of the old days, no man ever loved his wife more deeply than did Odysseus Penelope.

The ghost of Agamemnon had warned him not to love or trust any woman too much, but Odysseus loved and trusted Penelope, and he would have reason to do so again long after her death.

Playing in the sandy breakers with his baby son, Odysseus allowed his eyes to stray out to the sea. The voice of Athena at the altar had long grown silent: he had won the honor and undying renown she had sought for him, had fulfilled his pledge to the pan-Achaian kings, had set the course for a new generation who could think as well as feel, who dared to say no when the gods called, if they did not like the call.

He picked up the boy, little Pirithous, bounced him on his shoulders, let the hiccupping laughter spill over him like rain—but whatever joy it brought, it had no power to cleanse; whatever continuity it brought, it demanded nothing more than the life he had helped give it. Unlike his feelings for Telemachos, that he owed him a heritage, a father in addition to a hero, an island free of usurpers upon which to rule in his turn, Odysseus felt that this little boy had a course of his own to follow in the wide world, free of an aging father, a course for which his dependable brother could raise him better.

Odysseus thought about that feeling, walking, bouncing the boy, watching the horizon, easy of body, uneasy of spirit, with the salt air grasping at his lungs and pulling like unerring fingers.

Pirithous' brother and his king: so Odysseus conceived Telemachos, for after Penelope's passing, he no longer felt his beloved Ithaka his own. Not that Telemachos had in any way hinted a desire to replace his father—much the opposite, his son in fact made almost too pious, too solemn obeisance to his lord and father. Odysseus appreciated it, even admired such behavior in his dutiful son, but though he knew it right, he also felt it absurd. His *thumos,* the deep heart that fought and schemed so well and loved Penelope so well, knew that the first son—no longer boy, but grown man—more fully reigned as king of their island already than Odysseus could ever again.

Telemachos tended the fields; Telemachos met the traders; Telemachos kept the armory; Telemachos sacrificed at the shrines; Telemachos loved his baby brother as much as did his father; always seeking his father's advice, never overstepping his bounds, Telemachos yet made all the decisions that directed the life and lives of Ithaka. With Nausikaa expecting, Telemachos had grown to full manhood in every sense of the word.

Perhaps Telemachos heard the voice of golden-eyed Athena who had for so long spoken only to Odysseus, the man she loved for his wisdom and cunning.

Thinking so, breathing the air, knowing his new son in good hands, Odysseus allowed the panoply of images that danced across his mind to light upon the one he knew he must face and that he wanted to face. His fingers itched not to till and sew, but for tiller and sail.

In some men only death stills the lure of adventure.

Odysseus needed only an excuse. His mind turned with his nose to the salt of the sea, and his plans turned with his eye to the ships that carried away amphorae filled with oil and wine.

He played with his baby on the rough beach and taught his grown son the last that he knew of growing and tending. Nausikaa shortly made a grandfather of Odysseus, and the old soldier wept with joy to see the next generation to rule Ithaka, holding him up to the blessing of Apollo Shootafar just as he had done with his own Telemachos, who laughed and wept at his side.

What more could any man ask of the world?

Yet as that day passed, and another, Odysseus in his heart longed more keenly to sail again with a crew, swords belted to their sides, helms burnished for battle—or at least with their wits wakened for new folk and new places, new shores and new challenges.

Not long after Penelope passed from the world above, so did Odysseus' father, Laertes. The hero found his body in the hut of Eumaeus the shepherd, where he liked to go early in the morning to watch the sun rise over the hills of Ithaka. The cold face shone with a gentle peace—what more can we hope for our passing?—but Odysseus wept anyway, for the long years in which he had seen neither parent nor wife nor child.

So Odysseus held also the funeral for his father, once king of Ithaka, who had given him such good counsel.

And all his will and all his sorrow could not quiet his loins, and no Ithakan farm girl would do, and a certain young princess, nearly a queen, recovering from childbirth, seemed to grow in beauty every day. Unable to muster an explanation for Telemachos, Odysseus awaited the excuse.

One day it arrived. Sailing from the mainland, bringing livestock to trade for Ithaka's famous wines and oils, came an old friend Odysseus would never have thought could be tamed to milk and plow: Diomedes. Who else but the last of the greatest warriors of the pan-Achaian army? At a distance Odysseus could see his old comrade smiling, shouting, leaning from the prow. They waved and called to each other as boys might who had grown happily together to manhood, meeting and defeating the same challenges.

Odysseus had him bathed and fed and dressed in clean robes of the finest linen. That night they feasted and drank and talked the stars into oblivion, recalling heroes as glorious as gods, a city that rose nearly to the sky, adventures that a thousand men in a thousand lives wouldn't dare to dream, driving cruel and harrowing slaughters into the recesses of their memory.

Diomedes: younger than Odysseus, yet himself of more than middle age, his muscles thick and knotty as tree roots, his hair still lush and curly—his eyes held the furtiveness of one who has killed, the longing of one who desperately needed something, and the glint of one who might, driven to do so or merely given the opportunity, kill again.

Odysseus wondered if his own eyes shone with the same dull gleam.

Only with the first light had Telemachos and the last of the revelers gone off to bed. Then the two veterans, swirling the last drinkable sips of wine from the dregs at the bottom of their cups, at last whispered the talk both wanted to hear.

"A rumor," Diomedes mumbled. "No more."

"But if it's true?" Odysseus hoped.

"It may be."

"Evidence?"

21

"Stories. Traders from the North, the far North, beyond the lands of the Achaians, tell them."

"And you wish to believe them?"

"Wish? I believe them."

"I wish to believe them," Odysseus said.

"Why?"

"The same reason you do."

Odysseus could always tell what another man was thinking. He knew his own thoughts so well, and he knew few men who could hide their own or would even think of doing so.

"Tell me again, old Dio."

"After the city fell, it was such a vast place, we couldn't touch every bleeding corner of it. Their allies, some strong men lived among them, petty kings though they were. Having lost their sovereign, they quarreled over who should rebuild the place. No Greek wanted it. We had taken what we wanted of Troy, so no use fighting any more. Fucking Menelaos got his Helen. Sorry: that's your cheap wine talking. We took our vengeance and our spoils and went home. No Helen for us. Yes, I know you had Penelope, and I heard about your journey home. Who didn't? You've eclipsed Achilles, you know, in the eyes of the world, at least until you die. Who knows then? Agamemnon was murdered. You knew that? Klytemnestra and her pimp did it, knifed him in the bath. Never did much trust them myself, baths that is. Nor Klytemnestra, either. You'd think that when we left, they'd have fought it out. I heard they drew lots, winner take all—don't believe it though. But then I didn't believe it either when I heard you'd got home—had to come see for myself.

"So the best of the satellite kings made like comets and took off to find new kingdoms. No going west unless they wanted more of us, and no going south unless they wanted Egyptians or dust, so some went east—I don't know what happened to them—and some went north. They're the ones I'm telling you about. They had so much wealth even after Troy that wherever they went, especially those knock-kneed barbars up north, people thought they were gods. They built a following, took what they wanted, pushed on, found lakes and forests and, so I've heard, golden-headed girls, and set themselves up in a place where ice covers the ground for nine months of the year, the gods know why."

"Golden-headed girls, you say?"

"So they go and set themselves up as a new Olympos. Who but Trojans could ever think of such a thing? And all the tribes pay them tribute and make them sacrifices and defend their borders out of fear of some fancy clothes and shiny trinkets and bronze swords. They told folk there they come from Asia. They call them something like—it's a strange language, you know—Aesir. If we had any balls left in us, we'd go and find them and set them straight. We did it once, and we could do it again. We're not that old yet. Got to get up and—ow, help me off this bench. My knees hurt."

"So when do we go?"

"When can you be ready?"

"In the morning?"

"May I sleep off this Aias of a headache first?"

"No. The sea air will make you feel better."

By the time the sun had made a third of its course through the cobalt-blue Mediterranean sky, Odysseus had sharpened his weapons, cleaned his armor, packed a bladder with fruit and cheese and olives and bread, kissed his children good-bye, placed his baby in the arms of a stunned but ever-willing-to-please Telemachos, and set sail with Diomedes for the Greek mainland. He carefully wrapped and stored in the ship the enormous bow that had once saved his life and regained his kingdom.

As Diomedes' men rowed and prepared to hoist sail, Odysseus glanced back at the shores of Ithaka with a moment's twinge of love and longing. He thought of his beloved wife; he thought of his devoted mother, whose stamina failed before he could return from war, and whose face he had seen among the Shades; he thought of the father to whom he yet owed a filial duty. Then he turned his eyes across the Corinthian Sea toward Calydon, the first stop on the route north to hunt down that last remnant of the empire of Troy.

2

CALYDON

As morning broke olive-green over the rolling sea, Diomedes washed his mouth out with resinous wine, cleared his throat, and told Odysseus of his own homecoming. Every story, as we know, folds itself among other stories.

"Aphrodite never quite forgave me for that day on the battlefield: you remember. She screamed like a babe and flew straight to Zeus when I touched her with my spear. Would have had me skinned and burnt alive, I think, but the old thunderer just laughed: he'd promised the day to Athena, who loved me then, I think, almost as much as she loved you. And I did just what Athena told me to do—no love lost with Aphrodite, you know."

All night the Great Sea had tossed and rolled the freshly tarred ship, bobbing it like a toy. The fire in the center cauldron had leapt and flickered like a drunken firefly. Now light filtered around them, gradually submerging the stars and blanketing them like a morning doze.

"You'd have thought Ares would have been the one," Diomedes continued. "When Athena bade me strike him as well, he exploded, belching black smoke to the heavens like some volcano spurting Hades' wrath. I tell you, once Athena's battle-rage left me, it shocked me, the enormity of what I'd done. But he never bothered me much, though I

25

feel as if some of my desire to fight left with that Stygian smoke, snaking its way into the sky.

"You know when Latinus asked me to fight Aeneas of Troy, come to Italy at Aphrodite's behest to found his new empire—Aeneas who'd practically sailed the whole earth because he couldn't find his way to Italy, which sticks so far out into the sea you'd think it would have kicked him in the ass—well, when Latinus asked, begged me, for help, I just hadn't the heart for it. Might have been the goddess protecting her son, or might have been Ares denying me the glory of finishing off that branch of the race, or might have been the Father himself building times to come as he sees fit. Felt to me, well, that I just didn't care to do it. Ares wasn't with me, unlike now, when the thought of those lesser men who skipped the last battle at the city, turning north to all that gold and all those blondies, it makes my blood burn."

With the morning the pitch of the ship eased, and the nausea to which the men had long become accustomed eased and sank away. Diomedes' voice hung in the air like a seagull: following, rising, falling, rising again.

"Yes, I went to Italy, but for my own ends. Old Daunus, just for my telling him stories, gave me most of Apulia and one of his daughters for a bride. They couldn't get enough Trojan War stories, of the swift Achilles, the mighty Aias, who hacked to lint a whole field of sheep then threw himself on his own sword, the wily Odysseus who made the great wooden steed, and god-like Diomedes—their epithet, not mine—who fought the Lord of Battle himself and lived to tell about it.

"Oh, I didn't tell you this: I know you had a tough time of it, but when I got to Argos, right quickly by your standards, my wife had betrayed me, practically whoring herself. Well,

26

who could blame her, I suppose, as long as I'd been away, and I exaggerate a bit. Not everyone's a 'patient Penelope,' as the stories call your wife. And don't get me wrong, I believe them, but they don't apply to me.

"Aphrodite, I suspect, had a share in it: I fairly loved the old girl still, once I'd seen her again. But years chew away even the best of loves, so they say: even Orpheus turned buggerer at last. And there's no going back once she's lost that spark in her eye. So I just went looking for a new kingdom, not even any serious vengeance, and I found a new one, and maybe a better one, and a woman, too, more of a darling girl, actually. Had a mind to name our son Aias, just for laughs, or maybe Odysseus, eh? No: I called him Areades, finally, which is maybe why the god relented and we're sailing together now. Once you've started, you just can't get adventuring out of your blood, as you know, until a sword or age or disease drains the last drop of it out of you.

"So as I said, I'm in Italy, and I did help the locals clear up the east coast a bit, and never heard a thing from Aeneas, even after he'd killed the Latins' hero, married Latinus' daughter, buried his suicidal mother-in-law, and settled in right comfortably to build his little empire around Latinus' ears. If Aphrodite took care of him, Athena took good care of me, and unless she tells us otherwise, maybe we'll pay that Trojan a visit on our way home. Who more than Odysseus knows the ways of the gods—right, old man?"

Odysseus thought of Aeneas, so close, and yet so far—he felt, too, that Zeus turned his mind elsewhere, drawing him to the northlands rather than the western sea. A brush of wind, like a kiss on the cheek, sighing with the quiet, laughing voice of Athena, seemed to breathe assent.

"Fate moves even the gods, so the poets tell us," mumbled Odysseus, shaking gray morning from his speech. "How can we expect to be spared it, or even to understand it? So whom do we meet at Calydon?"

"You've guessed already, at least some of them, I'll bet," Diomedes answered. "While I'm thinking of it, old Nestor—yes, the man's still alive, wrinkled old flotsam and thin as a scepter, hardly talks any sense, if he ever did—but he did send you honors and regards, as well as two of his sons. That's right: Antilochus and Thrasymedes will join us, and they're waiting at Calydon with the others. 'Who better to teach them how to stay alive than Odysseus'— that's what he really said. What's that? How did he know you were coming along? Ha! Well. Antilochus is quick-eyed, swarthy, jittery, eager to move, his mind like a hawk on the hunt. Thrasymedes, though younger, will remind you of the father: ponderous and weighty of speech, deep, resonant voice, slow, but steady and stern. Put them together and you have a young version of the father. And no, neither yet has the veil of age that clouds the mind without stopping the words. Have to love the old fellow, but after hours of stories I do get the desire to take a wine-plug and stop his—why do you laugh? He'd have come himself; we had to go before he could hobble his way up the gangplank."

Again Diomedes washed his mouth with wine, swirled it over his tongue, and spat it into the stilling sea.

"Well, there are others, too, and you'll feel glad to see them, as glad as I was when I left them eager for your arrival, not that I promised exactly. Idomeneus—that's right—much the same happened to him as to me, though worse, I'd say. Leukus—did you meet him?—seduced his wife, then butchered her and her daughter and took over most of Crete for himself. When we meet Ido at Calydon,

don't ask him about this: he killed his own son. Same mistake as Agamemnon—come to think of it, few of us came out of that war unscathed—he promised Poseidon in the midst of one of those raging storms that if he made it home, he'd sacrifice the first thing he found in the god's honor. Of course they made it through—the Sea Lord didn't hate Idomeneus as he hated you—and wouldn't it happen that his son was out fishing on the shore as they arrived. He didn't even know the boy, young man by then, by sight, and once he found out whom he'd killed, it was too late. Leucus would have thanked him for it, but he had no need, since once they learned of the son's death, the Cretans drove the father right back whence he'd come, into the waves again: no more ceremony than that.

"So Ido cast back to sea with his bedraggled, unhappy sailors, who, with no better choice left to them, sailed on to Calabria. If they could find the place so easily, why couldn't Aeneas? There the folk, all Greeks, you know, took him in and wanted to make a bard of him: people just can't get enough of the damned Trojan War. Well, wait till they hear about this new venture of ours, but they won't hear it from Idomeneus: contrary to the general wisdom, poor fellow can't play a note, though I guess he can weave a tale as well as the rest of us, if he felt like, which he doesn't. That's why as soon as I found him, he grabbed a cloak and a bagful of bread and cheese and led me down to my own ship at a run. Funny how few of us have been able to tear ourselves far from the sea.

"Yes, there are more yet. Dictys, Idomeneus' poet who proved himself a pretty fair fighter, too, at Troy, he's waiting there, and believe me, he's the one who can tell a tale when he wants to. And more: Philoctetes of Thessaly, whose folk also drove him out—thought him bad luck—and whom I found wandering in Apulia, he's there. No, I don't believe the bad luck business, or I wouldn't be bringing him. You should see him cast a spear: reminds me a little of Achilles. Now get this: a little lad by the name of Achilles awaits you. Guessed it? Neoptolemos' son, grandson of the greatest of all warriors: Neo left him for me to raise, bound north on his own adventures, too dangerous for the boy, he said. So he ends up with us, right? Brave for a little fellow, and smart and quick; wish I could call him my own son, but I wouldn't do that out of respect for the memory of his grandsire.

"And one more: you're not going to like this idea at first, if you can even believe it, but you'll get used to it. Ah: the sun's getting warm already. Feel that on your skin, so that the spray feels cool and good? Here, drink some of this: it'll clear out your throat. We'll see land soon and get food there. Look! There's the first of it already. Not far to Calydon now.

"Oh yes, about the last of us. We could very easily not have come for you, considering all the trouble you got yourself into on the way home. So don't hold his troubles against him, though some people differ on how much he should take the blame. Well, it's Orestes, you know, and . . ."

At that point Odysseus, having heard some of the story of the unfortunate lad, had to interrupt.

"Don't you think, Dio, that whatever gods are left who don't hate me—blessed Athena aside, of course—will hate him? How can we possibly take him anywhere? I can't even believe he still stands anywhere above Hades, and that if he can manage that, he's right enough in body and mind for adventures."

"Right enough in body," Diomedes answered, "but not so right in the head, as you intuit. Rather more than a bit

rocky, in fact. How much do you know of him?"

"I remember what I heard. Agamemnon, great commander that he was, never had the sense to avoid obvious trouble. You laugh, but my troubles were not so obvious. *I* didn't take Helios' cattle, and *I* survived, thank the mercy of the gods, with their help and my own wits. But brave Agamemnon, smart Agamemnon, cautious Agamemnon, having when he got home spotted Aegisthus lurking in the rear, still dropped himself into the nice, warm bath Klytemnestra had prepared for him, where she massaged his back and, when he nodded, buried a knife in his chest, then did the same for Kassandra, minus the massage. Klytemnestra, so the story goes, pled vengeance for her daughter, but everyone knew she had become Aegisthus' mistress—don't laugh at my speech: I'm hardly awake after that monologue of yours. So Orestes, long gone to keep him out of Clyty's clutches, with the approval of the Oracle returned home and slit the throats of his murdering stepfather and mother.

"Having seen what I've seen, I can believe the next part," Odysseus added. "The Furies couldn't wait to get at him, burnt his heels all the way to Athens, where Athena herself, bless her advocacy, got him off, which is what Apollo wanted anyway. Sounds as though it ended well enough."

"Then you haven't heard the whole of it," Diomedes interjected. "Athena got him off at trial, yes, but even you, old sailor, haven't been pursued by the Furies. I doubt many of us could survive it. I actually saw a frieze of it in Athens, and if they look anything like that, they'd freeze Medusa to stone. Orestes survived, yes, but he's mad as an old sibyl. Oh yes, they drove him over the precipice where even your dick wouldn't follow Helen, and I doubt he'll recover. Now don't rush me. His head's in the stars, but his lungs breathe with life, and the whole ordeal has given him the body of an athlete, strong and sinewy as the knotty root of a mountain and fast as Zeus's eagle in a fight—oh, I've seen him do it. On our way back from Athens we got waylaid by pirates—you know the sort: tough, but no endurance for a real fight. We had few with us, mostly sailing crew, and they wouldn't have known Orestes or me, and the fellow wore a long cloak and a clouded expression and a shock of wild hair that made him look, well, mad, and as they tried to board, he just sang some wild song with no melody that I could find. Well, when he saw me pull a sword, he just patted my hand, pulled out a short sword he had hidden, threw off his cloak, and leapt to the gunnel, where he perched on one leg and swayed and sang his lungs out. I thought they'd kill him, or he'd kill himself, but I nearly fainted with laughter, he was so damn funny. They came on as grimly as any shade, but he just kept singing, grabbed a hawser, and started swinging back and forth, cutting them down one at a time as he swung by them. I tell you, I laughed so hard I hurt myself.

"He finished them, at least all that got close enough. After six or seven of them had gone down, each barely half the man he'd been, they shoved off as quickly as they could; I didn't even get a shot at one of them. As they sailed off, he howled at them until they were no more to us than a dot on the horizon. I'll bet that to this day they think they saw a singing werewolf.

"Then he came back to me just as docile as could be, almost like your favorite dog. Well, I'd been good to him: given him food, a decent pair of sandals, patted him on the head when he looked sad. The Athenians were afraid to have anything to do with him, so they were glad when I took him—wanted to pay me for doing it, but that sort of thing doesn't please the gods, and I had a feeling as if Ares were telling me to take him on our venture: part of my penance, maybe, or just because he fights like Achilles—may the gods bless his memory—after, you know, Patroklos was killed. Then things got even funnier. He came back and plopped down next to me as if nothing had happened. Just patted my sword arm, then started singing softly again, until he noticed I had pulled a muscle in my side. He cried for days, every time I winced or even moved slowly, until I could assure him that I was as good as new. The gods take, and they give, and I couldn't be fonder of the boy if he were my own son."

Images of the men he'd known from the war and of those he'd never met began to take shape before Odysseus' tired eyes, growing from the warp of imagination to the woof of expectation.

"Almost feels like we're on some kind of training mission, raising these boys to fight the next generation of Achaian wars, may the gods keep them from it—unless of course it's our idea. I suppose I shouldn't say *boys,* at least not for all of them: Antilochus has a touch of gray at the temples, and Thrasymedes has a bald spot on his crown. You'll find no gray on this head—what, you see some? Where? Well, this old body's still as good as anyone's, even yours, and don't make me prove it." Diomedes slapped his old comrade on the shoulder.

"There's the port. We'll dock there and reach Calydon before the sun hits zenith. You know why I've come here, why we've come here?"

"Safer, I guess. Your father's old house. Who rules here now, your uncle?"

"His son, my cousin: he's a good man, discreet, and he

33

knows I have no interest in his city. Rumor visits here even less often than Apulia, and we will be welcomed, fully provisioned, and sent on our way with nary a breath of it to the wide world. Since the boar ravaged here—you know that story?—we killed it, yes, but few visitors come, which leaves the place in blissful quiet. Come: a quick stop at the early morning market, and on our way, Ody!"

Odysseus was ready to walk off the wobbly legs that go with a ship's journey and to ruminate a bit by himself on his friend's tales, but Diomedes had arranged before he'd sailed for horses, so, having barely taken time to assure minimal comfort, they rode like heroes up the coast. As they reached Calydon, a shortish, boyish, but athletically-shaped figure stood on the wall, perched on one leg like a crane, his arms stretched to full length above his head.

Diomedes leaped from his horse. "Good boy! Come to greet father?"

"Owoooooo! Father One and Father Two, or Father Two and Father Three! Each one kind and each one true; brave as Troy he'd better be!" Orestes called out half-singing, then chirped scales like a small flock of birds. Then he leaped from the high wall. Odysseus, despite himself, caught his breath. The boy—hardly a boy anymore, up close—landed lightly as a sparrow and bowed before them. Odysseus, well traveled in the world, had seen such things before, though rarely, how the gods, taking one gift, give another: the blessings of Tiresias, the curses of Kassandra.

"What are you doing, my fine sparrow? Welcome to Father Two? Come meet Father Three."

"Meet! Meet? All the world knows Father Three, who he's been and who he'll be! Wrap yourself around a tree and listen to his odyssey! Ha-ha. Oooooooo."

Diomedes took from his cloak a small bag. "For you,

lad, from the market in Calydon: your favorite."

"Fall on my pate for sun-sweet dates! Kind Father Two, always; and what from Father Three?"

Odysseus had to think quickly. Dio should have prepared him for this, but his old friend might have construed it as a test, to see if the resourceful one still had a few of his many resources. He allowed a broad smile to cross his lips and scratched his chest. He watched the hint of anticipation on Orestes' face barely begin to fade, then he waved his arms several times back and forth before the boy's eyes.

"What's this behind your ear, young man?" Odysseus said, reaching. He snatched into sight, seemingly from the air, a fine crystal key, which seemed to have materialized in his hand, and which he now held before the boy's eyes.

"For me?" The key glistened in the afternoon sun, twisting colors right and left as though from a wild, serpentine rainbow.

"Of course for you."

"Ha-ha, ho-he, a kind and generous Father Three. Hard as a rock, but glistens like oil, but where does it work, and how does it toil?"

"My beloved wife sent it just for you. It is the key to Elysium. Someday, when we all seek that place together, you will open the door with it."

It was in fact the key to the chest where Penelope had kept many little treasures, love gifts from Odysseus. He had forgotten to give the key to Telemachos before he'd departed Ithaka. The chest would have to remain sealed until he returned, or forever.

"Who is she, Penelope? Where is she, Penelope?"

"Waiting for me there, in Elysium, if I'm good, and waiting for you now, too."

"Hoooo. Must I be good then?" Orestes gently took the

key from Odysseus' hand with an enormous paw.

"Yes, you must."

"And must you be good, too, as Father Two, and will you so be, Father Three?"

"I must, and I will try."

"Run, my good fellow," said Diomedes, "and tell Uncle that we've arrived. He and our friends are eager to see us."

"A quick leap, and off the floor; never a sparrowhawk needs the door." Orestes, finding footholds with amazing speed and facility, climbed the wall as rapidly and quietly as if he were a spider. Once he'd cleared the wall, his head rose briefly again from the other side of the parapet, showing a wide, mad grin. He put a finger to his lips to indicate silence—how did he hold on with one hand?—and disappeared as quietly as sunlight.

"Poor fellow," said Diomedes.

"Gifted fellow," said Odysseus, "but can we really take him with us? Is it right?"

"Considering what you've seen, how can't we? And by the way, do you plan to be good?"

"Plan or expect?"

"Either."

"Never."

"Where do you suppose they've got to?" said Idomeneus. "If I've understood Orestes aright, they came to the gate, and so should have been here long ago. Philo, should we have a look for them? You don't suppose they've stopped to seduce some girls already?"

"Tricksy one of many turns, he's a gamer; and with him Argos' hero, best horse-tamer!"

"Yes, let's go look," said a voice like Philoctetes'.

"Right. Shall we start at the gate or the whorehouse?"

"Who said that?" Philoctetes asked, annoyed.

"I did, you rockheaded Thessalian," said a voice like Idomeneus'.

"Who said that?" asked Idomeneus.

"You did, Ido, and rockhead yourself!" replied Philoctetes.

"I did nothing of the sort," answered Idomeneus.

"And if it's a rock in the head you want, I'll be happy to oblige you."

It sounded like Idomeneus, and Philoctetes was beginning to get angry.

"Will you now?" Philoctetes said, taking to his feet and cracking his knuckles.

"And Dio and I will have to take a rock and crack the skull of both of you," said a voice that for all the world sounded like Odysseus'.

"Who—could it be?" stuttered Idomeneus. "I should have known it, you old sea buzzard!"

Odysseus and Diomedes had slipped unnoticed into the tent where the famous heroes sat lingering over lunch, waiting for the most famous of them all. They leaned upon a wine cask, Odysseus just finishing a large bowlful, having thrown away their cloaks, and awaited the embrace of their friends and colleagues, old and new.

"Here we are now at last," said Philoctetes sometime later, after many tall tales and many bowls of wine. "Diomedes, I believe, has an adventure in mind, and from what he's told me of it, it suits me well. Next question: how do we do it? The 'when' I already know: as soon as we can provision a ship."

"In such a hurry, Philo?" asked Odysseus. "No wish to enjoy a few drinks with some old friends?"

"Funny thing," answered Philoctetes, "I feel smitten with wanderlust so I can hardly sleep, hardly even sit still. Look at me: I'd have been out wrestling with Ido if your joke had lasted a bit longer. I want, need, something to do, and I think the gods dropped Dio in my path because they want us to hunt Trojans. Not even Trojans proper, but what's left of them. And I say we start with Aeneas."

"Too strong," said Antilochus. "I've enquired. He's built quite an army among the Italians. And from what I've heard, it's as though he hasn't aged, his mother's power is so great upon him. The Oracles say he's destined to found an empire."

"Haven't you heard?" said Idomeneus. He tuned his voice to a whisper. "Haven't you understood our friend Orestes' story? The Furies are no more! They are the Eumenides, all kindness and dedication to Athens, to whose future they have turned all their powers. Men, learned men—as my friend Dictys here—have heard, and I believe them, that something new rules the people of the world now, if *rules* you can call it. What is it? I don't know, and don't shush me: I'm as pious as any man."

"Imagine that," said Thrasymedes. "If fate no longer dictates our paths, who does? Or what? How will we know the span and breadth of our lives, the course of our actions?"

"We still have the gods," Odysseus broke in, "and they still have us. Maybe for the rest, we can choose, the way we'd choose one wine over another, this cheese, that bread, those fruits."

"I have the key to Elysium, ha-ha," purled Orestes, to nearly everyone's astonishment.

"I don't know about the rest of you," said a voice little lower than a boy's, "but I want to swing a sword and carry a shield. You've all had a chance, and now it should be mine. Come along or not, but I want to find some Trojans and earn my birthright."

More than a little of warrior Achilles' tones rose and fell in the unsettled pitch but firm assurance of the voice of Neoptolemos' son, a living, growing icon of his grandsire. Recognizing it, the men had to laugh.

Before the boy's face could cloud with anger, Odysseus spoke. "Forgive us, young soldier, Achilles by name, blood, and worth. We don't laugh at you, but because we hear the echo of our old comrade, the best warrior the world has known, and we share your eagerness to begin."

"Then what's keeping us?" the boy shot back.

"A plan," answered Diomedes. "We need a plan. No worry for provisions, my cousin?"

"None whatever," answered Calydoneus. "What's mine is yours to take and use as you please, short of what we need to survive. I of course can't go, nor can you have the best of my soldiers: a prince's city is his first care. But I'll help as I can."

"Thanks indeed, and you're quite right, Prince Calydoneus," said Odysseus. "If you can offer materials, I can offer a plan."

"I thought you might," said Diomedes.

"And no, my friends, it does not take us to Latium, but through the great sea and beyond, where no one has gone before, if what Dictys has told me is right. We must start by building something."

"Not another horse."

"No indeed, not a horse, but a ship such as no one in this world has ever seen and such as our age has scarcely imagined. The Troyans have gone north by means of the East; we, to catch them, must go north by means of the West."

39

Growing darkness with the death of day had by then nearly engulfed the Greek heroes, lost in their talk. Odysseus, with a quick scratch over his flint, lit a fire in the central cauldron to illuminate the deliberations that would take them most of the rest of the night.

3

PLAN AND EGGS

"What Troyan dug a tomb by, Three must learn at Cumae. Oooooop." The heroes, tired with a night's argument, had sat for a while in the silence of stalemate, when the sing-song of Orestes, still wide-eyed while the shiver of Eos passed into the warming of first light, woke their words anew.

"What's he saying?" Odysseus asked Diomedes. "I don't get it."

"No wonder—we've argued the night to sleep. Say it again, son, or tell us more, if you can, my good boy," Diomedes pleaded.

"What Troyan dug a tomb by, Three must learn at Cumae. Oh-ho, ha-ha. Far above the golden sand, caverns measureless to man. Oooooo—deep, and more to learn than sleep."

"I know of Cumae, I think," said Dictys, rousing himself from sleep. "It may be important. New tales from the west of Italy tell how a colony of Greeks years ago founded a temple to Apollo at Cumae. An ancient sibyl still lives there, they say. She gives penance and prophecy according to the god's wishes. They say Aeneas went there, and the sibyl led him into a cavern where, deep in the earth, he found the Golden Bough, made safe journey to Hades, and found the key to a new empire. Sad thing to say of a Trojan, if one can trust the tales."

41

"As a teller yourself, you must trust them, at least partly, or you deceive us in the telling," Diomedes said, yawning.

"*Trust* may be the wrong word," Dictys answered. "I hear them from other makers, and if I like them, or I think someone like you will like them, I tell them, too."

"That's all?" Odysseus asked. "*Like* them?"

"No," Dictys admitted. "Have you ever slept without dreams? Of course you have. All men have, right? Well, not all men. I do not and never have. Sleeping tires me more than waking. Places, people, scenes, events, sometimes brief, sometimes in long tapestries that seem to weave themselves all the way from evening's fireflies to the last glimpse of the Morning Star: they unfold behind my eyes, with their noisy tramping and frenetic scurrying and endless talk—well, I can hardly keep myself from telling them, as though Lord Shootafar were poking me in the back with his arrow. A pain strikes above the ridge of the hip-bone and won't go away until I tell it to someone, not just anyone, but usually someone in particular."

By now all the heroes' eyes had pushed up heavy lids enough to turn to Dictys, whose speech gained volume and insistence like a runner moving from his poised crouch, waiting to spring to full stride, then rising to the manhood of his full speed.

"Yes, Odysseus, I see the question in your eyes. I had a dream. I saw you sailing, with Idomeneus and Diomedes and all the rest of us, over a broad sea and up a blue mountain. There a hag, blue and old as the mountain itself, laughed, kissed you on the cheek—don't shiver like that—laughed, and pointed north. We sailed again. To the east, where we should have seen land, stood a vast wall of mist, and from it warning voices echoed. We went north to a river's mouth. Mars stood astride the banks with a sail in his hands. He replaced our sail with his, pointed north with a grim smile on his face, not of threat, but of command. We sailed into a golden cavern or tunnel, where I heard the most miraculous singing. It stopped when I awoke to the sounds of our poor friend howling. A long blue sea it was, bluer than sapphire, then it turned into a river like a tunnel or a cavern. That's all I recall."

"Then north the sacred river runs, west of all lands touched by Huns: ride roan steed to rind-gold mead. That's Apollo for you." Orestes chanted his song, then trilled like a bird and shrugged.

"West I had thought myself," said Odysseus, "far west to a sea greater than the Great Sea, broader than anything anyone has ever seen. Yes, Dictys, sometimes I have dreams of my own, though I think the black death-like sleep more peaceful than one filled with dreams. Well, then, maybe not the broad sea at the end of the world for us, at least not yet: Shootafar has spoken to both of you, it would seem, and maybe I have finally learned to listen to the gods. Yes, Dio, and maybe I haven't.

"Thrasymedes, are you awake? Do you have that drawing you made last night, of the lands and seas to the north? Ah, here it is. If Thrasy's information is right, we can sail this sea, Tyrrhenian I've heard it called, to the land north. To the north are mountains taller than Olympos, so tales tell, and more than a man can count, but if we go west, not as far as the broad, endless water, no farther than where people dwell, maybe by some water, a river or inland sea, then we can pass north."

"To the north, I think, is where we'd find Cumae, and if I'm not mistaken, Aeneas' Trojans not far away," said Dictys, looking at Thrasymedes.

"That's right, I believe," said Thrasymedes, "at least according to the drawings I've seen, and I've copied them exactly for you. If we go that way, we may not be able to avoid them, by our wish or theirs, and one never knows what the gods will do."

"Well, let's think over it a bit and wash," said Odysseus. "I need some breakfast and a hot drink. You too? Dio, can your servants get us something? Then we can have Dictys tell us the story of how the Trojans got north and what happened to them there."

The heroes breakfasted on hot bread, leftover cold meat, dried fruits, fresh eggs, and hot water steeped in lemon and mint. At length Dictys told his tale.

"Not all of the allies of Troy favored them in the War of the Achaians. One tribe, called the Anchae, offered tribute in the form of war supplies and food, but would send no soldiers: they believed that the gods had told them not to join Troy, since they had not blessed its defense, the cause of the conflict rising from the kidnapping of Helen, lawful wife of Menelaos. Those people, from the north-northwest of Trojan lands, but south of the Black Sea, followed a king named Memnes, who had married one of Priam's daughters and carried her back to his homeland. While they had ever kept peace and good relations with Troy, they valued their peace with the gods even more than that with their allies.

"Memnes had a son he named Trorash whom he sent to be raised by Loricus, lord of the Thracians. Trorash was said by the shapers of songs to be the finest man to look upon of all those of that age. I suspect they had never seen Achilles. Loricus trained him better than if the boy were his own son, or at least on a tougher regimen. One story says that, while they were out hunting, the lord's party was attacked by marauders from the east, and while the lord was killed, Trorash fought valiantly, killed the invaders, and at

44

his return was elected by the people as their new king, to serve in the old lord's stead.

"Another story says that Loricus, jealous of Trorash's beauty, and of his many gifts that surpassed those of his own sons, had arranged for the attack so that Trorash might be killed and thus disposed of beyond the reach of law or vengeance, but that instead Trorash had defended himself like a seasoned warrior, killing his attackers and, learning of their mission, he executed the man he had naively believed his benefactor.

"A third tale, less sympathetic to the allies of Troy, tells that in due time Trorash, desiring a kingdom of his own, killed lord, lady, and advisors, taking the Thracian throne as his own by the sheer power of his will and the evil of his heart, and he built a new city to which he gave his own name. That tale says that the gods in vengeance destroyed that city and drove him north with a flood, punishing him for breaking Zeus' one sacred law, that of guest-hospitality. That sounds more like a Trojan to me, but then the gods separated those men from the Trojans before we came there—for their blessing or ours I can't tell you."

"That's no problem by me, if the fellow killed Thracians," Odysseus interjected. "I have a score to settle there with the Cicones. My men—against my advice, let me say—*negotiated* a few of their sheep. The locals caught them sleeping after their feast and killed nearly a hundred of them. We obliged by ridding them of nearly twice that many, but we hadn't the numbers to sustain a fight."

"Someday, maybe, you'll return, but for now we have other business, Ody." Diomedes patted Odysseus on the shoulder.

"Still other stories," Dictys continued, "say that having won a kingdom by courage and strength of arms and having been denied a chance for heroism in the greatest war the world has ever known, Trorash tired of the peace of his own kingdom, roused a small band of stout warriors, and traveled north over the far reaches of the world, adventuring and winning honor and a vast treasure. Those stories tell how he crossed the steppes on foot and followed the many rivers by boat to all the settlements unknown to us in the south. In the far east he slew a dragon so large and fierce that their three-day battle nearly tore the earth in two. Then he met a mage, the most powerful in the world, who deceived him, led him miles away, then hid his court beyond the reaches of this world to avoid the hero's vengeance. They say he sailed a sea east to the end of the world and, finding there a whirlpool as large as Crete, rowed back with all his might lest he be sucked into Tartaros.

"Crossing the vast forest, he explored the west, where he subdued the wild men who had lived as little more than beasts, and he taught them how to build a citadel and forge metal, so that when he left, they worshiped him as a god. In the far north he fought Frost Giants, creatures as tall and cold as ice mountains, driving them as far as the top of the world, where nothing lives but bears white as wave-caps. Many of the giants fled as far from him as they could get, to the very southern tip of the world, where they built massive castles of ice, from which they plot one day to attack and overthrow him.

"In the northeast he met among the sturdy, grim-faced hunter-folk a golden-haired sibyl of such amazing beauty he thought her not to have sprung from those people, but from the loins of Apollo. They married, and one poem tells how in a magic ship they flew to the great, golden waves of light that are said to flow like a sea across the northern sky. Such stories only mad makers will tell.

"Together they had two sets of twin sons, Loresh and Lokesh the elder pair, Modi and Magi the younger. They have all by now grown near to strong maturity, and they will fight for their father like Furies. Trorash and his bride, Sib or Sif they call her, as if she were a sibyl Apollo had let go, had also a fifth son, called Peldeg, who like his mother had the light of Apollo in his face, and upon whom no woman may look without falling in love.

"Trorash had gone first from Thrace with only a small band of the best and most loyal of his warriors, but after many adventures he returned to his adopted home and gathered to him, along with his experienced soldiers, the remainder of an army that could have rivaled the Hellenes at Troy—so said one Dares, a bard who survived our war and accompanied Trorash in all his journeys, so he claims. From Thrace, Trorash took all the Trojans who escaped our war and who made it there alive.

"With them the Trorites also took Keimtales, who carries their warning horn, a single note upon which will fetch friends from great distances and send enemies scrambling in fear. They took Hothines, a great strategist and commander of soldiers: their Odysseus, one might say. And also they took Para and Preya, brother and sister, children to farmers from the Thracian borderlands, who had grown up fighting side by side to defend their lands and who would never part far from each other, devoted siblings. One must not underestimate them, though one be female, since they have mastered the powers both of bringing life from the ground and sending it back again.

"By Trorash's side stands ever Skef, greatest king of the northwest, who turned over his army to the invader and pledged his life and that of his followers to join Trorash in whatever quests should please him best. Such loyalties he

47

inspires, they say, even in those he conquers.

"Besides those notable names, with a hundred soldiers from the north and a hundred more from Thrace they returned north, gaining lands by winning loyalties or battles, increasing their numbers and strength, all the way through the regions called Germania, Frankia, Reithgotaland, and Rus. People after people joined them or fell before them, but they avoided slaughter, leaving behind them what arts they knew, learning more, and moving on. Barely a generation passed before they became first legends and then gods, and people told stories of their beauty, strength, and prowess—may the gods spare me though I say so.

"That's how stories work. There must be islands in the Great Sea where they speak of you, Ody, as one of the immortals, vanquisher of Troy by the great horse, counselor to Agamemnon, friend of Achilles, favorite of Athena, with the resourcefulness of a hundred men, eyes of piercing fire, and a manhood the size of a mid-mast."

Diomedes howled with laughter, and Orestes cooed, then spoke one of his odd rhymes: "Fathers, fathers everywhere, with wives they eat and drink; fathers, fathers everywhere, so bellies never shrink. Hooooo." Diomedes howled again, and several minutes passed with a number of sheepish and finally angry glances from Odysseus before he could calm everyone. Even then Diomedes, thinking he had stopped himself, ejected his next sip of lemon tea out his nose, sending everyone but Odysseus and Orestes once again into waves of laughter.

Thrasymedes, ever the best able to control his spirit under ponderous brows, spoke first what they all were thinking. "Dictys, you're a story-teller, and tellers—I won't say *lie*—tend to enhance their tales. Do you tell them as you heard them told, or do you tell them as your Muse tells you, or do you tell them as they please you? How much of all that, if any, do we believe? I ask not to provoke you, but for information."

"All that and all that, toils obscure and all that," Orestes moaned.

"I suppose I can't blame you for asking that, Thrasymedes, but I know the seriousness of our plans. I haven't embellished at all, but I suspect those who told me did so. Stories are stories and tellers are tellers, as you would say. I speak not from my Muse, but to report everything I heard, so that we may make informed decisions. One day I'll spin you a tale, maybe a tale about you, with all the trimmings—then you'll know the difference. Or maybe the Muse will spin me, and then you'll really know the difference."

"I ask so that I may know, not to offend."

"No offense taken."

"We must take care indeed," said Odysseus, "not to offend one another, as we are few, and by now our enemy may number a great many. But we must also try to distinguish likelihood from tale. We must share everything we can learn about them and discern them shrewdly if we are going to achieve our task. Such men may live who love Trojans less than I, and I am older than I was, and Athena visits me less often than she once did—in her eyes, I suppose, I have won my fame and accomplished her desires. That means we must think all the more and plan all the more on our own and use what resources we can muster *together*. Now, Dictys, as Thrasymedes wisely asked, how much do you trust of what you've heard?"

"I won't say the men who told me spoke under the power of a Muse, but I will say that their eyes and their carriage told me they spoke what they knew or thought they knew. Though I trust it as honest, I don't know if we may trust it as *true*. Where there's mist, there must be water is all I'm suggesting."

"I hope," Philoctetes said, yawning, "that you're not suggesting we go north to hunt the ghosts of Trojans based on the belchings of a few hungry would-be bards. I'm as ready to fight as anyone, but I've used up a great many of my days, and before the rest depart, I want to swing my sword at Troyans, not legends."

"When I say they may not be *true*," Dictys responded, "I don't mean they're *lies*. The Trojan leftovers have definitely traveled north and have gained power, land, and soldiers. They have gained enough fame that if we seek them, we will find them. The rest may lie somewhere between truth and poetry, though I feel confident that if we fight, we will fight men and not gods."

"Quite so," said Thrasymedes.

"That good enough for you, Philo?" said Antilochus.

"Not yet," said Philoctetes. "I want to hear Odysseus' plan. When that most resourceful of men is satisfied, then I'm ready."

Everyone looked at Odysseus.

"Almost ready, not quite ready," said the wily one, and he was answered with several tired sighs. "I had thought to go far to the west, farther than any one, save the gods themselves, has ever gone. Dictys, you speak of dreams. Since I got home from Troy I have dreamed of a sea broader than all the world we know. Even on my first night home, as Penelope slept quietly in my arms, the weariness of long loving having stilled us both, I drifted in and out of dream, and I thought I heard the low, droning, melting voice of Poseidon, urging me west.

"Oh, I know that voice, from days in his cold waves,

when I spit salt water from my beard and kicked away sea-beasts the size of fishing boats. Yes, I know they could have had me if they'd wanted me, but, just the same, *you* try to stay still with their scaly massiveness scraping the skin from your feet and knees.

"Well, long I lived at odds with Lord Earth-Shaker, and I wish never again to do so. I think our first task, mine if not yours, must take me to his feet, where I must ask his mercy, beg if necessary. Yes, Dio, you did hear that right, Odysseus begging. No, young Achilles, I don't think your grandfather would have done it, but this old man must."

"Sicilia and sea-god's shrine, and Cumae sets the balance fine: hay-up-high, the lion sleeps, doo wop."

"Orestes, you sing from my own lungs—that's the name, Sicilia, that Poseidon whispered from his crashing waves. Thrasy, isn't that west, around the toe of Italy?"

"Yes, Odysseus, so I have been told, and so I have drawn it."

"And so say the stories of Aeneas," added Dictys.

"I wish you'd stop talking about Aeneas," Diomedes said.

"Sorry. As Odysseus said, better to be complete."

"No need to get that complete. The more I hear about him, the more I feel the need to pay him a visit and finish an unfinished job."

At that Orestes fell at Diomedes' feet. "Oooh, Father One, obey the Sun; clear out west—that's the best." He began to groan loudly and paw at Diomedes' feet.

"I wish he wouldn't do that," Philoctetes said. "It's demeaning, and it unnerves me."

"We'll every one of us need every bit of nerve we have before this is over," responded Odysseus. "I think that's why he speaks so. Lord Shootafar seems to bless us, though

I would welcome a sign from Athena. 'Let no one scorn a gift from the gods,' goes the old saying, though they often cut not far from where they heal."

Odysseus stood and stretched his arms far above his head, then yawned, massaged his lower back, burped, then sighed a long, low breath. "Boys, let me walk a bit. Things are starting to come clearly to my mind, but I need some time by myself to let them settle in. Don't worry: I won't be long. I need to shake off drowsiness and Calydoneus' sausages. No offense to a fine host."

"None taken," said Calydoneus. "Shake as you please. There's a path down there from within the walls, a bit steep, but a short way to a grove where the breeze blows gently in the morning. It's too far to the strand, but that grove always has the tang of sea air, as if you stood on the beach itself."

"My thanks indeed. One could ask for no finer host. I only wish you could join us on our journey."

"You're welcome, to my hospitality and to your journey. I for one don't wish to make it. I feel quite sufficient duty in defending my home and quite sufficient honor in welcoming Odysseus to it now and when you return, should you wish it. Meanwhile, Dio, shall I provision a couple ships, or will you be staying on a bit?"

"From the look in Ody's eyes, I should say prepare the ship. Ah, there's the smile. Yes, I suspect we'll be sailing soon now."

Odysseus meandered for some time among the rocks on the winding path down toward the grove. By the time he reached it, the chill breeze of morning had given way to the warm wafts of noon, and he bent his head to his footsteps and his ears to what seemed the sound of surf.

Their path, Odysseus thought, was clear, but only a sign

would give him the comfort of believing his feelings right. The gods seemed to be driving him west and north, but the pull of the World-Sea beyond drew him as strongly as sex or food, almost such that the mere thought of it set his crotch astir. He had got near to that sea once on his way home from Troy, so that he might call the shades of Hades to his aid. Something in him ached to go farther, beyond the edge of the world.

He found the grove, rather larger than he'd expected, with copses of trees and open spaces forming a simple labyrinth. Even as he walked eastward with the sandy wash tingling distantly in his ear, another thought crossed his mind, that he in fact felt his member rising, and he suspected instantly an experience that he had not had for many months and that he greatly desired. He immediately knew a twinge of fear and covered his crotch, raising his eyes slightly to assure his glance without staring:

The unmistakable laughter, like a soldier who knows he will win his battle, but with smoothness of olive oil and a musky warmth almost too much to bear . . .

Athena!

"Forgive me, goddess. Some things a man can't control, even before his best benefactor."

—Odysseus, I know you by now, wily one. What from another would provoke me to use my bow, from you flatters me, though few females, divine or human, fail to draw this from you, still a man among men.

"I have long desired your wisdom."

—I know, though, that doesn't look like a request for wisdom.

"I am sorry, goddess."

—I know. Now do as Apollo and I shall tell you.

"He is with me as well?"

—I am with you; you need no more. You may not task me; even Father Zeus seldom does.

"You come from the Father more fully than does thought from the mind or love from the heart, goddess."

—Always the flatterer. Well. First in this new journey you must flatter, and you have already guessed that correctly. On the east coast of Sicilia you will find a shrine to Poseidon. There you must stop and give sacrifice and do such penance as the Lord of the Sea asks of you. You will find, I am sure, that his wrath has softened toward you, for he too seeks the task you have begun. No, he does not bless you—that would be too much for you to ask—but at least he does not curse: be glad for that and for the fact that in doing his will you please your gods.

"And from there?"

—Two steps ahead: that's why I have loved you so long, Odysseus. That too you already know: to Cumae, where the sibyl will speak what you need to know. Be sure to take with you figs from Poseidon's shrine. Seeing that gift she will know you and serve you. Don't be surprised: others have already landed there and begged favor in the name of Odysseus. Ah: you thought no one would dare to use your name and your fame for himself? Remember this well, my mortal: pray in earnest, carry your figs, and hear the sibyl with your deepest mind. And get control of that thing in front of you before I forget my love for you and make you half the man you used to be.

"Dear goddess, don't be angry with me. You see and know what it is for a man who loves . . ."

Odysseus had gained the courage to raise his eyes to the goddess' face, but she had already gone. A warm breeze like the sound of knowing laughter washed over his back and thighs and disappeared up the path toward Calydon.

Imagine that: getting stiff for the war goddess—at his age!

When Odysseus returned up the long hill to camp, he slapped a dozing Idomeneus on the back, nearly knocking him from his chair.

"What there? Oh, it's you. Well?"

"Ha, get your gear, old Ido: we're on our way to—yes, I hear it in my head, Siracusa."

"Siracusa?"

"On Sicilia, a shrine of Poseidon, where we will get, if I humble myself properly, smooth sailing to Cumae."

"My palms are itching, my friend."

"And very soon you will scratch them. We can load the ship and start in the morning."

"The weather sits gently and snugly over us, and the moon will make the water shine like silver. Why wait till morning?"

"Why, indeed?" said Odysseus, belting on his sword and throwing his cloak over his shoulder. "I'd just like a few more of Calydoneus' eggs before I go. I had a couple with breakfast. They seemed to help me think. Maybe he'll have a servant pack a few. Nothing like fresh eggs under the broad moon to keep your belly calm over the waves, and any calm we can get will serve us well."

4

SIRACUSA AND CUMAE: FIGS IN THE DARK

What a blessing, smooth sailing under a full moon . . . Odysseus did not spare prayers to the gods, Athena first of all, and the Greeks sailed uneventfully across the long expanse of the Ionian sea in weather better than any man deserves.

With a hint of wind behind them and the energy of Calydoneus' provisions inside them, the heroes rowed steadily in shifts, covering one hundred twenty leagues from the coast off Calydon to Siracusa in three and a half days. They took with them only twenty sturdy young men ready to sail, but they had little training in—though much eagerness for—battle. Young Achilles himself rowed with the power of twenty men and without complaint: he enjoyed the exercise of his physical strength.

The heroes slept when they could, but mostly told stories of the old days, to which the young men listened with gleaming eyes. They tried, as well as one can on the pitching deck, to teach the young sailors the rudiments of weaponry, but soon understood why Calydoneus could spare them, good sailors though they were. They taught them then to assist in the sacrifices to all the gods, leaving out none—who knew how the quest would turn?

Orestes would hardly let Odysseus disembark: Diomedes and Idomeneus had to hold him back and try to calm him. As Odysseus stepped into the canoe to go ashore, Orestes called after him, "Beware the eyes that marched! Nasty dealer, the waveshaker!"

"Don't worry, son. Regardless, I must go. I owe the god a debt, and I haven't used the last of my wiles yet."

Having arrived in the afternoon with plain white sail and no show of force, Odysseus quickly found coast guards and gained their permission to land in Sicilia, then with the offer of a few small gifts he won entry from the votaries to Poseidon's shrine. The others remained aboard ship, aiming to arouse no ill will, and knowing that the task ahead lay to the Resourceful One and no other.

Odysseus slung a goat over his shoulders, its front and back legs tied separately. The goat, perhaps sensing its fate, struggled repeatedly, so that the hero had to spend much energy to hold it tightly.

Poor fellow, Odysseus thought, wondering for the first time if the goat had any idea of itself, of its life and impending death. Many times I've felt myself at the mercy of the sacrifice, he thought, drifting on the sea, about to be given up by the gods or the Fates to Lord Earthshaker. I doubt he will spare you as he spared me.

The shrine stood open on a high promontory overlooking a stretch of golden sand upon which the waves tumbled with the voice of distant thunder. Inside the gate grew a circle of fig trees with the largest, richest, sweetest-looking figs Odysseus had ever seen.

A long, straight stair descended directly to the edge of the water, such that the last fingers of the breakers licked its tip smooth as the water itself. Climbing is for young men, Odysseus thought, then realized he'd better not complain, with far more strenuous tasks soon ahead.

The struggling goat made the descent more difficult, as a steady wind and light spray made the steps even slicker than they might have been. Odysseus trod carefully and in an effort to calm the goat began singing a lullaby that his mother had sung to him and which he had sung to Telemachos. It didn't work. Nonetheless he sang on, finding in the simple tune comfort for himself, if not for his victim.

> Father and baby
> down by the sea;
> Mother at the window
> waiting for me.
> Bringing with baby
> fresh fish and oil;
> sleep on my shoulder
> after day's toil.

Reaching the bottom of the stair, Odysseus found the water rising to meet his feet, noticed the waves growing and gaining force from farther out, rumbling as hills do when they quake. Taking care with his footing, he slung the goat down, and with a last gentle word his deft and experienced hand cut the beast's throat.

The body quivered in his hands, but bracing himself with a wide stance, Odysseus held the animal above his head, the blood dripping down, and he called out, his own stentorian voice nearly matching the fury of the pounding breakers.

"Lord Poseidon, I beg you, hear me! This sacrifice I bring in the sight of all the gods for you alone! Let this body and this blood stand for me, my body, my blood, and let me be reconciled to you! I pray, a pious man, to you, great god, brother to Zeus and Hades, father of all waters, that you forgive me, and for my voyage grant safe passage!"

Odysseus reared back and with both arms threw the bleeding body of the goat as far out into the water as he could.

The sea surged as though it would rise and engulf him, as it did engulf the goat, and a voice, deeper than the earth, hung about his ears, heavy enough to pull him to his knees, so that only with the greatest strength of will could he avoid falling headlong into the waves.

—Not enough! the voice rang.

"What more, then?"

—You must offer much more.

"What do you want of me?"

—You must trust me.

"How? What must I do?" With all his strength, Odysseus rose again to his feet.

—Stop resisting. Let go. You must fight my waters no more. Give up your desire for lordship over my element.

Odysseus clung with the last sinews of his failing strength to the slick steps beneath him. He had either to find the strength to scramble back up the stair and lose the chance to mollify Poseidon or find the will to lose himself in the will of the god.

—You think I ask too much of you, a hero. Do as I command you.

Odysseus leaped.

Not much of a leap: his legs had little strength, and the slick footing left him no leverage, but he gave up his will and his life into the hands of the Sea.

Along with the water, Poseidon's laughter, cold and stony yet fluid and tractable, filled his ears and his lungs, and the suck of the tide pulled him under and, before he could gather his bearings to try to swim, out toward the deep sea.

Odysseus flailed with all his strength, but he only managed to deplete what little air the god had left him.

—Once again, Odysseus, you find yourself at my mercy.

You have never shown mercy before, thought Odysseus, but full of water, he could say nothing and continued to sink and roll deeper into the tide.

—You fear that you are going to die and that you have made your sacrifice in vain.

Odysseus, unwilling to die with no dignity at all, stopped flailing, but couldn't stop the rising burn in his lungs and his brain.

—I accept your sacrifice, but it is not enough. It has no consequence. You must give me something greater than that, something that will make you, too, my son.

As Odysseus sank and rolled, he could glimpse at the edge of his sight or the end of his consciousness a large, black shape emerging from beneath him.

—You must offer what you have taken from my son: an eye for an eye.

The shape beneath him emerged into an enormous stingray. It floated gently toward him, then around him. Just as it seemed to float away, its tail flicked like a whip, and the tip struck Odysseus flush in the left eye.

He had never felt such burning, greater than the point of a spear, greater than the fires of simmering Troy, greater than the pain in his airless lungs. Odysseus thought he would pass out, that at least death then would still the burning jelly of his eye that shot through the socket and through the air-starved brain and that paralyzed his limbs with tingling fire.

Warm blood oozed and froze against his drawn cheek.

—You think this is the gentle death by sea prophesied for you; not so gentle though, eh? Nor is it your death.

Odysseus thought he would pass out. Then he must surely die, and his body would disappear into the broad, dusk-blue sea. The body, unburnt, must turn in the waves until the small fish picked his bones clean, and his soul must sift into thin air, never to reach Hades, but to float on the waves and walk the earth restless for all time.

—No, you shall not die yet. You have a task to finish, one that I want you to do as well, I and Athena, who for no reason I can understand loves you. And now you may go with my aid.

Odysseus felt himself propelled, as though by strong hands grasping his sides, upward. When he thought no breath could reach him in time to save him, he broke the surface.

At first the air hurt even more than the water, and the burning socket of his eye still threatened to suck waking from his brain. He descended, then again felt himself propped up, buoyed on a wave. Full of water, he could barely draw air. He bobbed and spat, struggling too hard to curse.

—Swim now, my son, for I have made you my son, and your brother Polyphemos may rest avenged. Swim with all your energy to another sacrifice that you must yet make. Praise Apollo, for he will give you a gift that will more than compensate you for what my creature has taken. You will see farther and deeper than you have ever seen, and you will learn and understand what no one before you has known.

Odysseus bobbed and spat, disgorging water and taking tiny breaths of air.

—And one more thing: call me Step-papa. Come now, let me hear you say it. "Step-papa," say it just like that. I know you can do it, son.

Odysseus would have cursed the god, but luck or fate enveloped him once more beneath the waves. He heard the rumbling of Poseidon's huge laughter. From its force came a huge wave that crested as it passed Odysseus, catching him and propelling him toward the shore three times as quickly as a man could row, directly toward the stone stairway in the rapidly darkening air.

Just as he thought Poseidon had saved him only to dash his brains against the stone, the wave slowed and deposited the hero almost gently on a firm step, withdrawing and leaving him safely aground. The surf seemed to echo a deep, rolling, fading laughter.

A voice like distant thunder mumbled:

—First you must go to Cumae, where Apollo will instruct you in his gift.

—Then you must avoid what you will think you want beyond all else. You must not offend your new gods.

—And remember: you will have that golden-haired girl you dream of; ha-ha, you shall have her, and a handful you'll prove to each other, ha!

A small well of blood stained the water beneath him like a pool of oil, then dispersed. The bleeding stopped, cauterized by the salt of Poseidon's waves. The pain turned from sharp and burning to dull and hard, as one might experience from being hit repeatedly with a hammer.

—And one more thing. Do not tempt Scylla and Charybdis again. Sail west, around the island, then north and east, where my waves will guide you. Listen to your papa! Haaaa . . .

Oh, go away, Odysseus would have told the god, had he the strength. Safely, but hardly happily, Odysseus rose to his knees, pulled himself beyond the cold, flicking waves. Until darkness fully covered him, Odysseus hacked and vomited water and bile from his stomach and lungs, more it seemed to him than could have filled the whole enormous body of Polyphemos. The pain in his now empty eye-socket might have induced shock in a lesser man, but the Man-of-Many-Turns crawled, step by hard step, up the stairway.

In an hour he reached the top, where he sat, peering through his lone eye at waxing moon. The chaste Artemis had never been his goddess—he could expect nothing from her—and Athena, however much she loved him, seldom bothered to spare him pain.

Odysseus' mind began to seethe and turn despite him, despite the pain and the weariness: a vision of a golden-haired, golden-eyed girl—no, not a girl, but a woman, young woman, strong, shapely with a stern brow, but a laughing mouth—filled his mind.

Even in his pain, Odysseus felt his member moving, bobbing, rising, at the thought of the girl, woman.

Poseidon had said that with his pain would come a new gift. Had the vision truth? Had he already gained something of what Orestes and Dictys could see, the best and most frightening of Apollo's gifts?

The hope struck him that he had not, as Dictys expressed, with the gift he gained lost the ability to sleep, the sleep that knits the torn sleeve of pain.

Even as he feared it, he felt a wave of sleep threaten to engulf him, but he knew he must press on, return if he could at least within shouting distance of his shipmates: they must have feared by then that his sacrifice had gone amiss.

It had, and it hadn't. And he knew that he could sleep, but that he must not yet.

In another waft of sleep came a hint of dream, and in the dream came the golden-haired one with the smooth, cold forehead. She smiled at him, and his loins burned, a different pain than the cold hammering in his own forehead.

As he stumbled to the top of the hill and through the grove, he almost forgot to collect the figs, as Athena had urged him. He ripped cloth from his tunic, made a small bag of it, and by the light of the moon filled it with the brown, rich figs of the sacred grove.

With his makeshift sack brimming, he placed it on the ground, tore free another slim piece of cloth, and made a headband to cover the horror of his empty eye. Bag in hand, he fought off pain and sleep and descended to his ship.

With the first light of rosy-fingered dawn Odysseus' companions heard a muffled shout, jerked themselves from sleep, and saw their leader from a distance beckoning. Idomeneus and one of Calydoneus' young sailors jumped onto the sand from the spot where they had moored the ship, near where Odysseus had left his canoe.

The young man fainted when he saw Odysseus' face.

"Get me to the ship, Ido," Odysseus said. "I don't think I can eat, but I intend to drink an amphora full of the strongest wine we have and sleep for a full day to still this pain. When I wake I will tell you all about it. Before then if you ask me anything at all, I will strangle the life from you. Set sail and oar for Cumae. Do exactly as I ask. Go first south, and then west, and then north, around the Sicilian coast. Straight north in the straits wait Scylla and Charybdis. I've tangled with them twice and intend not to do so again."

Taking one look at him, and seeing Idomeneus wave away their questions, the companions turned their gaze aside, letting Odysseus pass. Orestes disappeared to the far end of the ship, where he curled up, moaned and cried quietly. Achilles, with all the spirit of youth, wanted to take the shortcut through the straits, but the others agreed reluctantly to take the longer way.

"I would see them for myself, and challenge them if they would have me," said the man still in the fire of youth.

Odysseus allowed Diomedes only to wash the crusted blood from around the headband Idomeneus had made for him. "I know you would, Achilles, but you must not, at least for now. I will speak when I have slept." He started away, then paused. "Do this one thing for me, and I ask as one who has seen comrades disobey the gods and die for it: don't eat the figs in this bag; don't even touch them. I collected them for Apollo's shrine. I do not command you; I ask you as my friends and comrades. Let no temptation woo you. Leave the figs alone. Remember Aeolus' winds, and leave the figs alone."

The hero drank, and then he slept, fitfully, with dreams full of pain, not the mindless nepenthe he'd wanted.

Again, miraculously, the wind rose behind them, and the ship made in a day's time nearly fifty leagues west, turning north around the western tip of Sicilia. In a day and a half Odysseus rose, shook off his drunken, painful stupor, and told his comrades of what Poseidon had taken and given.

"And that, my friends, is why we will not tempt the Sicilian straits. I will not offend the god again, at least not by choice." Nor will I call him "papa," he added in thought alone.

Philoctetes with a physician's skill had fashioned him a proper patch, which Odysseus accepted with a nod of thanks, and he also received a salve that would numb the tissue that had once given him a light to the world. Odysseus washed his face first with seawater, then with fresh, and, turning away from the others, donned the new patch.

"You look ghastly," Philoctetes said.

"Not so bad-looking," said Diomedes. "You were too pretty before, even for an old man. Many women, even the young ones, like a man with scars. Gives them the notion he's done something exotic and important."

In Odysseus' mind the vision of the blond woman returned, with her cold blue eyes, broad, smooth forehead, and hint of a smile. He turned his back to his companions and sat, legs crossed, in the stern of the boat, fighting to bring more of the image into focus.

"When he's ready," said Dictys, "we must get from him what he expects to learn at Cumae. I think I know, from the way he's sitting, what he's thinking now, but I don't see how that fits with his pain, and I don't know what it has to do with the sibyl."

" 'WOOooooooo why then I'll fit you,' Poseidon says. Take that! An eye, ho hi, and then a girl to fit you, you fitchew, I'll give you. So he says to Father Two, who with one eye sees what to do for his fathers." Orestes spoke, then bounced his way to the bow, whistling.

"I don't know what to think of that boy," said Thrasymedes.

"If I really listen, I get the echoes," said Dictys, "but the theme comes slowly in its own time. Apollo hurries for no man."

When they had crested the northwest of Sicilia and turned east, the wind eased—it no longer helped, but at least didn't hinder them. Achilles rowed like a man possessed, and he may well have been. From him the young sailors took their cue. Odysseus spoke little, but occasionally came to the tiller, guiding them ever north by northeast over a sea calm and smooth as a stormless summer field. They had good fishing, and their provisions held, and in four days they traveled from the northwest of Sicilia within sight of land, the west coast of Italy, south of Aeneas' Latium, the coast off the shrine of Cumae.

"Can *that* be that place, Thrasy?" asked Diomedes.

"Hard to say for sure," Thrasymedes answered, "but the distance and direction seem right, according to the drawings, and the place looks right."

"And feels right," added Dictys.

"Yeah, yeah, wop, do-wop, feels so right," sung Orestes.

"But we got here a little too easily for my tastes," said Antilochus. "It strikes me as eerie."

"Ask Odysseus if he thought it was easy," said Idomeneus.

"Right," replied Antilochus, nervously rubbing his hands.

Odysseus joined them, calling for Achilles to take a break. "Come here and have a drink, and I'll tell you why we avoided the enemy that you hoped to see for yourself."

Dozing in the bow, Odysseus had seen a vision old and new. Twice on his way home to Ithaka he had challenged the monsters of the straits: Scylla, who feeds on flesh, Charybdis, who whirls and sucks sailors to the cold sea floor. The old vision he knew too well; the new vision ended with a headless Achilles and a crew plunged into a roaring, ghostly sea-burial.

"The facts that you have heard me and sailed by the longer way and that you have not touched Apollo's figs gives me hope that we may find our Trojans and finish our battle."

"The consummation I have devoutly wished," Diomedes said.

"Now let us look to Cumae," said Idomeneus.

"Anything resembling a port?" asked Thrasymedes.

By the time they had moored the ship, evening had

fallen, so the heroes came ashore, built a fire, found a rustic supper, and rested free of the rocking waves—if not free of pain—and free in their belief that they followed a blessed quest.

As dawn rolled out her wine-bright sky, Odysseus, Idomeneus, and Dictys, with Orestes loping along behind, followed by Diomedes who feared for the young man's safety, climbed the hill to search for Apollo's grove and the sibyl. With some difficulty, they found both.

"Dictys, I thought you said that she's an old woman," Diomedes said.

"Father mustn't father more, nor Father Two, that's for sure, though he's sticking out the door. Hear the voices and be pious, then his Lordship won't deny us." Orestes sat on the ground before the entrance to the sibyl's cave, inside a grove of tall trees. He crossed his legs and intoned: "Ooommm."

The sibyl, a lithe young woman with long brown hair and enormous brown eyes that looked as though if one got too close, he could fall into them and disappear into midnight, peered uncertainly at Orestes then looked distrustfully one-by-one at each of the others.

"Young woman, where is the old sibyl who was?" Idomeneus asked, tired of waiting for Odysseus to speak.

"Retired, my lord."

"Surely that isn't the usual practice."

"No, my lord. But she served so long, our god found her a living. Comfortable she is now, if a bit shriveled."

"And you are the new sibyl?" Odysseus asked.

"Certainly," the girl said defensively.

"You are alone here?" Diomedes asked.

"Not since you've arrived, nor am I ever. I attend our god, who makes his presence felt always. And several soldiers from the town watch out for me at the god's behest."

As she spoke, several tall, rustic-looking young men, well-armed, appeared from the woods, trying to look menacing. The seasoned soldiers would have had no trouble with them, but the gravity of their business overcame their loneliness, and Odysseus focused his thoughts.

"You know why we have come?"

"To consult our god through me?" The girl seemed direct and guileless, almost innocent. "Have you brought a gift?"

"We have." Odysseus pulled out a small bag of gold. "This is for your upkeep and your guardsmen." The girl looked unmoved. "And this is for you and the god." Odysseus unveiled the figs from the grove of Poseidon.

The girl's eyes grew wider than Odysseus would have thought possible, until he almost felt as though he must fall into them, and they shone with a hint of awe and of fear. She bowed deeply. "Yes, you must come to the cave's entrance. We must not keep the gods waiting, yours or mine."

Carefully she took the bag of figs from Odysseus' hands, then backed toward the cave. At its entrance she ate one, then a second. "These I will take to the god. Please wait here." She entered the cave. Odysseus could just see her as she retreated into the dark distance of the passage. She placed the figs on an altar, then lit a fire and began to dance and wave a fragrant branch over the fire. Soon its pungent smoke poured from the cave, tickling his skin and burning slightly in his nose with a smell of sour grass. Shortly she began to weave and moan. Odysseus could hear Orestes, seated behind him, mimicking her cries. After some time of swaying back and forth, holding the branch before her, she turned and marched, wobbly, toward the heroes, her face turned toward the ground.

As she reached Odysseus, she turned her eyes directly to his, with a fey light encircling her face. A deep voice, mellifluous, powerful but perhaps cruel, tumbled from the girl's throat, though her lips barely moved.

—Keep back! But follow into my shrine. You have won entry to the visions that will answer your questions.

They followed warily, since the smoke wanted to curdle their stomachs. When they had all entered the passageway and formed a semicircle just within the entrance, the voice, like the deep strings of a lyre, sang again. Odysseus noticed that the figs had disappeared from the altar.

—Stop. Listen and see. You, wait outside with the boy and keep him calm.

Diomedes turned on his heels and left.

—Follow my words with your thoughts. Do not stray. The far-traveled one must see, and his friends must gird him.

While they felt their feet riveted to the ground, Odysseus, Idomeneus, and Dictys saw an image of themselves following the sibyl into a tunnel that channeled deep into the rock and desperately downward.

They seemed to plunge headlong down a sharp, rocky, curving path cluttered with withered trees that rose and twisted like knotted fingers, deeper, deeper into the hazy caverns, until something like sleep swept over them with a cold mist.

Walking, following. A light in the distance, above the path. Nearer, it shone golden, unsteadily.

—Aeneas came here. That is his bough, regrown. Break a small branch from it and follow.

Again walking, amidst a smell of dust and sulfur. Wild shapes, contorted, floated through the shadows. Ahead, a river, blacker than a starless sky, than new pitch heated for the hulls of ships, but moving, moving with a sound like wind.

—Stop here and wait. They will come. Speak with the one who seeks you.

They stood, and opposite them, across the foul, oily water, swirling smoke resolved into forms. Odysseus felt something cut his left index finger. The sibyl took his hand and held it out over the water. She held out her own, too, which also bled in small drops from a fresh cut. The drops fell atop the water, maintained their character, floated on. Human forms, grotesque, drawn, but recognizable, peered at them from the gloom. One stepped forward to the edge of the opposite shore and offered to speak.

"Odysseus, you know me."

"Father?"

"Laertes, but not father."

"Laertes, and not my father?"

"I believed myself your father and loved you as my son. I do still. But hear what you must know and do."

"I hear, beloved spirit."

—Hear, for you must know and do.

"On our wedding night, before we could consummate, your mother Antiklea, young, inexperienced, was seduced by another man, Sisyphus, son of Aeolus, wind god. Wily man, he told the truth to Asopus, river god, that father Zeus had abducted his daughter. Zeus, to get even, sent Death to claim him. When Death found him, Sisyphus caught and chained him, and he only released him when Death offered health and long life. Even when, years later, Death took him, his stratagem, begging to return to his wife to say good-bye, freed him from Hades, and he returned to earth to live yet more. Some say that, having seen Persephone, upon his wife's death he sought with words to sway the dark

71

goddess from Hades. Now in blackest Tartaros, lit only by the fire that marks his path, he rolls a boulder up a slope, whence, reaching the top, it rolls down, and he must start again. He, Sisyphus, is your father by blood, though I by love."

A second shadow, insubstantial, no more than a wisp, emerged from behind the ghost of Laertes and spoke to Odysseus.

"Odysseus, you cannot rescue me from Tartaros, but you can ease my pain. Go to the place called Ascerbergium. There you will find a steep mountain with a great boulder at its base. Build there a shrine and pray to the gods for the shade of your true father. If you pray piously, they will hear you and grant me respite, if not grace. Do this for the father who gave you, if not love, lifeblood, and with that blood resourcefulness, courage, and the willingness to see afar."

The thin shade folded into itself and disappeared. The other, stepping to the brink of the water, watching the last of the fresh blood drip away downstream, spoke again.

"Great Odysseus, do not fault your mother or me, or even yourself. Do what the gods ask you, and you will achieve a better quest even than the one you believe you seek. Let an old man who loved you as a father guide you now, along with the will of the gods."

—You will go north, past Latium: you must not stop there, though sirens and your own spleen will tempt you. Go to the place where river opens into sea from land shaped like a woman's hips. Row north to the place I will show you. Your journey takes you first there or nowhere, and from there everywhere.

Overcome by smoke and shadows, and perhaps by pain and loss of blood, Odysseus believed he swooned, trying only not to fall into the relentless black water. Water, rocks, smoke, pathways, mycelial, umbrous trees, shards of light all bled together into a mazy mist—unsteadily, Odysseus felt his spirit moving, with or without his legs, until gradually a light rose, and Odysseus knew he was standing, wobbly, at the mouth of the sibyl's cave.

The young woman took his hand. Idomeneus and Dictys stood beside him, their eyes wide, their senses just returning to them as well. Her hand felt small and warm and wet. She touched the skin around his patched eye socket.

"Come outside, Odysseus. You must drink fresh water and breathe fresh air and consider what you have seen. The god has spoken, and I can tell you where he means for you to go."

The three men followed the sibyl into the failing sunshine. Her deep, brown eyes allowed no debate.

73

5

NORTHERN SIRENS

Orestes hopped on one foot in a circle, making bubbling and cooing noises. "Fathers One and Two shall build, since they proved at Troy they're skilled; Father Two shall fathers name, freed of guilt and freed of shame."

Diomedes sat and watched with tired, wondering eyes, knowing he could do nothing else.

Both turned as they heard Odysseus and the others approaching. Seeing Odysseus, Orestes jumped repeatedly straight up from the spot where he stood, higher than Diomedes would have thought possible. He bounced, sung a strange bird-call such as Diomedes had never heard in all his travels, then another.

"Rossignol they call the one; thrush the other, Father One. Both to you I think are new; soon they'll sing for Father Two." Orestes cooed, leaping about again on one foot, with one arm thrown above his head and the other pointing down at the ground.

"What did you see in there, Ody?" asked Diomedes.

"Much to tell," said Odysseus. "Let's take our leave of the sibyl, and I'll tell you as we hike down the slope."

"Can't say I'd mind staying a bit," said Diomedes, looking over the sibyl from head to foot and back again.

Just then the local young men re-emerged from the woods, this time with reinforcements.

"But you know you must not, kind gentlemen," said the girl. "You are too smart to offend Apollo, and your journey must not wait. I will tell you how to find another kind of entry more important to you, though I believe, Odysseus, that you have seen it in your mind already—is that not so?"

"So it is," said Odysseus, his eyes meandering out over the sea, as if visions were already guiding him. Turning to the sibyl he said, "North and west it lies, past great islands, two hundred leagues or more, to the mouth of a great river? Then a long way from there, months perhaps, depending on war and weather."

"You see well, my lord Odysseus."

"May your god and all the others bless, young woman, great sibyl, and may they protect you from such men as we are."

"I believe they will, though I think you are all becoming better men than you ever believed you could."

"I hope not," said Diomedes.

—See to my young one. I let him rest in your care. Though he has many powers, yet you must save him at need.

The voice seemed to Odysseus to come from the girl, and yet she hadn't opened her mouth.

"Who said that, you?" Diomedes asked.

"Not she, but her god—am I not right?" asked Odysseus.

"Right again, hero. And this last warning I must give you: as you pass Latium, your men will hear what will make them wish to stop. They will believe, if they hear those voices, that their quest lies there. You must protect them, and you must not fail them, though weariness plague you. You will know what to do. Temptation will be strong for them and you, but if you fail this next test, you will fail in your quest. I am spent now and can say no more."

Then Odysseus noticed her pallor and realized that the journey to the Underworld had tired not only the men, but the sibyl as well.

—*Norns* the Northmen call them, and you must stay clear of them, for they would keep you from your task.

Odysseus heard the god's warning, but remained polite with the sibyl.

"May I leave you no other gift?" he asked the girl.

"Only this: obey our god."

Her eyes rolled back, and she began to sway; Odysseus would have caught her, but her young soldiers moved quickly to her side to support her and carry her back to her cave. One looked back at the heroes.

"None of you must touch her. Only we may, and then only to save her injury. Otherwise, the god will abandon her and us. Please go now, honored fathers." He added the epithet more as an attempt at good manners than as a peaceful appeal, for the heroes themselves looked worn and weary, little likely to do harm.

"Well, then, if we'll find no love here, let's get about our business," said Diomedes with a yawn. "I could use a meal, and you three look like you could use drink and sleep. Ody, at this rate you'll be an old man in no time, if you aren't already. Let's walk, and I want to hear every detail of what you saw—no malingering, now." He patted Odysseus on the back, and the men started down the slope.

By the time they reached the ship, Odysseus had told as much of their visions as he could remember, supported by additions from Idomeneus and Dictys.

"Of this I'm not sure, though, Dio: did we really go anywhere, or did we see everything passing before our eyes as we stood there by his altar, clothed in the ritual smoke?"

"Hmmm. That I can't tell you for certain, Ody. As soon

as I stepped back from the opening of the cave, I could barely see inside. I thought I saw outlines, but when I got up to see for myself, a voice told me to sit still, and I felt as though a hand rooted me to the ground. So I sat and waited and listened to Orestes. At first he laughed, then he told several strange half-stories—no, not about you, but about golden rings and lost treasures and vengeful brides, as far as I could tell. Then he sang the oddest song I've ever heard. I had him sing it over several times, so that I've almost got it now, though it's in some language I've never heard. If I could sing, I'd give it up for you now. Maybe he'll sing it again if we ask him.

"But first, I can't answer your question, though I do have one more for you: what did you do with Aeneas' bough? Ugh: I hate to say that name."

"Oh . . . I don't know. Did you notice what happened to it, Ido, Dictys?" The two men shook their heads.

"That makes me think you went nowhere other than the cave entrance," Diomedes reasoned.

"And yet look at the bottom of our sandals: red dust, like clay, and with a hint of sulfur in it," Dictys sniffed, "such as we saw in the passageway."

"Odd," Idomeneus said. "I feel as though I've walked for days, and the visions stay with me more than would any dream."

"Surely not a dream," Dictys added, "more like the grace of Apollo, or, if I dare say it, of some greater god yet."

"Shh," hissed Idomeneus. "A man shouldn't say such things and had better not even think them if he wishes to keep the favor of all the gods, which we will need if we are to succeed. I want to know, Odysseus, what gods we must face at Latium, and which we will find on our side. But here's the ship. Ugh: I must have a wash, some food, and some strong drink, and I hope I can stay awake for some talk. We have another test ahead that may prove our most difficult yet. No offense, Ody."

The heroes washed quickly, climbed aboard ship, and fell to food and talk. After the others had talked themselves to sleep, Odysseus lay exhausted but wakeful. Antilochus, the last to give up speech for the night, sat cross-legged, mumbling. Achilles, with the ability of the young to tire the stars, peered at the old, one-eyed soldier with a look that Odysseus understood, but didn't quite like. You have kept me from my adventures, old man, it said, and I will not let you do so much longer. You have kept me from Scylla and Charybdis, but don't think you will keep me from fighting Trojans, even if you wish to shake them off by calling them Latins. Calydoneus' sailors already had them rowing slowly on their way north, and Odysseus thought of what he must say to induce the last of his companions to sleep and to obey the gods.

"I know what you're thinking, father Odysseus, and don't believe you can buy me off with more talk of heads and whirlpools," said Achilles, hardly as near sleep as Odysseus wished he were. "I came to fight, and I will fight, if not for you, then for someone, and sooner rather than later."

Young men, Odysseus thought: you don't even have to convince them to fight with stories of glory and honor; if anything, you have to restrain them until the time is right.

"You are your father's son, and yet your own man. Your adventures, like his, bear the blessing of the gods. Have you seen what they want from you? I haven't. But maybe that is a sign in itself. I know you can't stand to listen to Orestes, but if you could, you would find wisdom in his wild words. He or I must have something for you soon. Your turn has nearly come: I feel it. And when I know, you will know, my young warrior."

"Know soon, then, Odysseus. My father and his father practiced war, not patience."

And the first Achilles paid with his life, and dearly he cost the rest of us, Odysseus thought, doing his best to keep his face impassive.

"Surely you've heard the story, Killy, of how the great Achilles kept an Achaian army waiting for his sword, until vengeance for his friend Patroklos returned him to battle? What do you think moved him to stay his hand?"

"Honor, not patience."

"And I ask only the same of you, that you wait for honor. To fight without hope of winning, against earth herself and her gods, breeds failure, not honor. You will have your chance. Can you imagine your uncle Diomedes on a quest with no battles worthy of honor?"

"I wouldn't have thought it of the great Odysseus, either."

"We are older now and have better learned when to fight and when not."

"You have your scars, and that you have new ones says either that you choose badly or that you covet the honor for yourself."

"Knowing your birth, the gods would not have put you in our path unless they had battles for you. As for this scar, you'd be welcome to it, but you'd better keep that handsome young face nice and clean for the girls."

"The only girl I want will take only a man with scars, and she'll probably have a few of her own."

So romantic, young folk, Odysseus thought—Achilles had probably never seen a goddess, even his grandmother, and he'd never see a goddess with a scar, nor turn down one without scars. "Fight well and earn them, then, and make the other fellow pay for his."

"I intend to."

"Do you want to row some more, or will you sleep?"

"Sleep for now, I think." Achilles, full of drive and will-fulness, could no longer fight off the deep, ready sleep that shields youth from the insomnia of middle age. Despite his desire to sound brave and independent, it fell over him like a wave as the Eos' first breath of life sighed over the horizon. Odysseus patted the youth on the shoulder, covered him with a blanket, and sought a jug of wine and his customary seat in the bow of the ship, where he drank his way to fitful but rosy dreams of a blond-haired woman with a wistful smile.

The gods had finally turned the wind against them, probably to give them time to still their eagerness and prepare for Latium, and the heroes needed nearly two days of strong rowing to draw themselves north off the coast of Aeneas' city, where they expected and more than half wanted at least a shower of arrows for their pains. Rain had begun early on the second day, and the waves kicked like Pegasus, tossing even their sturdy ship and roiling beneath them. Thrasymedes had warned them to stay well off the shore. Achilles refused to sleep, hoping to get a look at whatever the Latinized Trojans had built. Diomedes sat with him in the starboard prow, and even Odysseus slept with his one eye open. The others dozed uneasily, allowing the rowing to Calydoneus' steady sailors. Night huffed and smoked about them in a thin, stinging, steady spray.

Beneath the dead eye Odysseus dreamed.

He heard through the pounding waves the singing, distant, sensual, alluring, of Sirens.

Who better than Odysseus knew that sound? Gentle, warm, smoothly passionate, a musky sound between a grunt and a sigh, a soft *O* before heaving billows, that will draw his manhood right through a man's cloak seeking through the air, priapus-like, its fulfillment, a sound as old as men and women, older, the sound light and darkness must have made when they met before the birth of time, stroking, moving in rhythm, engulfing—

Odysseus woke instantly, hearing, he thought, Athena—he saw nothing, but leapt to his feet, placing them wide apart against the rolling of the deck, until he could get his bearings. He spotted Idomeneus dozing, safely covered from the rain and wind, and dashed for him. Orestes appeared before him out of the gloom with his eyes wide as moons and his index fingers thrust knuckle-deep in his ears.

"Wake up, old Ido: we may be too late."

"What, are you joking? Where are we?"

"No time to waste. Wake everyone. I feel us being pulled toward shore. Listen carefully, or rather don't listen carefully: if you hear anything that sounds like singing, stop your ears with whatever you have handy. Stir Dio and tell him to drive the sailors to row for their lives."

"For their lives?"

Before Idomeneus could ask a word more, Odysseus had returned with a jug of beeswax, which he began heating at the fire they always kept going amidships.

In seconds Diomedes appeared at his side.

"I have time to say this once: this stuff is good for more than just coating the hull. We must get every man's ears filled with this wax so no one can hear sound."

At that instant Diomedes' head jerked. Odysseus heard, too, the merest hint of low voices: female, sensual, chanting. Burning his hand, Odysseus jerked the jug from the fire.

"This will have to do. We'll dig it out somehow later. I realize we have no time for rowing now. Risk foundering if necessary, but get every man and boy here on deck, if you want to live."

—Norns, Odysseus, goddesses of the North who hold in their hands both fate and fury. Will you sleep and fail me for their deadly love?

"Athena!"

—Too soon for you to tire, my resourceful one, and bury yourselves in the sea. They prepare a whirlpool for you. You may yet survive, though you will pay a price. Take care: they are not your gods, but the Norns have power.

Before he could question her, the voice had gone.

Diomedes and Idomeneus were lining up everyone on the deck. Without rowers steadily at the paces, the boat shook and drifted east, a strong current pulling her.

The wind that drew the current kept the voices from the coast soft, barely audible—Odysseus' hope for salvation and fear of destruction lay in that wind.

The men shifted awkwardly, their heads turning from the direction of the shore to their feet and back again.

"Orestes, my lad: sing your song!" Odysseus pulled one of Orestes' fingers free. "Sing, son, with all your might!"

Orestes smiled wildly, nodded his head, and began to sing:

> Frère Jacques, Frère Jacques,
> Dormez-vous? Dormez-vous?
> Sonnez les matines, sonnez la sirena,
> din-din-don, din-din don!

"Sing, everyone sing!" Odysseus yelled. "Sing with Orestes, sing your desires! Sing as loudly as you can!"

Quickly but roughly, one-by-one Odysseus filled each man's ears with wax as the remainder tried to catch Orestes' song and sing along. Had they enough voice to drown out the Norns?

Odysseus himself joined the song with his rumbling baritone, stuffing the wax painfully, then yanking the next man forward. He placed gobs of the sticky wax in the hands of Idomeneus and Diomedes, who helped him fill ear after ear. When they had filled their own, and each had removed a finger from an ear of Orestes' and nodded to him, Odysseus took the last of the wax and stuffed his own ears until even the sound of the surf turned into no more than arrhythmic percussion.

He looked about with a sigh of relief. Then he saw Achilles, looking pale, walking toward them, but with his eyes fixed on the shore, as its outline emerged into sight in the distance far above the whirling water.

Odysseus could just read the boy's lips as Achilles turned toward his comrades and spoke: they want me!

Not you, old man, but me—they find me beautiful, more beautiful than my grandfather, and they love me, me! And they will give me victory, victory over that escaped Trojan, Aeneas. What we have all sought, I shall win!

In a flash Odysseus saw the horrified look of recognition in the eyes of Diomedes and Idomeneus. Odysseus gestured to Idomeneus and Antilochus, and the two men dashed the sailors back to their oars. Even as their rowing began to steady the ship and resist its flight eastward into the maelstrom growing beside them, Odysseus and Diomedes caught Achilles just before he could leap over the starboard bow into the raging current.

In the raging swirl of misty air Odysseus could see, as if floating above the current a spear's throw away, the hydraheads of a scylla: she swam, hungry sea-sister of the beast who had so horribly consumed his men years before.

Grasping Achilles with one hand, Odysseus used his free hand to clear one ear of beeswax. Immediately the Norns' song filled his brain, drove him nearly mad to leap himself.

—Come, men of Middle-Earth Sea, come and have me! Come, too, and win from your enemy all you seek of glory! His kingdom may be yours, from its towers to its floors, with the world's veneration, yours and your sons' for generations, with more gold than you can carry, and the golden-haired girl for you alone to marry!

Odysseus gripped Achilles with his legs in a wrestler's hold and with both hands grabbed the rail—he could barely keep himself from leaping.

He had once heard the Sirens' song and, tied by his crew to the mast, survived it. This song, too, had a strange, rhythmic, foreign power, different, but nearly irresistible: prophetic, fateful, luring—but Odysseus could feel underneath it a pulse of horror. The song promised what he wanted, to subdue escaped Trojans, Aeneas most of all, and to find the golden-haired beauty of his visions, but beneath, perhaps by Athena's gift or Apollo's, he heard the note of irony, of threat and death.

"Hear me, brave but foolish Achilles! The voices call you not to love, but to death! Resist them, as would your father and grandfather! Show your heroism now!"

Achilles writhed, struggling to free himself of the heroes' grip.

A wave breaking over the side of the rail sent the ship tipping sideways and thrust Odysseus, Diomedes, and Achilles in a tangle in the center of the deck. While Diomedes clung to Achilles with all his might, Odysseus disentangled, found Philoctetes to help with Achilles, and dashed to the head of the rowers. He could see the ship drawing closer to a great whirlpool turning slowly but irrevocably between them and the shore.

He stood before the men, whose foreheads glowed with a sickening pallor, now in a raging storm, and he pantomimed heroic rowing. He dashed to each man and boy, urging them with his fiery eye to row with the last thread of energy in them.

—Hear us, Odysseus: you need but kill Aeneas, and she shall be yours, the girl you seek, lithe and supple, and all the Latin beauties with her! Come to us, come with us, and you shall have her as you shall have us.

Fixing his mind, Odysseus himself grabbed an oar and rowed with all his might, praying to Athena and Apollo to clear his mind. He opened his throat and his lungs and belted out Orestes' meaningless, foreign song:

> Frère Jacques, Frère Jacques,
> Dormez-vous? Dormez-vous?

The rain pelted his eye so he could barely see, and his heart wept for the boy Achilles.

Just as the ship began to sway hard starboard and twist into the maelstrom, the rowers with titanic effort jerked it free of the current's death-grip, and the ship bolted forward with what seemed like a leap.

Odysseus could hear the scream of the Norns, as though they had been cheated of their prey by something loathsome and stronger than they.

—Hero, do not disappoint us! We long for you!

He rose from his oar and continued to lash the sailors with gestures, exhorting them not to flag, but to row till their sinews burst.

Idomeneus, Antilochus, Thrasymedes, Dictys each joined the rowers, spelling the spent sailors, working with the recollection of their lost youth.

They rowed until the Norns' screech disappeared in a fillip of wind, and the rain calmed to gentle droplets, washing the sweat from the limbs of the weary companions. Morning's first vermillion brought color back to fevered faces.

As soon as he saw them clear of danger, Odysseus realized that every man who had heard even a hint of the Norns' song had had an erection—every man except himself. That worried him: was it a gift from the gods or a curse?

Odysseus bounded back amidships. He saw Achilles huddled to himself, the men beside him with hands on his shoulders, the boy rocking back and forth, his wet hair thrown back and his eyes wild. His lips shaped a soundless howl, and his body moved more like a mechanical thing than of breathing flesh.

Odysseus crouched beside Diomedes, who looked over at him, pulling the foul wax from his ears and straining to hear. "Clear?" he asked.

Odysseus nodded. "And what about the boy?"

"I fear we've lost him, not the body, but the wits."

They had passed Latium without the firing of an arrow or the glint of a sword, Odysseus realized with a twinge of regret. Then he realized he owed the gods a debt that he could even think such thoughts, that the Northern Sirens had no power to steal them, as they had from Achilles. He would have joyed to take Aeneas' city, even to see it, but the gods had not given him that adventure, so he had to accept what they were willing to give.

And accept what they intended to exact?

You will pay a price, the goddess had said, and Odysseus realized that Achilles was to pay that price for the elder hero's sloth and for the Achaians' persistence in their quest.

Troy continued to exact her revenge, and no man, not even the great Odysseus, could free himself of it until events had sped their course.

Philoctetes covered Achilles with a blanket, but if anyone tried to talk to him, the boy pushed him fiercely away and continued his maniacal rocking.

Soon Orestes sat down behind him and joined his rocking motion. Together the two looked like compact winches drawing endlessly upward an enormous, invisible sail.

The rowing moved slowly, in easy shifts, and gradually all the crew filtered back, glanced at the mad boy, took food and water, and shuffled off.

No one, not even that most articulate of men, had a word to say.

A breeze pushed them north by northwest, but provisions dwindled, and they traveled two days before they spotted land ahead off the port bow.

Despite silence from the gods, all agreed that they must try to dock and seek supplies, though they had no clear idea of what or whom they would find.

"Where are we, Thrasy?" Diomedes asked.

"Hmm—I guess, you know, but considering how far we have come, I think we must have found the coast of the island they call Corsica. A larger island sits to the south, but I judge that this wind has swept us past it. We should I think find safety if not welcome here. I don't know that anywhere short of Olympos we shall find a physician for the boy."

Gathering their strength and resolve, the heroes settled on a point to land. Diomedes stayed to watch over Achilles, and Philoctetes sought to tend him as he could. Odysseus with Thrasymedes, Antilochus, and Idomeneus formed a small embassy to seek the help of the locals.

Where they had landed, they found the island barren. They set sail, and on a second landing found a village, but no provisions. Thrasymedes, skilled in languages as well as lands, got from the people there the way to a larger settlement. With their third stop the Achaians found friendly greeting from speakers of their own language, a colony founded generations ago from Mycenae.

There the people had heard no news beyond the conclusion of the war at Troy. They wept at Dictys' tales of Agamemnon's death and the trials of his son and at Odysseus' accounts of a long and painful journey home. The heroes remained silent about their quest, and their hosts, happy for the presence and stories of those close to their own folk, and legendary heroes at that, showed the courtesy not to ask.

A local chieftain told the heroes of a settlement farther north in the island of folk who called themselves *Galli* and who spoke a barbarous language. "They tell," he said, "of the land of their origin, north, but farther west than north, across the sea to the mouth of a great river, the entrance to which—how shall I say it delicately?—takes the shape, from shifting soil extruded from its banks, of a woman's hips, open."

"No need for delicacy among us," Odysseus said, chuckling, and noting again the odd image of the rivermouth. "How many days, would you say, to sail it?"

"Depending on wind and weather and the strength of your sailors, five days or more if you're lucky. You have, I would guess, a hundred leagues to sail. And you will get on better there if you take time to learn a bit of their tongue before you arrive, if you wish to receive a reception of other than spears," their host responded.

"I have heard," Thrasymedes said hopefully, "of a Greek colony called Nikaea founded somewhere near that place."

The companions spent nearly a month on Corsica, meeting with the Galli, restoring their strength, collecting provisions, and ministering to young Achilles.

When they departed, much to their regret, they left Achilles behind, at the home of a pious physician proud of his heritage and of his Mycenaean medicine.

"I will cure him, gods willing," the old man told Odysseus, "but the other, Orestes you call him? I wouldn't try to cure him for all Troy's gold. The light of the gods dances on his brow, as it does in odd moments with you, my one-eyed friend."

The night before the heroes left Corsica, Odysseus dreamed of the blond-haired girl with the mystical smile.

He awoke with an erection so stiff it was almost painful. He sighed with relief and rose to load the ship for Nikaea.

6

FROM NIKAEA TO THE RHINE

For the first time since they'd begun their journey, the companions met bad weather as they sailed west around the northern tip of Corsica. While rain and a west wind slowed them, it dulled their spirits less than did the loss of Achilles. Diomedes particularly felt unhappy about leaving him behind, since Neoptolemos had given the boy into his care, but he agreed they had little choice.

"He was five times the rower of any of Calydoneus' lads," said Philoctetes, who had developed a particular affection for Achilles.

"Five times any of us," Odysseus added. "But we must let him heal. Maybe Corsican medicine and the troubles we can spare him will help make him whole again."

In the pocket of his tunic Odysseus covered an herb he had got from the Corsican physician: *oreganos,* he had called it, touting its virtue as a medicine and a spice. He had a sense, as if Athena were speaking to him, that it would come in handy ahead.

In the evenings Idomeneus told stories of sunny days in southern Italy, and Dictys recounted what he had heard of the strange folk of the distant corners of the world, a race of people who had only one leg but hopped about with the speed of runners, another who wore their faces in their breasts, and yet another of variable gender, so that sometimes they might be men and sometimes women—the heroes laughed at that, all but Odysseus, who in his travels had seen far stranger sights than any mere stories might tell.

In four days they'd rowed no more about fifty leagues, but finally spotted land a-starboard. Heavy winds kept them asea, and they saw nothing that looked like their appointed landing. Provisions held. They fed on the dried meat of some unfamiliar game bird, some bland, fleshy fruits, chewy bread, and a golden-yellow wine which the Corsicans said they got from Italians north across the sea, and despite the rain, the fishing remained good.

Thrasymedes had made drawings from what the Corsicans could tell him of the Gallic coast, but no one knew of a port shaped "like a woman's hips" or of exactly where they could find the reputed Greek colonists. Even the oldest sailors among the Corsicans hadn't seen such a thing; it must sit farther west, they'd said, if any such things existed at all. Perhaps the gods had merely given them a riddle to slow their course. Poseidon had certainly sent them unduly rough seas, and Apollo hadn't shone fresh light on them since they'd departed Corsica.

For two more misty days they rowed along the coast, following its meandering course, until everyone began to feel thoroughly drenched and irritable. In the early evening of the sixth day, Odysseus sat sulking in his usual spot in the bow of the ship. The golden-haired girl no longer appeared in his dreams. His mind itched, and his legs felt drawn and sore. He began to wonder if they should simply land, return south, and have a go at Aeneas, just for something to do.

Odysseus noticed that, some time before, the wind had shifted and was blowing with its accustomed force, but out of the south. The rain had stopped, and the air smelled clean.

Then he looked up and saw Orestes standing before him.

"Ho-ha, he-he, hee!"

"What is it, Orestes, lad?"

"Ho-ho-ha-he-he-he-he-he!"

"Have you seen something?" Odysseus asked hopefully. "Tell me now!"

"Father One and Father Two, both will wish to enter through; all like fathers, One-Two-Three, through we'll go and in we'll be! Ha-ha-ha-ha-ha." Orestes pointed forward, in the direction they were now sailing, for a sturdy breeze was pushing them forward and for the first time in days easing the burden of the rowers.

Odysseus steadied himself on cramped legs and ambled as quickly as he could, following Orestes to where Diomedes already stood, gazing ahead, in the prow of the ship.

"Wonderful!" Philoctetes said, joining them.

"Astonishing," Diomedes added.

"Just as in the dream," Idomeneus whispered.

"Bless the gods and their visions: I couldn't believe it if I weren't seeing it," Odysseus muttered.

> Me love is faren in londe—
> Alas, where has she go?
> And I so sare for me bond—
> Old man, may I find her so?

Orestes sang, again in a tongue strange to the Greeks, had they been paying attention to the words. But they were looking dead ahead, as the ship gained speed toward the coast to the north.

They saw before them two jetties with a narrow opening between them curling inland. They fell off into the sea from curving, gently rising headlands round as buttocks. The land ahead, which must have formed the banks of a river, curved like the small of a woman's back, as if she lay on her belly, sunning herself, with her legs extending out into the surf. Far on, a blue bank of clouds rose like shoulders, with a darker bank farther on that fell over them like long, wavy, blue-black hair. As they looked, the red sky of evening spread outward from the west to the north—the southern sky remained obscure, passing into nondescript grey clouds.

The crimson rays of the setting sun struck the currents and the banks where the odd mouth of the river puckered southward, and the rays shot silvery-scarlet heavenward, leaping from the banks like shimmering legs.

"Philo. Philo!" said Odysseus, shaking his companion. "Get the rowers busy. Even with this wind, we're entering the mouth—though it doesn't look like a mouth—of the river, and we won't get in there but under our own power."

"Oh, all right," said Philoctetes, reluctantly drawing himself away from the stunning vista.

The men stared at the land and the sky, moved inwardly.

> Dip and stroke, dip and stroke;
> Turn her over and kiss her twice.
> Dip and stroke, dip and stroke;
> How very nice!

So Orestes sang.

"Maybe he shouldn't be looking at this?" Diomedes offered.

"Whatever the Furies left him, he's old enough to be a man, and he'll have to grow up some time," answered Odysseus. He noticed in the eastern sky the evening star had risen, glowing dull red. "Mars has given us his signs, as the gods said he should; may he preserve the lad and those undoomed among us."

With everyone's eyes fixed dead ahead, the heroes sailed up the mouth of the river that in ages to come the Franks would name "Rhone." Odysseus thought he heard the river goddess sigh as they entered.

The crew rowed gently for a time, and the ship moved slowly but steadily upriver.

They hadn't got far when Odysseus pulled out of his reverie with a start. "Am I a fool, or does the river look undefended?"

"I'm wondering the same thing," said Diomedes.

Then Antilochus joined them. "I've seen, I think, some men along the shoreline. Look closely, you can see them, like sentries, posted periodically. There's one: I believe he's signaling ahead."

Odysseus could see him then, too, and others as well. The river stretched more broadly than it appeared as one entered from the sea, but ahead he noticed that it narrowed, and on either side a wooden levee jutted into the current, suggesting that ships must dock regularly there.

The sun was sinking rapidly, and as the darkness loomed, Odysseus, despite his aging eyes, could see numbers of men, who looked to be armed with bows, angling for the levees.

"We have company now, Ody," Diomedes remarked, quietly.

"I noticed. They have no particular reason to believe we aren't pirates, though perhaps travelers regularly row these waters unmolested."

"Since we have no way of knowing, I suggest you do something," Idomeneus added. "If the Corsicans are right, these people are Greeks, or once were."

Odysseus walked the length of the ship, ordered the rowers to proceed smoothly but slowly, observed the movements on the shore, then stood for a moment in thought over the amidships fire. Just as he addressed a prayer to Athena, an arrow whizzed past him and over the port side.

—You must speak to them!

"Will they understand my speech?"

—You have no choice but to try. Remember: they were Greeks once, and you are still. Show them what it means to be Greek.

Not waiting for a second volley, Odysseus took a torch, leapt to the railing of the prow, drew a breath, held the torch up before him, and prepared to call out.

Another arrow flew past his head, just grazing his hair, and disappeared off the starboard prow.

"People of Gallia, hear me: we are not pirates, nor enemies, nor ghosts, nor whatever you may fear us. Know, if you can understand my words, that I am no other than Odysseus, King of Ithaka, son of Laertes, son of Sisyphus, messenger of Athena, Apollo, and Poseidon, builder of the Great Horse, sailor of the seas. We intend no harm, and the gods come with us. If you believe in the gods, desist, for you assault us at your peril."

"Only the great Odysseus," Diomedes whispered, "would threaten bowmen he can't see in the dark. If they've ever heard of you, Ody, they'll either back off now or shoot the lot of us."

Odysseus stood firm, holding the torch above his head. The rowers, frightened, had slowed nearly to a stop, waiting. Odysseus wished then that they had Achilles with them; he alone would have rowed with a will to outrun the arrows.

Odysseus believed he saw, on the portside bank, archers raising their bows.

A hiss penetrated the night air, as if a hundred men at once had caught their breath, and all eyes turned skyward to watch a shooting star, brighter than anything but the rising moon, race overhead from east to west.

Silence filled the air as all movement came to a standstill. Not even a breeze dared interrupt the darkening quiescence.

"What sort of man would call himself 'Odysseus'? He must be either a liar or a fool." The voice came faint but clear from the starboard bank in heavily accented but understandable Greek.

"What other man would call himself *Odysseus?*"

"You're not the first, nor the fifth. The rest have died or wish they had."

"Let us stop to speak with you."

"Who goes with you?"

"Hear their names: Diomedes, Idomeneus, Philoctetes, Antilochus and Thrasymedes and Dictys. We have others. Those names perhaps you have heard."

"As you may have heard them and taken them for your own."

"Speak with us, and if we don't satisfy you, we will return whence we came."

"If you don't satisfy us, we will return you to the gods who made you. Land a-starboard, and disembark alone and unarmed."

"Agreed."

Diomedes whispered to Odysseus, "Should we arm? If they give us trouble, I'd rather die fighting, and who knows that we may not fight our way out? We don't know their strength or their mettle."

"Arm the others. Tell Thrasymedes to come with me. Keep Orestes back—they're unlikely to know what to make of him, and we don't want to make them nervous. They just may turn out friends, and where we're headed, we'll need all the friends we can get—and all the advice they can give."

With the help of the men on the bank, who appeared out of the growing darkness in intimidating numbers, they moored the ship, and Odysseus descended onto the levee, followed by Thrasymedes.

"I said 'alone,' " demanded the voice who had called to Odysseus from shore.

"Who demands of me?" Odysseus asked.

"I am called Demos, and I serve as Guardian of the shores here, river and sea."

"Demos, then, the man who follows me is Thrasymedes, younger son of Nestor, great king of Pylos and counselor of Agamemnon at Troy. Unless you are Trojans, you have no quarrel with him or me. He knows how to draw lands so that we may find them more easily in our travels, and he counsels me in affairs of business and travel. Will you allow me counsel or require that I speak alone?"

"All the stories say that Odysseus needed no counsel, not even that of the gods."

"Even I have learned that a man cannot do without the counsel of the gods, no, nor in this new age of good men as well."

"And how do we know you are good men?" said Demos, stepping forward amidst a dozen other men who emerged from the shadows, lighting their torches, surrounding Odysseus and Thrasymedes, and behind them stood many more armed, but with swords sheathed.

"You don't yet, but I believe I can convince you, if you let me. I have a gift from those in Corsica who, I think, are your family, and I have much to share of news of the world."

"O, a good man is hard to find, and breaking them up is hard to do," sang Orestes, who unnoticed had leapt down from the side of the ship and followed in Thrasymedes shadow.

Hearing him, the swordsmen quickly drew their weapons.

"And who is this wild man, cursed by the gods: speak quickly!"

"Not cursed, but blessed by Apollo and Athena, his name is unimportant, but he brings with him luck and the gods' blessings and certainly no harm."

Orestes crept forward and placed his hands on Odysseus' shoulders. "Father Two speaks truth to you; hear and follow, as I do," he chirped. The swordsmen surrounded them as they spoke.

"You are in no position to do much harm, and I can see little good that pirates and madmen can do and little likelihood of their being blessed."

"Then you risk nothing but a passing hour of the evening to speak with Odysseus and his friends."

"I have never heard that Odysseus had lost an eye."

"You shall hear of that and more."

Odysseus heard shuffling amidst the crowd, which soon parted to allow another man to pass. He walked up alongside Demos and addressed Odysseus.

"I understand we have distinguished guests. Will you have a bowl of wine with me, strangers?"

"We will, gladly," answered Odysseus. "May I ask with whom I'll be drinking?"

"I am Herodotus, governor here. Getting wind of such distinguished names, I thought I should come to see for myself. Come, Demos, I believe we are safe enough. Is that not so—Odysseus?"

"True indeed, Lord Governor. To ease his mind, may I present to Demos this gift of the Corsicans, an herb of value as medicine and food. I think you will find it quite pleasant. They call it there *oreganos*. I present it respectfully to men who are Corsican, Greek, and also Gallic?"

"It does indeed grow there," Demos said, "as my family have shown me, for I have tasted it in my own youthful visits. You have guessed right, Odysseus or whoever you are. Let's see if your luck will remain so good."

"Come with me to my hall, and we will talk. Do you always take the wild lad with you, Odysseus?"

"Apparently he comes along when he will, at Apollo's will, or Athena's, rather than mine."

"Let him come then."

"Lord Governor, are you people not the Nikaeans?" Odysseus asked.

"Right again," answered the governor, "and I'm beginning to think you come here not by luck or ill chance."

"Right yourself, as I will happily explain."

Odysseus and Thrasymedes spent the night speaking with the governor, who had with him his brother, Hesiod, who acted as scribe and recorded all that they said. By morning the heroes had all disembarked and found proper welcome, lodging, and much needed land-rest. They spent the day at leisure among the Nikaeans, except for Odysseus, who recounted their adventures at length to the governor, selecting carefully, lest he tell too much.

By evening, at dinner, Herodotus drew Odysseus aside. "You realize I must ask you, and I hope I don't seem impolite, about your business here. Believe it or not, we do welcome travelers, particularly Greeks, and especially if they have something to offer, but we don't tolerate trouble, and we've been getting a bit of that lately, though usually from the north rather than the south."

"What sort of trouble?"

"Some new kind of worship that's going on up north, well up north apparently, but spreading. We've got only small bands so far, well-armed, but not violent, though they acted with great assurance and insistence."

Odysseus questioned Herodotus until he felt fairly sure that what he heard referred to the Trojans who had moved north. He hadn't expected the stories to be true, but apparently their power had spread even more thoroughly than Dictys' tales suggested—unusual for stories of that sort, which tend to overstate rather than understate. Finally Herodotus interrupted Odysseus to renew his own question. Odysseus decided he could, and probably must, trust the governor with the truth.

At first Herodotus simply stared incredulously at the hero. Then, when he saw that Odysseus' expression didn't change, he began to laugh, first a chuckle, then repeated gales of open-mouthed head-wagging, but with little sound in an apparent effort to suppress undue attention.

"You must in fact be Odysseus, either himself joking or a madman who believes himself Odysseus and able to turn Olympos upside-down. How many men have you?"

"We started with eight, not counting the sailors, but we have lost one."

Again came the gales of quiet laughter until Odysseus thought the man would choke himself. "Have you had any thought, my good fellow, of how many men you face, not just how many men, but how many armies? If half of what I hear is right, you couldn't begin to fight them with a thousand Odysseuses, each as wily as the first."

"Have you ever wondered how many men waited in the Great Horse at Troy?"

ODYSSEUS ON THE RHINE

Herodotus kept silence, again his eyes growing wider.

"Far fewer than you think. How big do you suppose the horse? Far smaller than you think. Tales inflate the size of men's deeds. Just ask your wife about that."

At first Herodotus began to look angry, then again he broke out into laughter, this time both loud and long. "Only Odysseus could say such things to a governor who with a wink could have him killed. I now believe you are who you say, but surely you must have some plan for meeting an army—they have sailed the World Sea to the far west, no? And they will meet you in the north, where you will mount a naval expedition against the Troyans, you wily one?"

Hearing the words from Herodotus, Odysseus felt for the first time the absurdity of what they were doing, a handful of middle-aged men and a couple of mad boys sailing north to meet the greatest enemy since Troy, maybe a greater enemy yet, if any of the stories held true. Why had that not struck him before?

"We left home, lord governor, to find and fight Trojans, and that is exactly what we intend to do."

Again the laughter . . . Odysseus waited, wondering what he must say to Herodotus, but first to himself. Herodotus broke the silence.

"Then Odysseus or not, you must be mad."

"If I am mad," said Odysseus, "then the gods are mad, since more than any time in my life I do their bidding."

"Well then, my mad friend with your mad gods, let us eat, and then you will sleep as long as you wish, since I have kept you a night and a day, and then we will talk again. Either I must dissuade you, or I must help you—either way, apparently, the gods will bless me: what will happen must happen according to their will."

EDWARD S. LOUIS

"Don't you fear the northern men, if you help me?"

"No, they will present no danger to us for a hundred years. Their scouts come, and a few of their traders, but from what we have heard, they concentrate their power far to the north and perhaps to the west. They will come here, but not in our lifetimes, though you, Odysseus, would seem to live the lifetime of many men, ha! Now rest, and tomorrow we will begin to see what we may do with you."

Waking or sleeping, Odysseus began to turn his mind this way and that for a plan, but how to plan before one has even seen the enemy?

The heroes stayed with the Nikaeans for a week. They traded their ship for provisions and a riverboat more suitable for inland travel. One of Demos' best men rowed north with them to the marches of Nikaean lands, and his brother Hesiod went along as well, recording their travels and stories. Herodotus had warned them they must proceed slowly. They would have to take time, learn the languages and the folk of the north, and wait out the long winter, unlike anything the folk of the Middle-Earth sea had ever seen.

Those the Corsicans called *Galli* represented many and varied peoples, with different customs and tongues. Dressed like their neighboring Nikaeans, the heroes accompanied their allies on scouting and trading missions to the north and east. Thrasymedes drew the lands they covered and sketched those about which he could learn something among other traders. Antilochus learned languages rapidly and picked up the fluid, lilting, nasal tongue of the Galli and the harsher, guttural tones of the Alpines, as they reached a mountain range greater than anything they had imagined.

"The caps," said Dictys, "white as an African's teeth or the eyeballs of a healthy child . . ."

102

"Surely the gods must live there—look at those peaks, rising like waves the size of islands! They must make but their winter home on Olympos," Philoctetes said.

"Beware blasphemy," Antilochus cautioned. "The gods have saved us thus far, at least most of us, and I shouldn't want to lose their blessings now."

"I was just speaking," Philoctetes replied.

"I would wish you to speak cautiously, Philo," Antilochus snorted.

"Look for yourself is all I'm saying," Philoctetes answered petulantly. Before dropping into silence with the rest, he added, "And by the way, has Odysseus decided on a plan yet? Has he even thought of one?"

Seeing the Alps, the heroes knew they must move west if not south for the winter. They camped as far north along the Rhone as they could, allowing for the vicissitudes of weather, stilling the itch for fighting with games, learning, and building, teaching the locals what they could and learning from them what they could. Some of the men found women, and by the time the first hints of spring scented the air and emerged from the ground, Odysseus had begun to wonder if he should ever get his comrades out of the rich river valleys and gentle green slopes of the Gallic land. They were growing older, he could feel it, and their travels into the snowy villages to the north had taught him some of what they needed to know: that the Trojans, called *Aesir* even that far south, had gained power and spread their influence, so that the mention of them brought respect and fear to the southern marches of their domains. Hesiod had left them just before the snows, which came that winter only in patchy showers, but before he went he warned them that they must plan if they wished to have any hope of achieving their quest.

"And you, friend Hesiod," Odysseus had said, "should sail to the south, beyond the island of the Corsicans, to your ancestors, the true Greeks, and tell them your stories of the gods and of the last of the race of heroes who sought the Northmen and rid them of their false gods."

"Some day I will, Ody of the One Eye, for I shall live a very long time" called Hesiod from a riverboat's bow, catching a cold current south to his brother's lands. "Tell the Northmen, when you get there, of the true gods. If anyone can make them believe, you can!"

"If we have our way," Diomedes said, "they will meet the gods before we do, at least those of the Underworld. We should oblige them to bring us a full report."

Odysseus heard Hesiod calling from the distance, as his boat passed quickly south.

"You must visit the Northern Sibyl, the Lorelei!"

"The what?"

"Lorelei! I have seen her in a vision. She will tell you what you must do. Remember: Lorelei!" The old man called again to the heroes until his boat had passed beyond hearing.

"What did he say?" Diomedes asked. "I couldn't hear plainly, or the words didn't make sense: something about a sibyl?"

"Who? Woo, me oh my, Lorelei, Northern Sibyl, without a quibble. Hear her words, and do her deeds; Rhinemaiden's lips shall spell our needs!" Orestes spun three times on his heel, then threw his arms out to his sides, cocked his head, and said, "Ah."

"What in Hades is a *Lorelei?*" asked Diomedes.

"I don't know yet," answered Odysseus, "but I do know that now we have a plan."

"Thank the gods for that boy's ear," said Antilochus.

And with the spring Odysseus remembered Hesiod and roused the sleepy heroes to turn north. They reluctantly said good-bye to the last of their Nikaean allies— Idomeneus had found a beautiful, buxom, violet-eyed widow with two children and was nearly ready to settle down with them and call an end to adventures.

First they followed the Rhone to its source. There they sold their boat, turned overland to the west, traveled as hunters and traders, seeking hints of a sibyl called "Lorelei." Following traces of the cult of the Trojan Northmen, they fared as far as a great lake with large settlements. From its north shore opened a waterway that the locals called simply "The Great Water," but that traders from the north called "Rhine." From one of them Odysseus heard a strange legend of a sibyl, called by the northern folk *volvu,* but in her own land known, he said, as Lorelei. They would find her at a place, the trader said, called *Ascerbergium,* but she was not, he said, a sibyl.

"She is a Norn, those people there say, and few will dare pass that part of the river except in the broad sunshine of mid-day. And even then men sail by with their eyes fixed on the water and their ears plugged with beeswax," the man said. He told Odysseus a dozen other stories, which Dictys duly recorded in memory, in exchange for the last of the heroes' southern wine, but only that one held Odysseus' attention.

Having become skilled over the winter in the hunting of that region, the heroes again traded their gear for a boat, and with no delay they sailed up the Rhine with the blessing of good weather and the renewed hope of fulfilling their quest.

7

LORELEI

The heroes sailed as rapidly as they could, allowing for the caution of not raising too many questions as they traveled. They let Antilochus do much of their speaking for them, though by now Odysseus and Dictys were nearly as handy with the northern language. They had for caution's sake taken to keeping weapons near at hand, but not in plain view.

The river, as they followed it north, twisted and curled like a serpent among beautiful woods and hills that smelled of fresh growth and cool air.

Wherever they went, they aimed to keep Orestes from public view as much as they could—they couldn't easily suppress him, and they wouldn't, and probably couldn't, tie him in the ship, but when they let him, he created a stir with his chirpings, singings, and antics, such that people would offer them provisions for the privilege of watching or listening to him. With a twist or cock of his head he would hum an unfamiliar tune or sing in a language none of the heroes had heard before, as if the gods sent him music from afar. Odysseus feared that the boy would gain too great repute, and their quest should get unearthed despite his care, but he could do little to change what must be, and by then he himself had come to find the boy's skirlings too entertaining for him to try to squelch them.

When they could, they inquired discreetly of passersby about the Lorelei. And as they traveled farther north, fewer comments they could get. Most people would say little, turn their faces aside, hold out two fingers toward them in some sort of magical gesture, and hurry away. Even crusty old sailing men who must have known the river better than their own veins would shake their heads, warn the travelers, and say little.

Odysseus had difficulty believing all those lands inhabited by superstitious cowards, so he began to gird himself for another crisis—as much as anyone can.

He also placed carefully amidships a pot of cloth balls impregnated with beeswax, in case the Lorelei should prove anything like her sisters who sang off the coast of Latium.

For some days they rowed the river safely, moving gradually north as the moon waxed clearly and boldly. Most boats, seeing the swarthy southerners, passed them as quickly as possible, or sailors moving south offered only cold nods of minimal greeting.

On the night of the full moon they met their first resistance. Keeping a watchful distance until a cloudbank covered the bright moon, a ship with a sharp prow with a tall, curving, dragon-like animal curling high above dove suddenly toward them out of the darkness and through the thickening waves that separated them. They could see that rowers had thick-muscled necks and shoulders; the men who led them wore leather jerkins and long, cascading coats of animal hides and tall, almost conical hats. The Northmen saluted the Achaians with each man on the foredeck holding one hand high and open above his head and the other grasping a torch.

Orestes, seeing the signal, returned it by whooping like a tropical bird and holding both arms rigidly above his head.

107

The boat pulled up with a rush beside that of the heroes. Antilochus held brief parley with them, then consulted with his brother; Odysseus picking up what he could of it, realized that the Northmen intended to board and joined his comrades at the rails.

"They wish, I believe, to conscript our boat for their mission south," Antilochus said, his brother nodding agreement.

"Tell them," Odysseus said, "that we travel north, trading, under the blessing of the gods."

Antilochus relayed the message, and the man who apparently led the northern party immediately grew heated in his speech, gesturing commandingly and menacingly. The man speaking and his cohorts had the look of seers, though they stood steady enough on legs trained for the water, and the rowers looked like relatively seasoned fighters or at least men set in their commission.

With a nod, Odysseus signaled Diomedes, who disappeared to collect and prepare the others.

"Tell them, Antilochus," called Odysseus in his own most commanding tones, "that we respect their mission, but that we will not be waylaid. We wish them good-night and safe journey." Odysseus looked about, could not spot Orestes, but saw his other comrades ready.

Odysseus could see immediately that the answer Antilochus rendered them did not satisfy the Northmen. In fact, the leader with an abrupt gesture brought men from their oars, and the others on the prow drew weapons of several sorts, from maces to cats-o-nine-tails to axes that shown silvery in the moonlight.

The Greeks did not wait to learn if they intended only to intimidate or to strike. Odysseus threw a dagger directly into the heart of their spokesman, felling him backward, then sprung for the rail to meet the next with his short sword. Diomedes had pulled a longsword and was in two bounds past Odysseus onto the other boat, cutting with practiced control.

From the darkness Orestes swung on a rope he had thrown over the Northmen's dragon figurehead, sweeping in an arc over the enemy ship, raising a long, thin wail and with a whip lashing the rowers who had rushed to the prow, snapping them from their feet. He seemed to fly past them like a harpy, returning again before they could catch their feet.

The other Greeks, all hardened soldiers, giving no quarter, did not wait to have their own boat boarded, but leapt to join the pre-emptive attack on the Northmen, each with his weapon of choice, cutting or striking. Philoctetes, famous spearman, allowed no one closer to him than a spear's length, missing nary a thrust.

The battle ended with little noise and in a few short minutes. Thrasymedes and Antilochus, raised as fishermen on sandy Pylos, had the Northmen who were yet alive wrapped snugly in fishnets. The Achaians hadn't sustained a scratch among them. Odysseus descended on their captives with the cold eye of a man who knows vengeance—and how to prevent the need for it. As well as he could, he spoke in their own language, halting in words, but unyielding in intent.

"Hear me. You have angered your gods. You will take your dead and continue your mission south. You will assault no other boat, you will speak with no others like you or unlike you. When you have reached the Broad Lake in the south, you will burn the bodies, sell your boat, and take other service, never returning here and telling no man or woman what you have seen. The demon who flew at you from our ship will follow you, and if you stint one oar-stroke, he will descend upon you and whip your hides straight to the freezing Lord of Darkness before you can utter a word of prayer. You have got my only warning. Go, now, and bless the gods that we have spared you this once."

With a flick of each wrist he released the captives from their nets, leapt back aboard his own boat, and croaked a call to his rowers to pull with all their strength. The other Greeks had quickly returned to their ship. Odysseus motioned to Diomedes to speed the rowers so they might get out of sight as rapidly as possible, and he remained at the rail, watching the remaining Northmen scramble to their oars and row southward for their lives.

He allowed himself a laugh as Diomedes appeared at his side.

"I needed that," Diomedes said. "We've sat idle too long."

"Yes, and yet we'll be lucky if it doesn't do us more harm than good. We don't yet need a reputation in these regions," Odysseus responded.

"I heard your speech to them. I don't believe Hektor himself could have been kept from rowing away like an Olympian."

"Did you notice something odd about them?" Odysseus asked.

"You mean beside the fact that, despite how tough they looked, they lacked fighting skill?"

"Their eyes."

"What about them?"

"No fear. Surprise, but no fear."

"Hmm. A bad sign."

"Yes, and that's true with what must have been the least of these people we'll be facing. Those poor fellows I suspect can't hold a pocketknife next to the real soldiers we'll find ahead."

"Do you think they really wanted us to worship their gods?"

"I think they were pirates. But we're getting a better sense of how far the influence of their gods extends."

The heroes continued north and heard no whispers of their first battle, much to Odysseus' relief. For a time they passed many fishing boats, until the river turned east, when river and the hilly banks turned nearly barren of signs of human life.

One last boat they met, a small one, with only a fisherman and two younger men who looked to be his sons. As the heroes passed, signaling peaceful greeting according to the northern custom, the older man waved them to stop, then pulled himself alongside the larger craft.

"You come from the south?" he said in an accent different from those the Greeks had heard before.

"Yes," Odysseus replied.

"You travel ahead where the river turns south, then north again, and the mountain turns to gold?"

"We have seen no such place," Antilochus said, "but we intend to follow the river."

"It is a dangerous place. No one safely sails there."

"You say so because you wish no competition in fishing."

"No offense, lords, but you don't look like fishermen to me."

"And what do we appear to you?"

"Not my business to say. From your voices and look I guessed you from the south, not the north. I have seen a boat like yours once, years ago, from the Broad Lake far in the south. I intend no disrespect. I only offer advice to strangers traveling into something of which they may have no knowledge."

"What do you know of it that you can tell us, you and your sons?"

The fisherman paused for a moment, looked at the younger men with a smile.

"Few men will fish here, so we do well. Go farther west, and you will find only soldiers and adventurers—only, I would say, the foolhardy. One may disembark back in the direction you've come, go overland, rejoin the river to the west, then take it north many leagues as far as the Great Water. I've never been there, but have heard."

"And what causes men to fear so much that they will take the trouble to go overland rather than sail a few miles on the river."

"I hear that folk in the south have a fine drink called 'wine.' "

"We have."

"A man may learn much in exchange for a taste of it. Such men as you can take no harm from the likes of my sons and me."

After two bowls of wine the younger men were beginning to snore in a corner, and the father had loosened his tongue to speak as much as he knew.

"Yes, sir, some call it that, *Lorelei,* others just say it's the River Goddess. Stories say that adventurers go there for the gold that shines from the hillside steep as a mountain. They say a voice like that of a woman, seductive, draws men to the spot, brings them ashore, where she devours them, or keeps them as, you'll pardon me, lovers, or leads them into a cave and down through the ground down as far as Hel's frozen lands beneath Middle-Earth, whence they never return, caught forever in ice and wind."

"You don't seem to follow the gods of the other folk of this region."

The fisherman laughed. "When I was young and a bit of

an adventurer myself, before I fathered these boys, I saw some of them riding through. Gods! ha! They were men, all right, not men like me, but like you. I would have called them 'heroes,' but I kept free of them. They gave great gifts of gold and treasure, bade men join them, conscripted them if they wouldn't. I was lucky: I caught a night boat sailing south for the Broad Lake and so kept free of them. Their power begins just north of here, then grows into the lands and seas of the far north, where snow seldom leaves the land and the winter nights, they say, last for all but minutes of every day until cold spring comes."

No, he told them, he had never seen the Lorelei himself, but had heard the first whispering notes of her song. Only the love of his wife had allowed him to scramble away, rowing with all his might—a moment more and he had not got away. About the Trojans he could tell little else, other than the rumors that said all the kings of the north had come under their sway, and more people than not believed them gods. In recent memory only those men had dared the River Goddess, and rumor said even they had not all returned.

"What is that place called, where the River Goddess waits?" Odysseus asked.

"I have heard no one call it by name. This place, ours, off the river to the north, we call 'Rudsheim,' after my own name. The men of the north, though, call it 'Bingen.' Beyond, to the north of that place you seek, blocking the way south to it, stands an old fortress called Ascerbergium."

"You are sure of that name?" Odysseus asked.

"A man doesn't forget an odd name like that. Now you have served me good wine, and I have told what I have to tell. I add only the same warning: don't sail west. Go back, go south, but avoid the River Goddess."

—Go alone, except for Orestes, to hear the Lorelei,

warrior-goddess of the river.

The voice seemed to have come from the fisherman, but he looked as astonished as the others. His sons, who had been drowsing, stood up straight, their eyes staring, and the Greeks felt their skin burning.

"Did you say that, fisherman?" Diomedes said through his teeth.

"Did I say what?" the fisherman asked.

"The voice came from you, but the words weren't yours," Odysseus answered.

"Whose? I've never said such things. What is an Orestes?"

"WHooooooo, who de man? I'm de man, uh-huh, I and you, Father Two," hooted Orestes from a dark corner.

"What's that?" one of the young fishermen exclaimed.

"A spirit who travels with us," Odysseus answered. "I suggest you return to your home for tonight. And when you fish tomorrow, row as far east as you safely can."

When they had gone, Odysseus turned to Diomedes: "That was Apollo, not Athena. I wish I knew the goddess' thought as well."

The heroes sailed until the river turned northeast, then anchored for the night to rest and talk. When dawn's golden eyes opened morning to the world, they sailed cautiously on, then around a sharp curve. Before they turned west, Odysseus saw that every man except for himself and, he decided reluctantly, Orestes, had his ears stopped with waxed cloth.

"Look," Odysseus said to Philoctetes, "how I've embedded a stem in the cloth, tight inside, loose outside. You can pull it out with this when we pass through."

"Remarkable," breathed Philoctetes. "Ody, you should have been a physician."

"I hope neither of us will need more of that today, Philo. Remember what happened to Achilles off Latium."

"We all do," answered Philoctetes. "This time I don't think curiosity will get the best of us—though I wonder what to do about our eyes, if what the fisherman says is right about the mountain of gold."

Suddenly, Odysseus felt a breeze rising; it felt at once both hot and cold. He shivered, and needed an act of will to stop the shivering. The breeze turned into a gentle, throaty feminine voice, singing softly, sensuously notes too soft for words.

"Quick, Philo—not a second to lose." Both men dashed with handfuls of the earplugs. The crew was already beginning to shiver and look to the north as the boat sailed around the bend.

Gold light poured down on the river, bright as the rays of midday sun, falling on the steep hillside that rose up the northern bank.

Odysseus cracked a whip over the heads of the rowers, pointed them on with a look bearing all his power of command. Diomedes and Idomeneus stood beside him, their faces turned pale and their eyes glassy. Diomedes grabbed Idomeneus' arm and motioned to Philoctetes for them all to join the rowers. He led them, motioning an even pace with his fists, then took an oar himself to keep his body busy.

Odysseus, rapt himself, barely noticed Orestes standing rigid at the edge of the starboard deck, staring up the hillside.

The voice filled his ear like a warm tongue, seemed to lick his body, and he felt as though he had been caught up in a golden cloud.

The slope shone as if with pure gold, and the light cascaded over it like a waterfall.

—Hear me, Lord Odysseus of Ithaka, come, come fly! Hear the song, feel the touch of lovely, loving Lorelei.

Before Odysseus realized what had happened, Orestes had taken a swan dive and was swimming toward the shore, his head bobbing on the water and his arms churning. Odysseus could barely shake off the song; he had just enough self-possession to lift the Great Bow from safe storage, the bow he had carefully packed and repacked throughout his journey, and to dive into the river as well.

The cold water struck him like a slap, pushing the air from him. Despite lack of breath, he swam as far as he could underwater: the cold gave him back his mind with precious seconds to think.

Each time he surfaced to breathe, the song encircled his head like loving laughter, but he thrust his head below again, and when he reached the shore, he came out of the water running. Orestes, young, strong, and wildly mad, ran well ahead of him, dashing up the hill of gold as if it were a flat racetrack.

—Don't worry, Odysseus; come on all fours! The boy is mine, but I am yours!

Odysseus felt himself weighed down, but fought, praying to Athena, and bound up the slippery, golden slope with all the strength he had. The laughter, sweet as cream and light as flowers, flowed over him like a balm, and yet he ran, the breath raising a fire in his lungs. The gold light pierced his eyes. Trying to shield his eyes with the long arc of the wooden bow, he saw ahead a cave nearly at the top of the slope and ran for it with all his strength.

Nearly fainting with the effort, his legs afire beneath him and his mind spinning with the Lorelei's sweet song, Odysseus threw himself flat upon the landing before the cave. Orestes already lay there, prone, his arms and legs extended, his tongue babbling. The sweet song had grown nearly to a shriek, but calling upon Athena, Apollo, Poseidon, and the spirits of his fathers, he rose to face the northern siren.

The golden-haired girl, the vision of glory and sex and victory, the embodiment of his longing, stood before him, shining with gold brighter than the sun!

No, not she—something harder, colder, without the musky warmth of human muscle and skin and blood, something metallic and frightening, consuming rather than sharing, something that he would at once have, could he have found the strength, worshiped with his heart and struck with his fist.

The glare of the light that shone from her pushed him to the edge of the slope. Without realizing it, he had nearly fallen backward, and he could muster not a word of speech.

—Accept his gift. We have sent him to you, and you may not turn him away. He brings the greatest gift he may give away, the Great Bow of his fathers, which I myself have blessed.

The voice! It came from Orestes, who had risen from his prone position and rested now on his knees with his arms thrown wide and his head tossed back. The voice of Apollo would save them.

The light of the Lorelei slowly diminished, and her song dwindled to gentle, almost human laughter. When Odysseus regained himself enough to step forward and focus, he saw that she looked like a tall woman, broad in the shoulders, beautiful, nearly human. And when she spoke, her voice sounded like a human voice.

"Odysseus, hero from the South, what have you brought for me?"

His voice croaking, Odysseus said in the northern tongue, "As the Lord of the Sun spoke, milady, I have brought you a gift worthy of a war goddess, the greatest of my weapons, the bow of my fathers."

"With this bow, you slew the would-be wedding guests who hounded your beloved Penelope?"

With the name of Penelope, Odysseus' heart swelled with grief and pain and shame, for all his thoughts and desires. "Yes, River Goddess."

"And you come here, I think, not for my gold, as do most men who have the courage to try me."

"I seek, milady, only to obey my gods."

"The whole truth?"

Odysseus could not then stop himself. "And to find and fight Trojans, and to do something to honor my fathers."

"You do not fear the gods of the North?" She laughed, her voice ringing in the cave and up and down the hillside.

"I fight no gods, milady, but only men, such men as I have fought before."

"And one more thing you seek."

"Yes, milady."

"The girl with the golden hair."

"Yes, milady."

"What would Penelope say?"

Odysseus could not answer, and the Lorelei laughed long and musically.

"Hero, I too hear your gods' bidding, and I accept your gift: I know how much it means to you." She seemed several steps away, but she simply reached out and lifted the bow from Odysseus' hands. "It is a bow worthy of a warrior woman as old as the gold of her hillside. You will miss it when you most need it, but I will give you something of even greater worth in return. I will give you your dream-girl, or at least the way to win her, and the means to find her, and I will tell you how you may honor your fathers as you rightly should. Follow me into my cave."

Odysseus and Orestes obeyed without hesitation. The music of her voice held and overwhelmed them, as though she had wrapped them in nets of honey. She hung the bow on her wall, stroked it appreciatively, then drew a sheet of vellum from one of what looked like a hundred boxes that lined the walls, and she laid it on an altar in the center of the cave. Over it she spoke in resonant tones a version of the northern language that Odysseus couldn't understand. She took the vellum, selected another box from her wall, and handed both to Odysseus. Then from another box she took a ball of gleaming crystal that when a chance ray of light caught it sent colors flooding the cave in all directions. She placed the ball on the altar and intoned another incantation over it, her voice rising in pitch till it seemed to search the ceiling of the cave for exit. The ball began slowly to emit a steady white light until its brightness became almost too much for Odysseus to endure. Orestes, motionless, stared at it with his mouth open.

"Odysseus, these gifts I give in exchange for yours. This drawing will teach you how to build what you must build, an altar to your fathers, and where you must do so: in the land where the Tencteri and Bructeri mingle. There you will gain something, though you will also lose something. And you, Orestes, cursed and blessed, I will offer you a gift as well, because you come here as has no other man, with an open heart, wanting nothing. Odysseus, shall I return the balance of his wits? You must answer for him."

With a shock Odysseus realized the implications of the Lorelei's offer to Orestes: he would regain the ability to reason as others do, but he would lose vision and regain the encumbrances of doubt and planning that slow others' actions, the recompense Athena and Apollo had given for his madness.

And I, Odysseus thought, may lose a soldier and seer, someone I may need if we are to complete our quest. He knew well that Orestes' quickness and unpredictability made him much more of an asset than a liability in battle, and his visions kept them close to the gods.

"Lady, you must not give that gift."

"Do you answer for his sake or yours?"

Odysseus tried to keep his thoughts from the answer. He argued with himself that Orestes would lose rather than gain powers, lose rather than gain the happiness of divine presence, lose gifts greater than the common lot he'd gain. But Odysseus, either because Athena would not let him, or because in the experience of his own gifts from the gods he had come to understand the pain that accompanied Orestes' blessings, could not keep his thoughts from the fact that our clarity of thought makes us ourselves, and Orestes had a right, if it were granted by the gods, to recover himself and know himself again. Does anyone achieve any greater quest, he thought, than to know oneself?

"Lady, you know I can't choose for him. He must choose for himself—and how can he? Can you allow him to choose?"

"I wished only to hear you ask it."

She took Orestes by the arm—he moaned softly—and placed his hand on the gleaming ball. His body went straight and rigid. His eyes turned first upward, then toward the face of the Lorelei, then toward Odysseus' own. Odysseus returned Orestes' gaze with fear, doubt, and something akin to pity, but far deeper and greater, and with the feeling that he had made an error in giving up the choice.

He read in Orestes' eyes that the blessed and cursed one had read his thoughts, and he saw there a moment's sadness.

You would betray me, though I have loved you, the eyes seemed to say, and in recognizing that truth Odysseus felt tears rising in his own eyes. Then Orestes' look turned into a smile, peaceful, knowing, resigned to a choice, a face that expressed a clarity of mind such as Odysseus had never seen before.

"He has chosen," the Lorelei intoned.

Orestes took his hand from the ball and stepped back toward the edge of the cave, his head down, his eyes on the ground, his body steady, dripping perspiration.

"Achaian hero, man destined from birth, if any man may be, for fame and glory, return now to your boat and to your quest. You have what you need to serve the gods and yourself. Descend my hill carefully, and do not look back to me, even should you feel a wish to thank me. The magic you hold in your hands must hold your attention. I will not warn you again. Keep and use those wits for which the world knows you, and do as I and your gods tell you. Few men have come here, fewer have departed alive, and no man shall carry with him a fuller memory of his visit to the Lorelei. Go now, and prove yourself worthy of your blessings."

Odysseus bowed deeply to the lady. At the top edge of his sight a scorching gold light arose from where the Lorelei stood. He kept his eyes fixed on the ground. He reached out for Orestes, but his companion had already backed through the door, and Odysseus could hear his feet beginning to slide down the breathtaking slope to the river. He followed.

The way up had taken energy and fortitude; the way down proved rapid and giddy. Odysseus followed Orestes down that slope at something between a slide and a run, golden light kicking and spurting from his feet like raindrops bounding in a storm or sparks from the smith's anvil.

As Odysseus neared the bottom, Orestes had already

reached the water, leaping in a smooth, lightning fast swan dive into the river, then bobbing up well into the waves. Odysseus fought a keen desire to look back for one last glance at the Lorelei, found himself mercifully losing his footing, and concentrated on meeting the water without losing the treasures she had given him.

The boat had sailed up river the distance a young man might walk in the time he would need to savor a large apple. When a wave brought his head higher, Odysseus could see no one standing at the stern. He hadn't realized until then the deep-down weariness he felt, and he began to wonder if his strength would hold him.

He also wondered how they would get along with a new Orestes, Agamemnon's son, restored to a clarity that would show him the utter foolishness of their quest.

Odysseus swallowed water, then again, but gripped tightly to the box and vellum, resolved to go to the bottom of the Rhine rather than lose them. He felt himself pulled to the surface, held long enough to get a breath that renewed his strength.

As he bobbed on the surface, he saw before him, bouncing just ahead, the smiling face of Orestes, the eyes as wild as ever.

"Wo, wo, don't let go; hero who, Father Two? Still the winds and hush the: ooo! Swim a bit before he nods!"

Orestes laughed, swam ahead on his back with his head up, eyes fixed on Odysseus. The hero renewed his strokes, held against the pain of exertion. When he believed he could swim no more, two arms reached down and pulled him onto the boat: Orestes' and Diomedes'. Diomedes had fashioned some kind of cap of cloth that fell down over his eyes.

"We've got you, Ody. Keep your sight fixed on the deck.

I'll set the rowers to a slave's pace." Diomedes disappeared. Orestes sat sprawled before him on the deck, breathing hard, but smiling. Odysseus had insufficient breath to keep himself from passing out. He'd lost his eyepatch, and water filled the empty socket as well as much of his lungs. One last thought appeared before the darkness got him: he couldn't believe it, but Orestes had chosen for himself, and he had chosen divine madness over human sanity.

Words followed him into his darkness, flitting in a voice that sounded like Orestes': "Serve the Fathers, serve the— ha! Then you'll never feel at odds!"

Odysseus dreamed. He saw take shape a shrine with an altar, built by his own hands of smooth, carefully shaped red stone. There he carved the names of his fathers— Laertes, Sisyphus, Apollo, Poseidon—and of his faithful guardian goddess, Athena. The shrine must stand near a beautiful town on the riverbank. It must stand seven cubits broad and five cubits high, with small windows high up, a smooth stone floor, and a copper altar with a golden bowl filled regularly with sacrifices to the gods. It must . . .

The dream faded, and when Odysseus woke, he was sprawled on the deck, covered in a warm blanket. The boat moved along slowly but steadily northward. The hillside along the river had lost its solar gold and shone instead brilliant green. Philoctetes sat beside him, keeping watch. He noticed Odysseus' eye had opened. He had sewn a new and better patch for the empty socket.

"We thought, after all you'd gone through, old Ody, that we'd lost you, but you're tougher than a barnacle. Welcome back."

"Thank you, Philo. How long have I slept?"

"Three days. Are you hungry?"

"Enough to eat a Trojan horse. Where are we?"

"Ido just told me a bit ago that we're nearing either a town or some kind of outpost. There it is: I can see it clearly ahead."

Odysseus rose on his elbow to have a look, then tried to stand. Dizziness overtook him, and he nearly fell—Philoctetes helped him sit.

"Best to go slowly. I'll get you some hot food and cold water—no wine for you yet, and we're pretty low on it anyway."

Odysseus ate, then dozed again, until he woke with Idomeneus shaking his shoulder vigorously. "Wake up, Ody: you need to see this."

Odysseus could just hear someone, Orestes, singing in a language he had not heard, something that sounded like a drinking song. He rose, unsteadily, but safely, and hobbled to the edge of the deck.

Along the north coast of the river stood ranks of men and women in long cloaks. Long hair fell uncovered to their shoulders. The men wore hair under their noses, but had no beards. When the people saw Odysseus standing before them, they bowed. The bowing motion passed north through their ranks, moving alongside the riverbank as a wave does in water.

"I've spotted a landing just ahead. Should we try it, Ody? I'm for stopping, if for no other reason than we're out of wine."

"Could be dangerous," Antilochus said. "We know nothing of these people or their intentions, despite their apparent obsequiousness to our friend here."

"I think, Ody, that you have little choice but to speak with them," said Idomeneus. "But do you have the strength?"

"Yes. Dio, put in there at the landing. Anti and Thrasy,

stand on either side of me as we disembark—I'd better not fall in the water before we even meet them. If Orestes is singing in their language, as I suspect he is, we may have trouble communicating with them, so listen with your whole heart if they speak. Thrasy, do you know where we are?"

"At the western edge of the drawings I was able to make: I don't know if these folk are northern Galli or Northmen or something we haven't met. They look different, but we shall see."

Some men slid a large plank from the shore to the deck of the boat to ease the Greeks' disembarking. As Odysseus and the others came ashore, the people there all bowed their heads and made low moaning sounds, but spoke no apparent words.

Odysseus stood for a moment and looked to them: as a rule, average to tall folk, some with reddish hair, some with flaxen, nearly all with light eyes; round faces with grave expressions that bespoke seriousness and patience. He spoke to them in Greek; they bowed again, but said nothing. He spoke to them in halting Gallic, and they responded again with silence. Finally, he tried what he had been able to learn of the northern language; he tried to say that they were travelers who sought rest and supplies. Then he heard an audible gasp. One of the men, tall, with a long shock of reddish-blond hair and a hair stretching from beneath his nose nearly as far as each ear, stepped forward and spoke. The words seemed cumbersome on his tongue.

"Welcome. Though you look like men, we believe you come from the gods. You say you are Achai Othis? We do not fully understand your language, though we recognize the words of the Northmen."

Nor do we know yours, Odysseus thought, but decided

EDWARD S. LOUIS

he'd better not say. He realized that the man speaking northern was not using his own language, either.

"We will speak together as best we may in the northern language, until you teach us what you can of yours. My friend will speak for me." He nodded to Antilochus.

"Who are you?" Antilochus asked.

"I am called Brucca of the Bructeri. These people are some Bructeri, some Tencteri."

"What do you call this place?"

"We call it Bructen, but the ancients called it Asciberg."

"Ascerbergium," Odysseus said to Antilochus, "that is the name the god told me."

"Then we have found this place not by accident?" Antilochus said.

"Little on our journey has happened by accident." Odysseus then whispered to Antilochus, who spoke to Brucca.

"We wish to come ashore and speak with you. We intend no harm, but wish only to replenish our supplies and share the blessing of your gods."

"Welcome. Nor do we intend harm, nor will we spare in what provisions we may offer."

"We thank you."

Brucca stepped toward Odysseus and tentatively moved a hand toward the hero's cheek. "We have expected you, Vanum," he said. "We were told one should come, sent from the gods, he with but one eye. We see now that the messengers must have been seers, for you have come."

Vanum, Odysseus thought: what could that mean?

The local folk, a joint settlement of two tribes, gave the Greeks all the welcome they could wish. They had little fear, believing that the Lorelei protected them from marauders, which may well have been true. In exchange they discouraged people from traveling south, even assisted them in returning

126

north or in turning westward overland. They showed amazement that the Greeks had traveled safely from the south.

"We came here only by the blessing of the River Goddess," Odysseus assured them—the answer puzzled but apparently satisfied them.

Antilochus and Dictys set to learning what they could of the language and exchanging selected stories of their journey, while the others set to barter for provisions. They had little to trade, until Odysseus remembered the gifts the Lorelei had given him.

The vellum, he saw, had detailed drawings of the shrine he had seen in his dream. The box held two bags, one a small bag of the purest, brightest gold he had ever seen, and the other held a smooth, perfectly shaped gold ring of a size suitable for a woman's finger. He safely stowed the box with the ring, then went ashore with the rest of the gold, figuring to apportion it carefully.

When he showed the gold to the Bructenians, they looked at him with terror. Several of the elders held heated discussions until they agreed to accept some in exchange for the provisions they offered their guests.

Later Brucca tentatively asked Odysseus about the gold. "Othis of the Achai, you got this gold from the Lorelei?"

"Yes."

"It shines as old tales say the hills do, her hills to the south."

"Yes."

The local man shook his head sagely, knowingly, his eyes showing a touch of wonder if not fear.

Once they felt sure of their hosts, Odysseus asked for a meeting with Brucca and the other elders. With care he broached his plan, explaining that the gods had sent him to build a shrine to his fathers.

"Yes," said an elder named Tencto. "That is right, that you should do so. A man should show his respect for his fathers and his—gods?"

"So we believe also," Odysseus said, "and I wish to begin tomorrow."

Odysseus, wary of saying too much, would tell no more of their mission than his intent to build and to seek knowledge of his brothers in the far north.

In a week Odysseus, with the help of his fellows and the locals, had constructed a shrine of polished red stone in the exact shape and dimensions as he had seen in his vision and as he saw before him in the Lorelei's drawing. It stood on a beautiful spot on the riverbank just below a line of white birches and just above the water. When he had constructed the altar of copper, he placed an oak bowl, lined with gold from the Lorelei, in its center. In the bowl he placed a dried fig that he had found in the pouch of his tunic, a remnant from Poseidon's grove on Sicilia.

On the outside walls, those facing landward and riverward, he carved in obscure signs that he knew, from south to north, five names: *Laertes, Sisyphus, Apollo, Poseidon, Athena*. On the roof he laid an icon of the sun, but beneath that icon he carved another name: *Odysseus*. The shrine had about it a sturdy look of permanence, or at least as much of such a look as anything of this world can have. *Amen,* he thought, and prayed to Athena that the shrine should bring peace to his fathers and to himself.

—Odysseus, You have honored your gods, pleased Laertes, and eased Sisyphus' pain. Are you now ready to meet death?

He heard Athena's contralto laugh.

"Not yet," he whispered. "I have Trojans to fight, and there's the matter of the blond-haired girl."

The laughter seemed to rumble along the ground and rise over the water and into the sky to the west.

Odysseus paused to admire his handiwork.

He paid a local elder who seemed to have the duties of a priest to fill the bowl regularly with a small offering to the gods and to the spirits of his fathers. The elder said that not only would he keep that task, but so should his sons and their sons, since their people wished ever to earn the blessings of the gods.

When the Greeks departed, the local people again lined the riverbank to bow them a farewell. Brucca stood before them, his hand raised, a hint of a smile warming his placid face. "May glory and joy go with you, Othis and his Vanum," he said, and the Greeks waved in reply.

"Apollo bless you," Odysseus said, again wondering what *Vanum* meant.

THE ENEMY

Gentle weather allowed the heroes to ease their way north, though fog shrouded their sleep and kept its hold into the morning. On the second day past Ascerbergium, Idomeneus rose early to examine some long, tough, slender bows Diomedes had got from an archer there. Diomedes, ever in the prow searching the waters for enemies, found his watch rewarded. A larger boat, probably as large as could sail the river, with two enormous red dragon heads curling from its prow, ripped through tufts of morning fog not yet burnt off by the summer sun, and Diomedes could see immediately that they were armed for war. He barked an order astern. More quickly than rumor Orestes stood by his side, his hand stretched above his brow, eyes staring mock-seriously through the yellow mist.

Odysseus, still obviously tired from his labors, trudged forward to see for himself, and the others took up ready posts, Idomeneus neatly slinging a quiver over his shoulder and slipping out of sight, taking just enough time to pitch another bow to Philoctetes. The rowers, unskilled in battle, hunkered down beneath their oars, though a few with more confidence grasped what weapons they could find at hand. As Odysseus strode to the prow of the vessel, he nearly took an arrow, which shot past him so close he could feel the breeze and embedded itself near his usual seat in the stern. Orestes had disappeared, but Diomedes firmly held his place.

The boat yanked itself perpendicular to the riverbank, blocking passage and showing the Achaians its full length, armed with archers and swordsmen.

"Would you parley with us?" Odysseus called in his best Norse.

A man sturdy and knotty as an oak tree, with grey-gold hair hanging to his shoulders, replied in a series of fluid, percussively melodic grunts. Odysseus turned to Antilochus.

"I think he said, 'Stand down and be boarded.' Or at least that's what I'd say, were I in his sandals."

"He doesn't appear to be wearing sandals," said Thrasymedes. "Look more like animal-skin boots to me, with a rather nice fur trim. Colder in the north, you know."

"Odd time to talk fashion," Antilochus muttered.

"Nonetheless, I wouldn't mind a pair of those, considering where we're going," Thrasymedes answered.

"Ask him what they want, or say anything to them, while I get a look and think about what to do," Odysseus said, and another arrow passed him, sticking next to its fellow in the poop deck.

"They don't seem to be much in the mood for talking, Ody," Diomedes said, "and that doesn't entirely displease me, though we're a bit outnumbered," he added, allowing his eye to trace the rows of soldiers, who must have numbered in the dozens. Odysseus wished he were amidships with some cover and his great bow—not for the last time.

Antilochus spoke again in the northern language, asking what gods they served and why they sought to block the river.

The Northman spoke again in his gruff sing-song, but with a different accent. "Southerners, by the sound of you, and foreigners by the look. You may not know us, nor do we take questions about our gods. You will abandon ship now or get acquainted with our weapons. Now, not later." Odysseus realized he had only seconds to plan, and that wouldn't be enough.

"Did you understand him, Ody?" Antilochus asked.

"Completely," Odysseus replied. "I suggest we bow to them, as did our hosts at Ascerbergium, low and formally, then dive for the nearest cover and prepare for a fight. If we can drift a trifle closer, I can cast a blade into their leader. I suggest each man pray to his gods."

Another arrow whisked by Odysseus' face, grazing and drawing blood. The sound in his ear stung more than the welt rising on his cheek.

"Now!" the Northman commanded.

"Now," echoed Odysseus, "and may Apollo and Athena bless my right arm."

As the Achaians began a mock-submissive bow, Odysseus heard an unearthly cry, saw a body like an enormous bird flying from the stern of their ship into the ranks of the Northmen. The enemy turned their eyes to it too late to keep the first half dozen from getting kicked from their deck into the water, their limbs sprawling and their weapons flying. Orestes had entered the water, swum behind their boat, risen unnoticed to the deck, looped his whip around their mast, and swung himself feet-first like a battering ram into their ranks.

Odysseus used the distraction to pull a blade from his tunic and cast it directly into the face of the northern leader. His aim was true: the man took it in the eye and fell stone-dead, like a beast mercifully sacrificed. That gruesome death would seem a mercy, considering the slaughter to come.

Before the Northmen could recover their line, Idomeneus and Philoctetes, who had gained vantage points on either side of the boat, began firing arrows into their ranks with the new northern bows. Antilochus and Thrasymedes had dived for cover, drawing dirks and swordblades to defend the ship. Odysseus and Diomedes, with Dictys only a step behind, had taken the offensive, diving into the water, swimming under the surface, one toward the fore, one toward the aft deck of their attackers' boat.

Orestes dove among them shouting and whooping like a harpy, and before they could lay weapon to him, he had dived off the opposite deck. Turning their backs to the Greek ship to follow the flight of their assailant, the Northmen became easy targets for the Greek bows, as Idomeneus and Philoctetes now had help from the most intrepid of their oarsmen.

Odysseus boarded the enemy boat from the stern, Dictys from the far side, and Diomedes from the prow. As the boats drifted closer, Antilochus and Thrasymedes, accustomed to fighting together, bounded to their attackers' deck and engaged them hand to hand. Despite the element of surprise, each would have been overwhelmed by sheer numbers had not Odysseus and Diomedes, using their shortswords, cut their way forward from either end. Orestes had swum under the boat, and he boarded again into the center of the growing melee, snapping his whip with one hand and a cat-o-nine-tails he took from a fallen Northman with the other. The oarsmen, led by Idomeneus and Philoctetes, defended the Greeks' much smaller boat as boldly as they might, as Northmen boarded, eager for battle and uncertain about the number or quality of their foes.

Despite having lost their leader, the Northmen kept their composure, regained their lines, and hemmed the Greeks in the center of the ship. Though at close quarters, some kept their bows and took shots at the Greeks when a space opened in the fighting.

Finding his brother falling under the heavy blows of a Northman's enormous longsword, Antilochus leapt and struck the fellow with both feet, sending him sprawling into the river. Finding him slow to his feet, a Northman shot him, the arrow entering the right side just below the ribs. Thrasymedes rose to defend him, and Odysseus, seeing his comrade bleeding, pushed a crowd of warriors to cover the opening and obscure the chance for another shot. Antilochus fought from one knee at his brother's side, swinging his sword with what strength remained in his left arm.

But the Northmen were no mere missionaries of their gods, as were some of their fellows. Veteran troops, they encircled the Greek heroes and began to wear them down, the occasional bow shot reducing them to defensive posture. The Greeks' bold attack had worked, but they lacked the numbers to see it through against soldiers as resolved to death as they were.

Idomeneus and Philoctetes, having run out of arrows, abandoned their bows for spears and held their own deck for the Greeks, but their companions were thoroughly surrounded by soldiers bent on nothing but their victims' deaths.

A tiny boat with two shadowy figures had slipped in amidst the pitched fighting. The figures carried grappling hooks and had broadswords hanging from their sides. They boarded the Norse boat as quietly as morning interrupts night.

Odysseus and his companions had begun to feel the weight of aging limbs. They fought on with undimmed resolve, but with failing bones, and Antilochus, who had broken off enough of the arrow to take his feet and fight, was losing bowls of blood. No one spoke, nor did even Orestes utter a sound: the Northmen were not offering an easy death, and the Achaian heroes wouldn't have accepted had they done so.

Then suddenly a new commotion arose from the rear of the ranks of Northmen, as soldiers fell right and left. Odysseus didn't know what he was seeing, and he didn't know why, but he felt his spirits rise, as something like an easy laughter gripped his heart and filled his lungs. With a glance he saw that Diomedes' face shone with new life.

"He-he, he-he, he-he, he-he, he-he!" Orestes was laughing.

Finding themselves set on from behind, and feeling again the cut and thrust from the weapons of the antagonists they thought they'd cornered, the Northmen reeled beneath renewed and more severe assault. Odysseus saw that on each side of the circle a lithe, lightning-fast warrior, dressed in black from hood to soles, was whirling and cutting down rows of men as if they were no more than grain. He renewed his swordstrokes joyfully.

Orestes had leaped onto a platform amidships and was cheering, "Brothers, brothers, of different mothers, toil and swing—we'll take the others!"

Without knowing who had come to their aid, the heroes accepted the reinforcements that turned the battle in their favor. In minutes they covered the deck with the enemy. Thrasymedes held up his brother by his good shoulder, he himself covered with so much blood that Odysseus couldn't tell who had sustained the greater wounds.

"Dio!" Odysseus called, "our vessel?"

Diomedes nodded, took off at a run, and leapt from the Norse boat to his own. Dictys took Diomedes' place at Odysseus' side, cleaning his short sword on the cloak of a dead Northman.

Orestes landed beside Antilochus, helping Thrasymedes lift him.

Odysseus turned to one of the figures in black and said in Greek, "I don't know who you are, but if you fight for us, see that one of these Northmen lives." A youthful face, partly covered and that he didn't recognize, but that looked vaguely familiar, nodded and smiled. Turning to the other warrior, Odysseus found him cleaning his spear, his head covered in a hood. The old soldier gently pulled back the hood.

The face of the youthful Achilles smiled at him.

A long, liquidy laugh danced over the carnage like music.

"You should see your face, Father Odysseus!"

"Achilles? Is it you?"

"None other."

"And your companion, to whom we owe equal thanks?"

"No thanks necessary. It was fun. I've been waiting for this for a long time."

Blood pooled at their feet, and the calls of crows had already begun to echo across the river.

"May I ask who . . ."

"He'll tell you all about himself, but first we must get our comrade what help we can. Is Philoctetes still with us?" Achilles asked.

"He was when the fight began."

"Let's find him, and perhaps between the two of us we can save Antilochus' life."

Diomedes returned, nodded to Odysseus, and joined Dictys to search the dead for the living.

Philoctetes had indeed survived the battle, and with the help of a few stout oarsmen, the Greeks had held their ship. One rower had fallen from an arrow shot, killed instantly. Odysseus saw him, but had not even known his name.

Philoctetes was overjoyed to see Achilles, but the two men fell immediately to the task of trying to revive Antilochus, whose stertorous breathing drew painful gulps of air into his lungs, but blood, now that the flow had stilled from his side, was dripping from his mouth. Thrasymedes, the blood he bore being more his brother's than his own, held his hand, while Philoctetes worked to stop the bleeding, and Achilles applied a hasty poultice to his wound and directed his associate to prepare a medicinal draft. Odysseus knelt at Antilochus' feet.

"The Corsican has much skill in medicine," Achilles said, "or I wouldn't be here. We must work quickly, though."

"No need," Antilochus breathed. "The gods take what they wish. I'll meet you, brother, when you cross over. Killy, welcome back. No more strength. Ody, kiss the golden girl for me. I . . . our father's name . . . Let me rest at Ascerbergium. Dictys, you will compose a poem for me?"

Orestes, who had carried Antilochus aboard nearly by himself, howled with pain and bounded away aft.

Odysseus, the man who more than any other had known death, had until that moment kept from his mind the shadow of death that stalked their quest.

He had already become aware of the absurdity, the impossibility of what they intended to do, but he had not allowed himself the thought that any other than he could actually die in accomplishing it.

Antilochus' eyes glazed, and a yellow pool mixed with the red one beneath him.

"Too late," Achilles said, "though I don't know that we could have done anything anyway. With that wound he shouldn't have been able to fight as long as he did."

"The men who fought at Troy had that ability," Odysseus said, "at least those who survived it."

"Obvious, that," said Idomeneus, trailing into silence.

"We must return to Ascerbergium," Thrasymedes said, still holding his brother's hand.

Odysseus kept silent a moment, loath to lose ground, but knowing Thrasymedes right: they must grant Antilochus' last requests. "Yes," he said.

Odysseus glanced at the stranger who had accompanied Achilles, found that his carriage and movements looked oddly familiar. He rose, saying to the others, "I must learn if our comrades have found any of the Northmen yet alive. We must know what they know." Holding his knees, he hobbled across the deck, eased himself onto the other ship, the stranger two paces behind him.

Odysseus found Diomedes and Dictys standing with a Northman sitting between them. He had blood dripping from the corner of his mouth and from a cut in his shoulder, and a parti-colored knot rose from his forehead. He looked dazed, accepted a bowl of water from Dictys without offering thanks.

He looked perhaps thirty years old, with a slim but muscular build and the typical yellow-brown hair falling to his shoulders. He had lost two fingers of his left hand and was holding a torn cloth to the wound. Without Antilochus' help, he would have to rely on Dictys' and his own skills to question the man. Odysseus nodded to Dictys, hoping the man would respond best to the enemy who had tended him.

"Who are you?" Dictys asked.

"Gartheow is my name."

"From where do you come?"

"I am of the Svarians."

"All of these men, are you of the same race?"

"Same tribe? Same people? Not anymore."

"Did you come from the same tribe, the same place?"

"We came together, but we were born in different places."

"Who sent you and on what errand?"

When he didn't speak, Diomedes poked his foot against the wounded shoulder. The man winced only slightly and made no sound. "He can offer you more than that," Odysseus said.

"Let him, then," the man replied without expression. "If you are gods, you must know without asking me."

Diomedes kicked him in the same spot, with more of an air of business than of malice.

The man's face paled further, but if he made a sound, Odysseus couldn't hear it.

"Let me speak with him," said the stranger, stepping forward from behind Odysseus. His face looked boyish, bright, familiar.

The stranger knelt by the man, placed the poultice he had been preparing for Antilochus on the wounded shoulder. For the first time the man uttered a sigh, a sound that indicated more grief and relief than pain. The stranger spoke softly in a tongue that Odysseus didn't recognize, something like the gruff music of the northern leader's speech, but gentler and more melodic. The sounds immediately changed the expression of the injured man from one of cold resignation to one of disarmed surprise.

The two conversed for some time, the stranger in tones

friendly, almost hypnotic, and the Northman as though he were speaking to a respected elder whom one may not countermand. As tersely as he had responded before, so much he answered loquaciously after.

About the time Odysseus had grown restless, the stranger rose, patted the Northman on the good shoulder, and turned to Odysseus. As he did so, the Northman heaved a long sigh, as if satisfied with what he'd said, and passed out.

"Dead?" Odysseus asked.

"Sleeping," said the other, and for the first time Odysseus got a clear look at his face.

Part Telemachos, part Circe, he thought, boyish, brash, golden.

"You have guessed, then?" the stranger asked.

"Tell me."

"My name is Telegonus. I am your son."

"And Circe's."

"Yes."

"Mortal?"

"Yes," Telegonus responded hesitantly.

"But?"

"With much of my mother in me."

"Does she love you?"

"Yes."

"Does she hate me?"

"Not at all," said Telegonus, laughing. The laughter reminded Odysseus of fresh, ripe, sweet fruits dangling from their limbs, wafted by a breeze. "The eye: mother didn't tell me you had such an injury. Usually she likes her men whole."

"I was whole then. I'll tell you about it later. You have powers of speech, among others?"

"Yes. Will you sit down and talk with me?" The words filled Odysseus' ears with something between polite request and fatherly command, and his legs suddenly felt unmanageably tired. He bent his knees to sit, and nearly collapsed on the spot, but with an effort of will straightened his legs, shook his head, and stood firm. "Ha-ha," laughed Telegonus. "Mother didn't exaggerate your own powers. Dare I say you are the first full human to have resisted that tone of voice. Ah! I tire myself when I use it. May we sit and talk—we have much to discuss. You need not worry. I have not come to do harm, but only to seek my father. Nor is Telemachos—nor any of his family—in any danger from me. I found him on Ithaka and have, since Corsica with Achilles' help, traced your journey here, and good thing for you I did! Oh, I'm tired—you see, you have wrought the spell on me that I sought to work on you. Please let's sit and talk. We can clean this mess later."

"I am an old soldier, son. Let's clean up first and talk later." Odysseus felt the need to show that his son's voice could not subdue him.

"I told the truth: I'm deadly tired now. I'll do my best to help."

The Greeks found two other men alive. One, even with tending, lasted an hour and died. The other, relatively uninjured once he had regained consciousness and reviving after a conversation with Telegonus, woke his compatriot and, granted Achilles' small boat, rowed slowly south, commanded by Odysseus that they dock the boat just north of Ascerbergium, set off south on foot, and never return to those lands nor tell anyone of their fate.

"I have learned much from our friend Gartheow, all of which I'll share with you when we've rested," Telegonus told Odysseus. "Normally men of this sort would dock,

141

then speed north as fast as they could to report to their lords, but in this case I believe you will have no trouble."

"Overconfident?"

"I think not, though you're right, I must be careful, not having dealt with people like these before."

The Achaians had no choice but to ground the ship and, against their wishes, burn it along with its cargo of corpses—though a better ship than theirs, the stench of blood and death had permeated the Norse vessel. Fire and smoke rose into the night sky, which did not please Odysseus. After they'd salvaged what supplies they could, Odysseus bade the men sail south to Ascerbergium. Working by the light of the burning Norse ship, they wrapped Antilochus and the dead oarsman in white shrouds and turned back whence they'd come.

They sailed slowly, Odysseus and Telegonus spending an entire day talking, heads together, in the stern of their boat. While the others tended their wounds, slept, and mourned their comrades, Dictys sat at the prow, calling on the gods to send him a poem to praise Antilochus.

Odysseus summarized for Telegonus the Greeks' adventures to that point. He noted as he spoke that his son, while tall and beautiful, looked in the face little more than a boy.

Telegonus gave greetings from his mother, despite her disapproval of her son's plans, recounted his own journey, and discussed with his father what he had learned from the Northman.

He had come in fact from those he called his lords and his gods. He served under a great king by the name of Skef, who had given him in a company of a hundred and twenty men to serve the god Trorash or *Tror*, as most call him. He told Telegonus how Tror had come from the east, people said, with a family of dark-skinned, dark-haired gods who had swept up into their forces all the great kingdoms of the north as they brought with them wealth, power, wisdom, and knowledge of crafts that had made the lives of the savage tribes easier and better. He and a sibyl had a troupe of sons who fight the sun and the moon if they try to get out of line. An old soldier-god, they called him Hothines, taught them strategy in battle, so that they fight more with wisdom than with brute anger—apparently he hadn't taught this lot enough. The art-god, Keimtaler, taught them music and building. A brother and sister, beautiful as summer orchards, taught them to grow plants and husband animals and to provision armies. A smith god, Wela, taught them metalwork. Gartheow, seeing the Achaians fight, had thought them gods related to their own until they started asking him questions.

"I wonder if he has ever seen the golden-haired girl," Odysseus muttered, more to himself than to Telegonus.

"What golden-haired girl?" Telegonus asked with a hint of resentment.

"Oh, nothing, sorry. Anything else you can remember?"

"I remember everything," answered Telegonus. "He also said that they have won the loyalty of nearly all the peoples of the north. They have immense power and resources and great wisdom. And among them, I understand, you expect to find Troyans?"

"They, we think, *are* the Trojans, or at least what's left of their allies."

"A small task, to find and kill them. A sport. A leisure. An afternoon's adventure before a bowl of wine."

"You have, I note," said Odysseus, "your mother's wit."

Telegonus then told Odysseus of the soldiers they had fought: one expedition among many that Trorash's forces traced regularly along landpaths and waterways, conscripting those they wanted for military duty, allying with those who controlled resources, converting those they could to their gods. When they confronted any bands who looked dangerous, pirates or strange soldiers, for instance, they could, at their captain's discretion, either win them over to the Norse gods or kill them outright—they seldom met substantial resistance, having blended already with any significant powers through most of the northwest.

"These men," Telegonus concluded, "though not the most skilled of their soldiers, were among the most eager to fight."

When Odysseus finally drifted to sleep, he sensed Telegonus watching over him and the river, glad to have found his father, warm in the fact that Odysseus listened to him not as to a boy of his loins, but as a trusted counselor.

They anchored north of the settlement overnight, but in the morning Brucca and his folk again lined the riverbank to greet them. The heroes docked, Odysseus explained their task and introduced their new companions, and Brucca readily assigned laborers to help them. They burnt the dead, allotting the dust of the oarsman to the Bructenian burial ground, and placing the ashes of Antilochus beneath a mound just upland from the shrine Odysseus had built. On the altar Odysseus placed a beautiful long, curving knife, its blade carved with the shapes of dragons, its hilt decorated with bronze, that he had recovered from the Northmen's store of weapons, and a cloth that held drops of Antilochus' blood, now dried to an uneven brown stain. On the inside south wall he carved a name, Antilochus Nestorides, and he shed tears for his friend as though they could bring back the life their expedition had taken.

Thrasymedes knelt for two days at the entrance to the shrine, weeping, praying, honoring the memory of his brother, leaving beneath his brother's inscribed name a small urn that held drops of his brother's blood and his own.

And for those two days the Greeks and their hosts held feasts and games, the Greeks teaching their hosts the games of the south, and the Bructenians teaching their guests those of the north. Other than Thrasymedes, only Dictys didn't participate: he secluded himself, parlaying with his gods, composing.

Much of the hard gear they'd got from the Northmen the Greeks left with Brucca and his folk as payment for their help and hospitality. Then once again they provisioned their ship and turned north, reluctant to leave behind even the ashes of their beloved comrade, but yet more eager than ever for the task ahead.

As they embarked from the dock of Bructen, Dictys stood on the starboard bow, straight as a fresh spear, and chanted this poem:

The Fathers' shrine claims its first urn.
Ares spares neither brave nor taciturn.
Antilochus was balding and slim,
but he saw Troy burn.
May this northern soil honor his dust
And remember he knew his comrades' trust.
I shall see his shade in Elysium.
Then the Greeks heard a voice coming from the shore;
it was Brucca's, and it sung out thus:
Men must endure
their coming and going.
May we have
a woman to love us
and friends to avenge us.

Thrasymedes, hearing Brucca, let out a deep shout of pain and thanks.

"We shall see you again, Achai Othis of the Vanum," Brucca called.

In Antilochus' death Odysseus had fully realized the folly of their quest; perhaps the gods sought yet to punish the sackers of Troy, or they found pleasure in the silly adventures of old men; still, he felt more intent upon its end than ever. If they pursued absurdity, they did so willingly, with a commitment more typical of youth than of sullied age.

In near silence, honoring their dead companion, the Greeks rowed more than fifty leagues north by northwest until they finally turned west for another thirty-five leagues, where they found the river widen, then open into a vast western sea. While he would miss Antilochus, Odysseus was glad for the return of one companion and the introduction of a new, and he felt eager to learn about his newly-acquired son. He realized, looking at the vast water beyond, that they would need a bigger ship, and he wished again that he had not had to burn the one the gods had put briefly in his hands.

9

TROJAN NORTHLANDS

"Look, Ody, at the symbol on these cloaks," Idomeneus said, poring over the materials they had acquired from their attackers. "I hadn't noticed that they all bear it. What do you think it means?"

"It looks like a large-headed hammer, maybe for smithing, but the gods know what it may mean to those people. Do you suppose it refers to their smith-god? Dio, have a look at this sign."

"The proportions look wrong for a smith's hammer," Diomedes said. "Ask Thrasymedes: he's good with drawn signs."

Thrasymedes had moved and spoken ponderously since the death of his brother. Since the heroes' departure from Ascerbergium, his mind had dwelt only on Antilochus' tomb and his family on Pylos. He stared at the icon for some time, then shook his head. "Army insignia or a cult sign? If we can find what it means, we may learn much more about the men who attacked us."

For several days they had drifted about the mouth of the Rhine, rowing tentatively north along the coast and then back, knowing they had reached a sea too rough for their vessel, unsure of how to obtain a better in those lands, uneasy about encountering greater forces of warriors than they yet had, but realizing they were drawing unwanted attention from the local settlements. The oarsmen particularly felt reluctant about the cold northern sea, and from the coast they had occasionally seen farther out long, dragon-headed ships of the Northmen, ships built more for difficult waters. They did not want to acquire a reputation and become the targets of every group of bowmen passing in the night. They took to quenching their amidships fire so as not to draw attention.

Having built his shrine and having reached, as far as they knew, the end of the earth, Odysseus had no clear plan for what to do next.

Odysseus suspected that major settlements on the waterway would support the warrior Northmen, either by choice or necessity, so the Greeks had little hope of succor or even useful information there. They found a secluded bank and docked their boat to take time to think. While the older men parlayed, the younger, Achilles and Telegonus, practiced combat by the hour with their spears over the widest part of the deck.

"I can see no other course than to take one of those long dragon-ships," Diomedes offered.

"And what then?" Idomeneus asked. "Where do we sail?"

"I think we must find a way to learn more about what lies to the north or even to the west," Dictys suggested. "We don't know that the world ends here. We must find knowledgeable people who can help Thrasymedes make his drawings so that we have some means of finding the Trojans we want without having to fight every Norse ship that sails by."

"Who should help us, and why?" asked Philoctetes. "We will look as odd to these folk as they do to us."

"That appears," Odysseus thought aloud, "to constitute our current problem. We need to learn more about them without their learning more about us."

"That will slow us down on our way north, and who can guess what winters we shall find up here," Diomedes added.

"Hear, hear," echoed Philoctetes.

Finally Thrasymedes spoke. "I feel as though I have done my brother's shade a disservice and that I have no more to offer you, my friends, though together we have seen many adventures. Telegonus can learn languages much more quickly than I, and my fighting spirit has left me—younger men hold up better than old." He paused, and the others hung their heads in the silence. "I must, I think, return to Ascerbergium and resolve myself what to do. Would you risk these boys, our rowers, on the high northern sea unknown to us all? Would you risk our quest on the chance that we will find more folk sympathetic to Achaians over the inland North? At Ascerbergium I can learn and pray. When I feel ready, I may move overland and join you in the north, or I may return to my people in the south. The weather here, cold even in summer, makes my bones ache, and I have lost touch with my gods. I have lost my sense of place, and I need a sibyl, someone to teach me what to do. Undoubtedly you think me now an old woman, but I haven't the will to go on, now that Antilochus has gone from me. I feel as though I have lost part of myself, and I fear in losing him I have failed our father."

As young men the others might have chided, teased, or even struck their reticent companion, but having journeyed together beyond their known world, and knowing that the brothers' spirits had been joined like two nuts in one shell, they nodded without even allowing their heads to rise, recognizing the justice in what Thrasymedes said.

Diomedes rose, patted Thrasymedes on the shoulder, and ambled to the prow to stretch his legs.

Odysseus turned to the boys in their spear practice. "Young men: you use the spear as I have never seen anyone do before. Will you teach me?"

"Gladly, Father," Telegonus responded. "We will show you what we know, but the movements take practice, and I warn you to go slowly: the tips bear poison. My mother and Hermes showed me its use. It comes from the barb of an uncommon sort of sting ray, light in color, longer and thinner than others. Have you seen them?"

"I have," answered Odysseus, "though I've had my problems with another sort." He practiced with them for much of the day, and the other heroes would often watch them, noting and commenting on this move or that. Even Philoctetes, after Achilles perhaps the best spearsman of his age, watched in wonder. The young men went on long after Odysseus had tired. When Achilles stopped for water, Odysseus asked Telegonus, "Achilles took quickly to your art of the spear?"

"Yes, and I believe it healed him, or helped. Few treatments work so well to heal the *thumos*, head, and heart as the devoted practice of an art."

"He has got better even as I've watched."

"Achilles has now matched my skill level, and he will soon surpass me. He is, after all, namesake and grandson of the great Achilles, whose deeds will last, like yours, forever."

"I'd like you to teach me that spin, where you twirl the spear about and around you—a defensive miracle!"

"Yes, if one can manage it: dangerous to try in combat or even to practice, even for the skilled spearsman, but almost impossible to breach if one can accomplish it. I will teach you, but with caution, when you and I have fresh energy."

The Greeks' supplies running low, they all retired to a spare dinner, and, feeling stranded, they talked little, willing the darkness to come as soon as possible as an antidote to the clarity daylight shed on their restlessness.

When night fell and Artemis shone silver, shooting her sparks from along the river and skimming them across the broad water beyond, Odysseus sat alone in the bow to think. He had been having trouble sleeping, and even greater trouble planning, and rubbed his ankles against the growing chill. As the sliver of dawn marks the imminence of first light, he shivered, realized he had dozed, and heard the echo of a once-familiar voice ringing faintly in his ear: Athena!

—You must abandon the water and yourselves for a time, labor and learn, face the ice and flatland wind. Become your enemy and so know him.

"Haven't I always been my own enemy?"

—Smart man. You have learned not to rely on expectations, and yet you must learn what to expect. Your journey is blessed, but you won't achieve your end through cruelty, and you cannot attack the Trojan Northmen outright—they have too much strength and too great numbers for you. And yet you may succeed. You have learned to use your mind and your heart; you must learn now to use your spirit as well.

"I don't understand. How can I join them and not lose my gods?"

—Most men could not; you, Odysseus, can.

"Shall I then lose myself?"

—In losing one self you will gain another. Destiny has marked you for fame, first in the South, now in the North. Go forward to claim it, but go with wisdom and neither rashness nor malice. Have you forgotten patience and surprise?

"How shall we proceed?"

—Do as you did on Ithaka, when you returned. The man of many turns may take a turn as another man. Hide yourself in plain view, so that you may meet your Trojans man for man with hope in your belly.

"You have always blessed me, Athena. How shall I begin?"

"To whom are you speaking, old father?" asked Telegonus, appearing quietly from the foredeck and shattering Odysseus' already fleeting memories. The dream of Athena that had been reconstructing itself as he lay on the edge of waking faded abruptly, and Odysseus turned his face from Apollo's light to his son's face. Morning creased the sky and bent it with a rising blue, and a cold moon held out her fingers for one last pull on the river. "My mother said you sometimes talked with Hermes and Athena, but I wouldn't have thought you the type to hold much commune with Artemis."

"We seldom see eye to eye, Artemis and I, yet she is a goddess and I a man, so I pay her respects," Odysseus answered. "She once blessed my bow, but I have given it into the hands of another goddess, so I don't know if she will favor me again. Athena remains true to the one who will seek wisdom."

"Do you seek wisdom? It looks more to me as though we are seeking folly."

"Do you see wisdom as doing other than the gods bid you?"

"We must steer carefully between what the gods bid and what we bid."

Odysseus laughed. "You're right, young soldier." He fought off a shiver, but allowed himself a sigh. "How far may a man go without losing his gods?" Having said that, he wished he hadn't, but since he was too late to call the words back, he searched Telegonus' eyes, wondering how much wisdom the youth had inherited from his mother.

"If you're asking me, I can't see into the future, but I know this: the gods will go as far as a person will take them."

"And will we find new gods in the north?"

"You will surely find men who have to some people become gods, but the great Odysseus should know how such tales work. Come and practice the spear with me."

"Now, before breakfast?"

"That's the best time, when the muscles feel fresh."

"To you, maybe, but not to me."

"Will I grow old, Father?"

"You don't know? If your mother doesn't know, I can't tell you, either. If I may make a suggestion: live long without growing old. But how about some breakfast? I wish I had some of good Calydoneus' excellent eggs."

"We don't have anything, eggs or otherwise—sorry."

"Might as well practice with the spear, then. I'll loosen up as we go. Slowly, then, until I can shake the night from my bones. Killy, come join us! How would spearplay work, Telly, among three soldiers? Now we will learn what we can about war; later we must learn as much as we can of the northern language."

Later in the morning Odysseus saw Thrasymedes packing.

"Let me but ask you this, old fellow: stay with us one week. I have an idea that I think may give us hope, but we will need your skills. I agree with you, too, that we must risk our young oarsmen no further; I propose that you take them south to Ascerbergium so that, if they wish, they may settle there or follow the river south. Though they have not seen the wars and the world as we have, they have learned much on our journey and may follow you, serve new masters, learn a craft, or make their own way."

Thrasymedes, kneeling on his haunches, sighed deeply and spoke in sad rumble. "A week seems long as eternity now, Ody, but since you ask, I will try. Yes, I will take the young men south: their numbers will no longer help you if you go overland, and they may slow you unduly. I came to fight Trojans, and have at least fought their allies. Who knows yet what I may learn from my brother's spirit. Perhaps the Lorelei . . ."

"I shouldn't have tried her myself, Thrasy. 'Men have little patience with the gods, and the gods have less with men,' goes the old saying. I say mourn Antilochus properly, study with the Bructenians, and pray to Athena and Apollo. One can hardly go wrong so."

"Good advice from the Resourceful One," Thrasymedes said tiredly. "Meanwhile, what do you want me to do?"

That evening, following some lucky fishing by Philoctetes, the heroes held a council. The next morning they sailed for one of the quiet settlements near the mouth of the river. Where they could find the closest thing to safe harborage, the Greeks hid their boat and, with the exception of Philoctetes and Orestes, who remained to fish and guard the boat, moved inland as quickly as weary sea-legs permitted them, dressed in the hammer-marked cloaks they had won from the Northmen. Odysseus hoped that Philoctetes could absorb Orestes in fishing to keep him away from common and probably superstitious villagers. Orestes had remained uncommonly quiet since Antilochus' death, drawing at once Odysseus' concern and, considering their circumstances, relief. Reluctantly the heroes left their own familiar weapons behind—all but Telegonus and Achilles, who wouldn't give up their favorite spears—carrying only northern gear, so as to arouse as little suspicion as possible. They spent some time in reconnaissance, but by mid-afternoon realized that they must make a move or lose another day, so they entered the village two-by-two from different directions. Odysseus noticed an ethereal grainy smell as they walked.

Seeing the foreigners, the villagers stared, but paused only briefly in their tasks. They worked busily at various crafts: carpentry, smithing, lugging water or wood, preparing food. Business looked to Odysseus remarkably orderly; the cold bite in the air must bring with it a greater sense of urgency, he thought. He, Telegonus, and Dictys listened intently to whatever words they could hear, but the villagers seemed either reluctant to speak around strangers or remarkably taciturn. Odysseus thought that, as elders, he or Diomedes ought first to address someone, but he lacked confidence with the language, and he knew Diomedes felt less eager than he. Telegonus could best handle the task, but how would the local folk respond to a troop of soldiers led by a boy?

Then the thought struck Odysseus: that might just work, a golden-faced boy whom they might see as a god, at once disarming and intimidating. He spoke quietly to his son. "Have you heard enough of the language to try to speak to them? Good. We must find just the right one—ah, let's try that smith: he looks as sturdy as Hephaestos before his limp. Here's what I'd like you to say to him."

They approached a tall, broad, muscular man working with hammer and stained tongs on poor quality copper over a smoking fire. His blond hair and beard were cropped so short that he nearly looked bald. His hands stretched broad as flatbread baked for hungry men. He appeared to be trying to refine a curved blade that looked as if it might be a tip for cultivating implement. While the others stood at a distance with their faces shadowed in the hoods of their cloaks, Telegonus and Odysseus approached him. The boy allowed his hood just to expose bright eyes and the golden glow of his youthful features. His voice tumbled gently as the sound of one's best wine poured carefully into a bowl, as he applied the speech that weakens the resolve of the hearer.

"Neighbor, may the smith-god bless you."

The villager responded with silence and a nod, seemingly impervious. Odysseus wondered if he had understood Telegonus' words.

"Our commander sends us for supplies. After long days at sea, we must reinforce a regiment to the north, praise the gods," Telegonus said in an assured but youthfully ebullient tone.

The man nodded again. Odysseus noticed just a hint of the man's knees bending as though he would sit down.

"Can you direct us, neighbor, to where we may find supplies in this settlement or another, and to soldiers like us, if you have seen them? As your fellows, we ask your help."

The man blinked, shook his head slightly as though brushing away a fly, then bent his brow and struck his blade several light strokes with his hammer. Finally he spoke. Odysseus could understand most of the words, though he wouldn't have felt confident trying to render the speech himself. "Few come here, except for mending or—yes, as you say, praise the gods, Tror and his gods—or for . . . drink, yes, that's it. We make that here, drink—perhaps you smell it in the air? But we have a small village, and it is said the gods protect us, as do I—I could use a drink myself, you know—and some others who have families and so do not sail. We protect it, too. What was that you said? Praise the gods, yes. And you needed something—yes, supplies, praise supplies. Go that way"—he pointed with his hammer— "and tell them Hans sent you, and they will give you, what did you want? I must sit a bit." He stood still as a menhir, pointing.

"May the gods bless you, Hans, and we thank you. Wela be with you."

"And you, yes, supplies, and a drink, that's it. Wela, yes."

Odysseus couldn't believe the effect Telegonus' speech had on the man; he imagined what the boy could do once he had fully learned the northern tongue and how to reach its speakers.

"Not so difficult, Father," Telegonus said, as the heroes together approached a grand tent in the direction Hans had pointed, some few hundred yards from the smithy. As they walked, Telegonus and Achilles whistled, and the people they passed, hearing the tune, seemed to walk a bit more trustfully and move more comfortably. Odysseus himself felt his joints loosen and wondered if that came from walking on land for a change or from some magic in the boys' tune. "I'd bet," Telegonus chuckled, "that smith hasn't spoken so many words in his entire life."

"An enemy of substance, and so a better friend," Odysseus replied. "This tent looks to be their marketplace. I suggest we try it. Each man have his bit of gold? Remember: show little, spend less. The northern warriors obviously win some gold, though each man must not retain much of his own."

They spent the remainder of the daylight buying and trading, but mostly talking with the villagers. They realized they must find a larger settlement: if they were to gain much information about soldiers' camps, they must seek out wrights in the larger settlements who would have regular commerce with travelers. Odysseus noticed that the people would watch them tentatively, but, if they thought themselves unobserved, intently. They would need their vigilance. The alternative, slaughter, did not appeal to him. The villagers weren't Trojans, and Zeus' law of *xenia* must, he thought, apply not just in the south, but everywhere.

As evening drew its way onto the evening sky like the whifflings of a well-fed hawk, Odysseus asked one of the more talkative merchants where they might find a shipwright. He directed them to the south side of town, assuring them the man there could repair any problem they had. Telegonus thanked the man, who looked pleased as his eyes took on a healthy, relaxed look. He sat down, looking satisfied with his day's work, and then looking as though he had just forgotten something that had had importance to him once. Seeing the look, Odysseus laughed silently and shook his head. The Greeks assembled and headed for the south of town, their arms full of supplies, mostly food and simple tools, eager to learn what they could from the shipwright, more about troop movements—of which he should know more than anyone there—than ship repairs.

As they reached the south gate, they noticed a man sitting there on a rock, dressed in a long cloak with hood, his torso bent slightly forward, as if he were concentrating intently. As they passed him on their way through, the man nodded and spoke in a low voice, "Gods bless you, soldiers."

"And you," said Odysseus. As he walked past he placed a small pouch with a little of the Northmen's gold on the rock next to where the man sat.

"Generous of you, Aki Othis of the Vana."

Alarmed at hearing the name, Odysseus nodded to Telegonus, who addressed the man in his soothing tones. "My good man, may you use the gold well. Hide it safely in your pocket and sit very still, so that no one may find it and take it from you."

The man rose slowly to his feet. "You need not use that voice with me, young man, since I intend you no ill."

"May I ask, sir, your name?" said Telegonus. Odysseus noticed that he could hardly keep himself from speaking his own name.

"Rather forward of you, I should say," answered the man, "and I don't believe I'll tell you until we have talked a bit."

"Then you have the advantage over us, friend, or at least over me," Odysseus said.

"And I should like to keep that advantage," he said. "Would you wish to sit down here, young man?" the stranger asked Telegonus. Telegonus took two steps toward the rock, then stopped himself. Achilles walked right behind Telegonus and bumped into him when he stopped, so that both nearly fell down. Telegonus looked at the man with surprise. Diomedes grasped a short sword under his cloak.

"We must speak more openly before someone gets rash," said Odysseus, wondering if the man were a god or if by some special power he had moved Odysseus' thoughts to leave him the gold. "As a gesture of friendship, let us see your face."

The man stood still for a long moment, then brushed his hood aside, showing a youthful but weathered countenance with active hazel eyes and a tall brow. His thick brown hair he had cropped just below the ears. His smile uncovered large, even white teeth, and the gesture suggested more confidence than friendliness.

"Where, may I ask, did you hear the name by which you called me?"

"A man's name may circulate even in the wild north, if his deeds precede him. Too much heroism does not often serve the wise. Shall we sit here and talk a bit?"

Odysseus heard in the stranger's tones a version of Telegonus' power. He noticed his companions looking about, as though they would sit down if they could find a place. He, who had heard the voices of gods and Sirens, Norns and sibyls, called to memory the feel of Athena's presence and the plying necessity of her words, and he knew himself in the presence of no more than a highly skilled man. He acted as though he was about to sit at the stranger's feet, but when he bent forward, he grasped the man's cloak, and jerked it forward and up, sending the stranger flying backward. In an instant Odysseus, aging, but still firm of foot, stood over the man with his just knee above the stranger's windpipe and his weight slowly pressing down.

"Yes," Odysseus said, "let's talk. We'll start with your name and see where we go from there."

The man looked at first stunned and fearful, then despite Odysseus' weight bending toward him, he laughed. "Shall I believe, then, that you are after all a god, Aki Othis?"

"Believe what you will. Your name?"

"Please let me up, and I will tell you more than that. I have sought you for some time. I am called Gangleri."

"It means, I think, 'traveler' in the northern tongue, does it not?" Telegonus asked.

"Did your father so name you, or did you take that name to hide your own?" Odysseus asked.

"Is Aki Othis the name of a man from the south, or does

he take such a name to hide his purpose in the north?" Odysseus pressed his knee down until he could just hear the man begin to cough, then he let up. "My father named me *Gylfi,* but I have traveled so long that people in this region who have come to know me have called me—how did you call it?—'traveler.' I have gone through the northern world seeking wisdom and knowledge, and so have taken that name as my own. I have sought out gods and men to learn what they may teach me. I have gained some skills. I truly intend no harm, at least not to you. If you will talk with me, I may be able to show you much that will benefit you, who apparently are travelers, too."

"And why would we, soldiers on the way to joining our regiment, need anything from you? What can you tell us?" Odysseus, now in no position to meet harm, dropped his voice, let it rumble as though it came from the earth but tumble gently from his lips, tried whether he might not use Telegonus' voice of control on his adversary.

"He-he-he," Gangleri laughed. "You are not as good at it as your young friend, unless you are a god testing me, to see how far I will offend you."

"Father, you . . ." Telegonus began to speak, but Odysseus motioned to him to keep silent.

"Father? Does he mean . . ."

Odysseus, interrupting, returned to his normal tone. "He means I am his father, and since I am now going to return you to life rather than crush your windpipe, you may call me 'Father' also. You may well help us here, if you feel willing to offer your goodwill." Odysseus rose and offered the man a hand up.

"I offer it freely. I intended to do so all along; I merely sought first to make sure that I allied myself with someone worth following."

"And you believe you have?" Diomedes asked him.

Looking at Diomedes, then back at Odysseus, he answered: "Yes, I believe. I suggest, though, if I may, that we return to your ship before darkness covers us. While I'm sure you can take care of yourselves, your comrades will feel safer with you than without you. The soldiers of the *Aesir* travel by land and water, by day and by night."

Idomeneus fell in with Gangleri, easing him into friendly conversation, as they walked through the growing darkness. Picking their way with Gangleri's help, the heroes returned, along with their new colleague, to their boat to find their comrades restless, but secure. They had their boat well-hidden, and Orestes held up a basket of fish fillets for his fathers' approval. "Well done, lad," said Diomedes, "and we have brought supplies that will make that fish go down easily."

"I don't suppose you have any wine?" Philoctetes asked.

"No," answered Diomedes, "but we've found a substitute. Not as good, but potable: I tried some in the village yonder, and if you need a bit more of it, it can at least wash down food and make your head spin."

"Let's have a sniff. Phew! Smells like rotting grain," Philoctetes said disgustedly.

"Give it a chance; it will grow on you."

That night the heroes ate well, and they talked until the last of the stars had tumbled to rest into the western sea. From Gangleri they learned much, both about him and about the north. In the morning Thrasymedes began new drawings of the lands and waters ahead of them. Gangleri taught them some variations of the tongues of the north, detailed for them flora and fauna, and told them how the northern folk had learned to deal with extreme cold. He also told them of his own family and journeys.

He had gone to the court of those people called *Aesir*, and he had seen in person the face of Trorash, called in the north *Tror*.

"They say he comes from the ancient city called *Troy*, in the Orient, where giants and gods fought with men called Akilly and Agmemna and Disthus and Demodes to recapture the most beautiful woman the world has ever seen," Gangleri said, yawning.

"Maybe so," Diomedes mumbled, himself drifting into sleep.

"What's that he said?" Gangleri asked, looking through one eye, the other already closed in sleep.

"Nothing," Odysseus said. "What did you think of Trorash?"

"A man, like other men, though perhaps not fully like. More like you, but not so much a—god?"

Odysseus hadn't yet decided how much he should tell Gangleri. "No," he said, "not a god, though the gods have spoken to me, and I hope they will again."

"Thought so," Gangleri said, and fell asleep where he sat. The man had drunk more of the villagers' alcohol than Odysseus had thought possible, and he had known men who, were the sea filled with wine, could nearly have drunk it dry.

Seeing Gangleri nodding, Idomeneus said to Odysseus, "I think, Ody, we have found exactly what we needed: a guide who knows the north. And I believe what he has told me of himself and his family: he has as good reason as we for questing. We must allow delay if delay helps us learn to succeed."

Odysseus had many more questions, but Gangleri slept through that day and night. He awoke the following morning with a headache. They fed him, and Telegonus urged him to drink all the water his stomach would take, which he did only at Diomedes' insistence. Odysseus plied him with questions until Gangleri insisted he would say no more until he got some answers of his own. "One more question first," Odysseus said. "What took you to the court of Tror/Trorash?"

Gangleri sighed and nodded. "My father was a warlord in the northwest. Tror's Aesir came to us and demanded our allegiance. He took all that we had, including my father and brother to serve in his armies. I went in disguise to question his people and learn what I could about my father. They had far too much power and protection for me to get to any of them, but as they did, one may seek allies in the world. Now my turn: you don't seem like heroes come from the far south for rest and relaxation. A voice tells me that your quest differs little from my own."

Odysseus looked over the faces of his comrades, who one-by-one nodded assent. "Go ahead and tell him, Ody," Idomeneus said.

" 'Ody?' Why do they call you that? Is it a southern ending? In these regions the rumors call you 'Aki Othis.' "

"We have come here, Gangleri, to fight Trojans. Your Aesir are the last of our Trojans. That man is Diomedes, your Demodes, I suspect, and I am Odysseus—I think you named me Disthus—once king of Ithaka, now wanderer, along with you, of the north."

10

FROM MENAPIA NORTH

Walking on the beach, next to her. That smile: he knew it,
her, that enigmatic smile. The skin smooth and youthful,
with hints of the color of the Corsicans' wine and of light
in the western sky as the sun sets and the smell of clean
musk and grain and flowers. Walking together, placed his
hand in hers. Breakers rolling, pounding, easing in and
out, the waves warm, massaging the skin. Her arm slipping
round his waist, his around her shoulder, desire for her
lips. They walk together, then run, find a spot of shade,
where they fall together. Her body slender and sweetly
curving, her eyes pouring out the light of the sky, her face
round, the nose small and fine, the lips soft and warm as
leavened bread. Now he on top rolling, now she on top,
the golden hair falling over him like grain, then he behind,
she submissive, shimmering, then active, fluttering like a
dolphin. He loves her with his mouth, then from atop
again he thrusts, she smooth as water, smiling, accepting,
drawing—essence shooting from him, she recedes, he
reaches too late, wakes.

Odysseus found himself alone in the cool morning in his
accustomed spot in the bow of the ship, having suffered the
indignity of a teenager. Gods, such inconveniences at my
age—must our bodies betray us first and last? he thought.

He dived into the river, shivered at its muddy cold,

stripped his clothes, floated, swam a bit, washed. As he pulled himself onboard, the air chilled him more deeply than did the water, and he hurried for a fresh tunic. He dipped a bowl in the hot fruit-and-honey punch that Philoctetes had learned to make and downed the whole of it in a swallow, feeling the warmth dip as far as his belly, but not to his loins, which in the weeks of travel had calmed with the cold—he had begun to wonder if they had done so for good, and if his love for the golden-haired girl, should he find her, must fill his thoughts alone.

Odysseus sat next to Gangleri to breakfast on some dried meat and fruits and goat's milk that they'd got in the village.

"Why," Odysseus asked, "do people here call us 'Vanum'?"

"Vanum?" Gangleri echoed.

"I heard you say 'Vana,' " Telegonus said.

"Oh, the ending differs, and that threw me off, but the root is the same. I heard it from someone traveling from Bructen. To them it means 'striving ones' or 'those who desire something'; to me it means 'those of the wounded one.' I thought it referred, Othis, to your lost eye—no offense."

"None taken. You say we must start to the south. My friends here would rather go north."

"We'd have a better chance among the folk called the Menapians: they have less willing trade with and little love for the soldiers of the Aesir. You can exchange this northern gear for some of theirs and sail north with them on a trading venture. In their garb you will look less like stragglers or deserters, and they will happily take you into service, since they have much to gain from good relations with those people, who trade with the rich south, and often need stout sailors who can fight. We may do best to live and work with them for a bit: they may have seen dark men like you before and so will find you less odd and dangerous. If they accept us, for they are wary, we may even be able to stay with them for the winter, which can come soon and last long. And besides: Idomeneus tells me you like eggs, and the Menapians have the best eggs I have tasted anywhere in the world."

"Ody, eggs or not, I'm not eager to waste more months in the cold north doing nothing," said Diomedes, who among the Greeks was growing the most restless. "My sword has tasted too little blood, and my eyes ache for the sight of Trojans to feed it."

"Ah, my patient friend, you haven't yet seen a real northern winter. I know you told me of the pleasant snows of the mountainous south, but I warn you that the ice and wind of the frost giants of the far north could make you wish you were hurrahing your way down your god-mountain sitting on your shield."

Diomedes had taken a dislike to Gangleri since he had mentioned Helen, and though he kept his opinion to himself, Odysseus could see the slow burn in his friend's eyes, and he could sense defensiveness in Gangleri.

"I know you're right, Dio, but Apollo already rests lower in the southern sky, and Athena warns me in my dreams. We must wait, I think, and take our adventures here a bit longer, gain confidence with this world, and appease its gods as we do our own. Spring will be our time, I think, though our beards show Autumn," Odysseus said, trying to appease in another the anxiety he felt himself.

"Sensible, Othy—do you mind if I call you that as they do? It has a friendly ring to it in the dialect of my folk—and by spring we will get ready. I know how to get us there, if you can show me what to do once we're in. There we will need all that your Athena can offer us. Ha! I can still hardly

believe that I will fight with the heroes of Troy at my side—
almost as good as the gods themselves! Yes, yes, I know:
'Hush.' Tell me: why do you call the other young one
'Killy'?"

"Achilles."

"He can't be."

"His grandson."

"Unbelievable."

"Believe it."

"And the wild one?"

"Orestes."

"What of him?"

"You don't want to know."

"I want to know."

"I don't want to tell you."

Before the heroes moved southwest, they saw off
Thrasymedes, who, having remained for some days while
the Achaians sent reconnaissance south, had waited as long
as he would. Leaving his friends on the southern bank of
the Rhine, and having turned over his drawings of the
northern lands to Odysseus, he wished his old friends the
gods' blessings and, along with most of Calydoneus'
oarsmen, guided their boat southeast for Ascerbergium. Reluctant both to see his companion depart and to lose any
strength from their small force, Odysseus knew that
Thrasymedes was doing the right thing. The men on the
quest had come along not by vow or necessity, but because
they had desired so. No one should follow a mad quest
under compulsion, he thought.

Two of the rowers remained. Twins, Ori and Agni,
young cousins of Calydoneus, had eagerly joined the expedition, and upon their companions' leaving, had begged
Odysseus to remain with him: they had come for adventure,

had experienced some, and continued to long for more. Odysseus, who until then had not known their names, reluctantly agreed. Those two had shown courage if not skill in the battle with the Northmen; one who has courage can learn skill, though even one with great skill may have a difficult time learning courage, he thought.

The remaining companions stood on the bank watching their old shipmates depart. Orestes dived into the river, swam behind the boat, for a time nearly keeping up with the rowers, calling out in high-pitched burblings. After a time Odysseus could see he'd stopped, his head bobbing in the current, as the boat finally outstripped his swimming speed and left him unable to touch its wake. Finally the head disappeared beneath the water, and a ripple appeared to show that a subsurface form swam toward them. Shortly after the boat disappeared to the south, Orestes resurfaced, sad of face, inattentive to the river flotsam that festooned his hair.

That makes eleven of us left, Odysseus thought, but all willing fighting men. He looked at the faces around him, from the young oarsmen to the godlike countenances of Telegonus and Achilles to the strong but weather-beaten brow of their new counselor Gangleri to the weary but resilient eyes of Idomeneus and the indomitable, ever-ready solidity of Diomedes' stony cheekbones.

"We have lost a fine and worthy companion, men," said Gangleri, breaking the silence, "but we have a long way to go on foot, and these lands, however gentle seeming, have their dangers, even for the heroes of Troy."

"I should be wary of using that name," Diomedes warned.

"Quite right, my prudent friend," Gangleri countered. "But my point remains the same and true."

"Agreed," grumbled Diomedes, and the men set forth toward the coast to the southwest with as much speed as might carry them quickly yet not waste their reserves of energy.

They traveled for two days before they noted in the distance the first Menapian watchmen, who hid at simple outposts that offered them little comfort. The Greeks spotted them easily and managed to dodge them. When they came upon one sentry unexpectedly, Telegonus used the voice on him, after which he babbled briefly, then fell into a quiet, untroubled sleep. Under cover of night they reached the outskirts of what looked by its size a significant village. Gangleri, having experience with their language and customs, offered to approach the guardsmen at the gate. The others, storing their gear at a safe distance, remained hidden in the brush, more difficult because the leaves were beginning to fall with the chilling weather. "If I succeed in getting us admittance, I will signal by whistling a tune. Telegonus should follow me, then Achilles and the young rowers, then the veterans later—we don't want to alarm them. I believe I know their chief here, a man named Iolu. He is shrewd, but cautious: he will know your potential value to him, but also the dangers that accompany your odd appearance—no offense."

"I am beginning to take offense," said Diomedes.

"None intended, my touchy friend," said Gangleri, who slipped into the road and strolled nonchalantly toward the gate.

"I'm not sure about that," Diomedes harrumphed. "He says that more often than anyone I've ever met."

"Easy does it, Dio," said Idomeneus. "We need him more than he needs us."

"I doubt it, but if you say so, Ido, I'll admit the possibility."

As Gangleri advanced to the gate with both hands raised

and palms pointing ahead of him, two sentries armed with long pikes emerged to bar his way. Odysseus could just hear Gangleri speaking and could see him gesturing with his arms. He talked for some time, occasionally looking back down the path, until the guards impatiently motioned him in the gate. He entered, making a final gesture, and then proceeding slowly. The guards called to two others to replace them, then strode attentively down the way toward the heroes, holding their pikes in front of them.

"Better go on, Telly," said Odysseus. "Something may have gone wrong, but we have no better plan, and any one of us can handle these two pikers if need be."

Telegonus hustled onto the path, then walked composedly toward the guards after the fashion he had seen Gangleri use, with his palms facing up and forward. The two men stopped in a defensive posture when they saw him coming. He talked to them, but seemed to be making little headway, so Odysseus sent Achilles along. He could just see Gangleri in the distance, having passed the gate and looking nervously back. As Achilles approached, one of the guards pointed his pike aggressively towards the boy, at which point Philoctetes, no longer willing to wait, stepped into the road and followed. Odysseus was wishing he still had Antilochus and Thrasymedes, both of whom looked more scholarly and deceptively less martial than the rest, and so made perfect ambassadors, when Telegonus made a small wave with his hand, and both the guards let their weapons fall to their sides, stepped away to make room, and Telegonus and Achilles followed Gangleri through the gate. Philoctetes followed, bowing to the guards, who absent-mindedly bowed in return as he passed. The others followed then two by two, until Odysseus came last and alone.

By the time Odysseus reached the gate, a number of

other sentries had appeared, armed and looking none too sanguine at the arrival of so many strangers. Gangleri had passed out of sight ahead, and Odysseus thought that had he wanted to, their new friend could have betrayed them. He wasn't sure whether to consider that thought ungenerous or prudent.

Odysseus then realized that the Menapians might be responding not to the Greeks' southern strangeness, but to their northern cloaks, uniforms of soldiers with whom they apparently had little sympathy. As he passed a tall, youngish guardsman, Odysseus, using Gangleri's language, tried the voice on him, but the man merely sneered and spat out a few words Odysseus couldn't understand. The man, however, did not follow him, but remained rooted where he stood.

Traffic in the village grew quickly, and as they followed its turning pathways, people stared at them, then hurried around corners. Just as Odysseus found Gangleri at what appeared to be a market square, he heard the sound of tramping feet in the distance—the sound troops make on their way to battle. At Gangleri's urging the Greeks had come bearing only light arms beneath their military cloaks. "You must do something quickly, Gangleri, or a number of people will die, probably you among them."

Gangleri looked surprised, maybe slightly hurt, but motioned for the heroes to follow him. "I am remembering my way now. Hurry and follow me. The path twists, but I know the way to the chief's house."

"Why didn't you whistle for Telegonus, as you said you would?" Diomedes asked.

"I forgot that I'm not a very good whistler. No time to argue now—hurry!"

The heroes followed Gangleri through a twisting marketplace, down some narrow alleys, then out into an open square at the other side of which stood the largest building they had yet seen in the village. "That's it!" Gangleri said, and dashing forward, called through a window in a loud voice, using a language that to Odysseus' ear sounded part Norse, part Gallic. "Iolu!" he called, followed by a long string of syllables. Odysseus heard the tramping coming from several directions, grasped his weapon beneath his cloak, and looked about for cover—the Menapian guard would almost certainly have bowmen at their vanguard.

Then a grizzled head poked itself out the window where Gangleri had addressed himself. A look of surprise, then of joy, crossed the face. "Gangleri!" it spoke, followed by more words Odysseus couldn't understand. The head withdrew itself from the window, but in seconds came through the front door with a body attached to it: a man rather tall and slender, with wispy grey hair and beard but clearly still hardy, dressed in a white robe with a shiny, multi-colored pendant hanging from his neck, ran directly toward Gangleri and engulfed him in a bear hug. Gangleri returned the gesture, and the two men walked arm in arm into the building. Gangleri signaled behind him with his free hand for the Greeks to follow him. The grey-haired man ushered Gangleri through the door, then motioned for the Greeks to follow, just as several groups of soldiers marched threateningly into the square. With a whistle the old man called them off, and the heroes entered a dark, close, wooden hallway, through which they followed Gangleri and their host into a large, well-lit room.

"My friends," said Gangleri, "let me introduce you to the honorable Iolu, lord and chief of the northwest Menapians." Iolu bowed and raised his open palms toward them, so the Greeks did the same. Iolu looked pleased.

"Does any one of you speak the Gallic language of the south? Lord Iolu lived there for many years as a trader."

"I do, a bit," Idomeneus answered, "and Dictys better than I."

Gangleri spoke again to Iolu in the Menapians' tongue, and Odysseus could understand only the last word he spoke: "Odisthus." He wondered once more if Gangleri were betraying them.

Iolu leaped from his chair with a look of disbelief and a long string of surprised, hurried words, then he began to speak to Idomeneus, who answered haltingly in the language of which he had learned a little. "Yes, that man is certainly Odysseus."

Iolu leaped to Odysseus and gave him the same bear hug he had given Gangleri out on the square. He began speaking words more familiar to the Achaian ears. "Surely it can't be? Can that man still be living, the one whom the great gods challenged with sea and wind and man and beast? And here in my own humble hall, the man who built the Great Horse, who blinded Polyphemos, who traveled to the Underworld, who made love to goddesses, who returned after twenty years to the most patient of women and cleaned his castle of thieves and wantons, surely not that very man—unbelievable, unbelievable! Do you speak this language? Can the man who fought with giants at Troy speak with me?"

"A little," Odysseus answered.

"Ah! Unbelievable!" Iolu danced about like a child who has just won a hard-played game. "No one will believe me when I tell! Oh, but I must not tell! You must have some trouble, or you wouldn't have snuck in to see Iolu, you who have walked with the gods. Come and sit down; I must have your story! Ah! I have something here that you must taste—

you must not have had it for some time. Did you drink that nasty beer up north? Pah! And that yellow wine they make in the south? Ugh. You must drink with me now something worthy even of Ah-kian heroes!" Iolu opened a low cabinet and rolled out a large amphora. "Djulo! Call servants to pour this for me!" The Greeks heard a voice calling, then two boys hurried into the room, whisked out fresh bowls, and poured from the great amphora a rich, red liquid that the heroes had not seen in many months.

"Red wine, heroes! Drink up, just as you would find in the south! A man knows no better drink than this, though the sun has not yet reached its zenith." Iolu tipped his bowl, then let his head fall back with a sigh.

Diomedes, waiting no longer, reached for a bowl and drank its contents in a swallow. Then refilling his bowl himself from the amphora, he downed a second. "I've had better," he said, "but I can't remember exactly when."

"Demodes," Gangleri said to Iolu, pointing to Diomedes.

"Ah! You, in the flesh? Unbelievable."

"They say that a lot here, I've noticed," Diomedes said. "Do they not believe their eyes or our words?" He drank off another bowl.

"Demodes, Odisthus, drink your fill, and—oh, I am a bad host—I will send the boys for food. You must not have had decent food either, and you must tell me your stories and what has brought you here."

Odysseus sipped the wine, found it at first ambrosial, until he wondered if it tasted so only because he had lacked it so long. His memory drifted through the mainland and islands, to his own island of Ithaka; he had tasted better, but had no need to tell Iolu so.

Gangleri spoke quietly to Odysseus. "Don't worry, your

secret is quite safe with Iolu; I trust him as I would my own mother. You must tell stories, though, of your adventures, whether they be true or not. He will reward stories, and with his aid, we can get safe wintering and passage north in the spring."

Dictys, who had overheard, whispered in Greek, "I believe I can accommodate him. I have many stories, stories I have told, and stories I'm itching to tell, and I think I know the southern language well enough to tell them. Shall I, Ody?"

"Yes, but use prudence. Tell enough to please, but not enough to rouse."

"Done."

For the remainder of the day Dictys regaled Iolu with stories of the gods, of Troy, of the heroes' journeys home, of their adventures coming north, and some that, in the heat of the creative moment, he simply made up on the spot. Iolu laughed, groaned, whistled, cried, and could not get enough of the tales. His lieutenant, Djulo, saw to the heroes' comforts, getting them food and lodging and fresh clothing, showed them about the settlement, warned the guardsmen that they should not trouble Iolu's guests, and upbraided them for allowing strangers through their front gate without drawing even a drop of blood.

After midnight Odysseus returned to Iolu's headquarters, where the chief and Dictys were still drinking and telling stories by torchlight like old friends. Gangleri had fallen asleep in a corner. Iolu rose unsteadily and bowed to his guest, pouring with Dictys' help the last of another huge amphora into a bowl for the King of Ithaka to drink. "I have learned much, Ody, and we have much to gain from these people and to offer them in return."

" 'Ody'? You call the great hero-king Odisthus, friend of

Athena and Akille 'Ody'? Ha! May I also? Yes? Unbelievable."

Odysseus felt tired enough, aided by real wine, to sleep without dreams. He allowed himself to drain the bowl, accompanied by the cheers of his drinking companions.

Late the next afternoon, when Dictys finally woke, he related to Odysseus all he had told—or all he could remember of it—of their adventures and all he had learned of the Menapians. They had been surprised to find soldiers dressed in the cloaks of the Aesir arriving by land. The Menapians were good sailors and successful traders both north and south, along the great Western and Northern Seas, and the Northmen, usually better soldiers than sailors, had aimed to keep them as allies rather than to raid them for recruits and supplies, but the Menapians preferred to keep their own counsel and had remained aloof, trading with them only enough to keep greater forces away and hiding the greater part of their resources so as to seem a less desirable target. Iolu had shared considerable information about Menapian history and legends, and he had related to Dictys all he'd heard of the southern world—stories had traveled quickly, but had changed, twisted, grown over years and large areas of land and sea. Dictys had told of Odysseus' encounter with Poseidon, of their passing the Norns, of their winter in the east, of their battles with Northmen—those bringing rousing cheers from their host. He had deflected questions about their goals in the north, except to assure Iolu that the Achaians had no designs on anything that belonged to Menapians, other than perhaps to learn their knowledge of the seas, at which Iolu had beamed with pride. Dictys had deferred anything further to his leader, Odysseus, who, Iolu would understand, must speak for the group. "Well done, Dicky—who could ever say that poets have no value?" Odysseus turned over in his mind what he must tell his host, and decided not to consult Gangleri, but to walk a bit and pray to Athena. "Walk a bit with me, will you, while I think, and tell me as much as you can of their language."

By evening Odysseus had decided. He and Dictys returned to find Iolu, and Odysseus asked for a parley. He told Iolu why they had come north, what they knew of the Northmen and the Aesir, and what they had hoped to gain from the Menapians. "Translate for me, Dicky, so that I don't err. Here is what I want to say. We wish to learn their arts, particularly all they know of sailing the northern seas and how they withstand winters. In exchange we offer our labor until spring, when we will go north to our destiny. If he has any fine soldier he can spare who wishes to quest with us to destroy Trojans, he may join our company. We offer him our thanks, and I do so personally, the Resourceful One who has spoken with the gods."

Iolu, who nodded his head through Odysseus' speech, had partially understood, but Dictys translated completely anyway. A smile grew on Iolu's face as Dictys proceeded. When he had finished, the chief said, "I will grant you all you wish and more for one boon alone: Dicky, will you tell me how you passed the Lorelei? Men here fear her power above all others."

Dictys looked at Odysseus, who had understood. "Tell him how we survived by the goddess' grace, not by our own powers," Odysseus said. Dictys nodded, realizing that Odysseus didn't want him to tell the whole story, and he immediately launched into a long tale that kept Iolu spellbound until nearly midnight, while Odysseus sat sipping wine, enjoying it, but wishing for better once he realized that Iolu's stores impressed more by the Greeks' lack than by his own wine's quality. It is fair wine, he thought, but good enough—good *enough*.

"Truly astonishing, I should say 'unbelievable,' Dictys, had I not come to believe your tales implicitly. Come see me in the morning, and you'll find I am as good as my word. I have been meditating an adventure, and now that I have the additional force of arms of Greek heroes, I will undertake it—no worry, I shall unveil your identities to no one, but I may enjoy our secret nonetheless. I may be the only man in the north who hates your Trojans as much as you do, for they close our shipping lanes and frighten our merchants, and I would happily rid these lands of the lot of them. Now before sleep, Dicky, tell me again of the death of Hektor, tamer of horses."

Iolu proved his goodwill, and in the morning the Greeks set off on horseback along weaving paths until they reached the great western sea. Through the autumn they sailed with Iolu's best men to a great island in the west to explore its green, rich, rainy lands farther than the Menapians had dared. On a vast plain, beneath a barrow, they found a cursed treasure, but the Greeks feared no curse as long as Athena remained with them. Diomedes killed the beast that guarded it and so won for them all the wealth they'd need to fund the journey north in the spring. From there they sailed north to the lands of the Frasi and the Chauci, trading farther up the coast than they had ever gone. When they encountered Norse ships, they steered clear when they could, and when they couldn't they fought. Had they dared to leave any of their attackers alive, they would have become known as the scourge of northern seas and the bane of the Northmen, but through seamanship and soldiering brought themselves back to Iolu's lands with more wealth and stories than that wealthy man dared dream. In the winter they followed the main paths south to meet Menapus, the overking of those lands, and spend the winter in his court, and they felt lucky to have done so: the winter descended long and deep, with snow and icy winds such as no one could remember.

The Greeks learned to sail the longer ships of those seas; they learned the tricks of the north to survive all but the worst of winters, though as southern men they feared the cold would nearly kill them. They learned local songs and customs, and found what comfort they could in a culture less barbaric yet more insular than they had found since leaving the Great Middle-Earth Sea. The Menapian women found the strange southerners appealing, and even the young men, who came to know sexual love for the first time, found themselves more and more at home in those lands, all but Odysseus, who beyond experience and reason had come to wish for no one but the golden-haired girl, who came to him only occasionally in dreams, but whose presence in his waking fantasies kept him as self-absorbed and melancholy as a teenager in his first love.

Dictys, at Iolu's recommendation, had become Menapus' court poet, having gained as great facility with native tales as with his own. Philoctetes had come to see himself as Achilles' foster-father, trading with the maturing lad whatever they could learn of medicines and spearcraft. Idomeneus, longing for the charms of the previous winter's violet-eyed widow, kept himself busy smithing weapons. Gangleri basked in his association with the heroes, gaining more knowledge of Greek and of their culture. Diomedes felt happier than he had since they'd left the south, for once again he had conquered and adventured, until the snows turned their limbs to ice almost too thick for burning hearts to melt. For him, as for the others, this land felt foreign, and when the first shoots of spring notched the still-white ground with green and yellow, he began assembling gear for the trip north. Orestes for long months had gone strangely silent. His face had grown pale, like a man too far from his gods. Around Diomedes he showed perked spirits, but often he would follow Odysseus on long walks in the snow, their hands stuffed deep in the pockets of their cloaks, their lips silent, their minds far away.

One brisk morning as the ice began to clear, the Achaians took thankful but abrupt leave of Menapus and galloped north to Iolu's settlement, Dictys the least willing to leave, having settled into his pension, but each man smelling in the cold spring breeze the culmination of their quest. They had long since traded the last of their northern gear, but with their share of what they had acquired in the fall's adventures—their hosts had refused any cursed treasure—they bought Menapian gear, boarded the largest trading ship in Iolu's fleet, and sailed north. Iolu, too, had further enriched himself and his folk through raiding and trading, and his best captain, Horsa, gained the finest crew the world had ever seen to engage his venture north.

Before leaving, Odysseus purchased all the red wine that Iolu would sell him, all but one amphora. He stored it in Horsa's great ship, off limits to the entire crew, including himself.

In a week they'd sailed farther north than had any Menapian trader before. Having reached the lands of the Aviones, their ship decked in such martial finery that even the best of the Norse dragon-ships avoided them, they docked to trade along the coast of the northern sea. For the short term they took on stray soldiers there, hardy but unintelligent, and paid them well to row tirelessly and shout and grimace at passing ships.

In a month, guided by Gangleri's memory, when the warm breezes began to blow out of the south and the coasts showed spectra of color among the evergreens, they had found, visited, and studied the major outposts of the seacoasts. Finally, off Bornholm Island in the Baltic Sea, they fought a battle with a shipload of Aesirian guard, devastated them, and turned their ship and the remnant of their gear, except for their trading goods, over to Horsa, with the exception of the pay they owed their mercenary comrades, sending them south rich and happy with ancient treasures from the cursed hoard, likely to get themselves slaughtered before they could reach home. Most importantly, Telegonus was able to draw from survivors intelligence of Trojans' strength and the location of the court of the Aesir, in the south of the land called Sveria, as Gangleri had remembered. He, along with Dictys and Odysseus, also learned as much as they could of the local dialect, not so different from what they had from the first Norsemen they'd encountered on the Rhine. Before word of their victory could spread, they landed on that coast, loaded themselves with gear appropriate for training, and moved inland, pulling their goods on sledges. After a day's walking, from a distance they spotted a city that in its breadth, if not its height, rivaled Troy.

"Yes," said Gangleri, stifling a shout, "that's it all right, Asgard, home of the Aesir, though I came to it from the west before. And if I followed any other companions, I should demand the first swordstroke."

"We shall have plenty to go around," Diomedes said.

They crouched together around a fire to cook a meal and affirm their final plans, then took up their way with renewed vigor. As they moved overland closer to the stronghold, they came upon a rise, and the younger eyes could see armed men dressed in courtly gear. Just before a sentry on one of the walls raised a halloo, Odysseus caught a glimpse, on a long greensward, of a healthy girl walking, carrying a basket, her hair dancing and shimmering gold as the sun that stroked it. He felt a shiver race up his spine, and beneath his tunic blood rushed to the forefront as it had not done in weeks of gloomy winter. He knew, even from a distance, who she was, and his heart and his hands and his face grew southern-warm, though not for battle. Somehow, perhaps by Athena's blessing, he knew even through aging eyes the golden-haired girl of his dreams.

11

THE AESIR

Odysseus returned the sentry's call, and he and the other
men with their hands free raised them, palms out, in the
customary greeting of the Menapians. Dressed after the
fashion of their previous hosts, the heroes, expecting that
the Northmen would recognize their gear, hoped for a cor-
dial welcome from a people who had long sought the
Menapians as allies and suspended any enmities. Where in-
telligent men have much to gain through peace, they can
sometimes avoid war, if the profits look good.

Odysseus prepared his men. "Friends, we have long
planned for this day. We have traveled sea and land, met
gods and monsters and armies, and now we have found
Asgard, home of the last of the Trojans. A little patience yet
will bring us what we seek. Gangleri and Telegonus, our
best with languages, will lead us as our ambassadors, and
Diomedes and I will follow them two steps behind. Achilles:
you shall now find your Trojans; follow the lead of brave
Idomeneus and Philoctetes, who have fought them before,
and you should bless the gods for Orestes at your side.
Dictys: you shall depart here with the second-best story you
have ever told. Ori and Agni, kinsmen to great Calydoneus,
while you bear burdens now, you have learned the art of the
spear from two noble teachers, and your diligence will pay
off should you need it. Heroes, you who follow here do so

184

as equals, for when we fight, each man stands up as his own lord. We who have got this far may get farther; we who have felled Trojans may fell Aesir, who abandoned their Trojan allies at the thought of us. Good cheer! The man who kills a king here may claim an empire. The work's done, and now the game begins."

"A man who has friends may go a long way, if luck stays with him, and he should count himself blessed," Gangleri said to Telegonus as they took their place in the formation.

Time may stand still as a stagnant pool; it may drip like runoff from a gentle rain; it may rush like a cataract poured through a funnel: having journeyed and waited, the Achaians found themselves at the brink of their success or failure. Breathing the bracing air of northern spring, anyone but such veterans would have charged the gate, weapons aloft, shouting their challenges. Each of the Greek heroes took a deep breath and calmed his eagerness, and with a lurch they pulled their sledges forward with the demeanor of men who have troubled greatly to bring their goods to market and who desire nothing so much as a hot drink and a long nap by a roaring fire. Odysseus felt pleased that they found the fortress of the Aesir, while secure, fairly lightly guarded—that showed men who, while cautious, believed their world relatively safe.

"Hay-up-hi, the lion, the lion," Orestes sang softly in the Menapian tongue. Heads jerked to him, and Odysseus was about to urge quiet, until he saw Orestes' face. They returned his gaze with the widest, wildest eyes Odysseus had ever seen, and the wily one could do no more than chuckle and pick up the tune that he didn't know, but that sounded, like so many of Orestes' ditties, oddly familiar. Odysseus glanced at Diomedes, whose face mirrored his own pleasure at the return of the fighting spirit of their gifted godson.

185

"Hush my Aesir, my peaceful Aesir, Achaians feed to-night," Orestes sang, and before long all the men had picked up the tune as they nearly hopped along, sliding their burden with a lightness of heart that must have scared the sentry, who, seeing them approach, shouted a deep and resonant "Halt!" A sentry, with other armed men aligned to either side, stood atop the parapet of the long wall that spread beyond sight in either direction.

Telegonus stepped forward along with Gangleri, who had shaved his beard, leaving only the long moustache that some of the Northmen wore, and who kept his hood up to hide his face, lest someone recognize him. "We have heard that you desire trade with us," Telegonus said. "We have traveled now some weeks in the south and in the north and have acquired some goods that may interest your lords." Telegonus spoke without using the Voice, but in clear Norse with a Menapian accent. His smile beamed despite his attempt to seem nonchalant, and he allowed his hood to fall away from his face, exposing features that to the northerner would seem, because of their golden youth, less alarming.

"Who are you?" the sentry asked. He had the shoulder-length blond hair and beard and pale skin and eyes of the Northmen and had his cloak hasped all the way to his chin.

"Menapians."

"Menapians don't trade with us."

"We have been long away from our home and king. We hope to return with such goods as will make him a better friend of ours and yours."

"What do we have that you want?"

"That remains for your merchants to teach us."

"What do you have that we want?"

"That we may only show your lords: it is only for people

who have traveled the world and known its better pleasures." In those words Odysseus heard a hint of Telegonus'
magic.

"Why does a young man speak while the elders remain
silent?"

"I serve them as ambassador: I speak your tongue more
easily than they, but where we come from they have power
and authority such that your lords will suffer no dishonor in
dealing with them."

"If they are lords, why do they travel with merchants?"

"Have you ever known Menapians not to travel with
lords and soldiers?"

"Are you then soldiers?"

"Only so often as we need be, when we must deal with
pirates rather than men of quality. Will you turn us at your
gates, or *allow us to enter and speak with one of your lords?*"
With those last words Telegonus turned on the power of the
Voice—a risk with so many men along the wall listening,
but he directed the words as specifically as he could to the
sentry who spoke. Odysseus noticed several of the men
wobble a bit on their feet, and the speaker on the wall had
to catch himself to keep from falling backward. His lids
drooped, and he blinked his eyes rapidly and shook his
head.

"May we come in the gate?"

Silence lasted for several long breaths, to the point where
the Greeks were becoming nervous and Diomedes began
fingering a dagger beneath his cloak.

"Open the gate," the sentry called within, "but take care
to search what they carry."

Telegonus looked back to catch Odysseus' wink, and the
heroes proceeded beneath the gate, a large, elaborate
wooden door with enormous hinges. It opened ponder-

ously, and inside stood a troop of men with large shields and either swords or spears. The sentry, looking slightly pale and confused, approached with several other unarmed men who looked official but unwarlike. Telegonus spoke again quietly to the sentry. *"You need not search us,* since we intend you no harm, but you may observe our goods—I would happily grant you a taste if I didn't fear the displeasure of your lords."

"I believe, my prudent ambassador, that we may allow this fine man a taste of our wares," Odysseus said, keeping his face covered. "My good sentry, have you ever *tasted wine?"*

"Wine," the man said uncertainly, "I have never taste—I have heard, I think, yes, heard." Anticipating and yet more confused, he reached out an unsteady hand.

Odysseus motioned to Ori and Agni, who unsealed a small amphora and brought it forward along with a bowl. "Then *you must taste* and see for yourself, to determine whether or not your lords will approve. *I'm sure* they will trust your judgment." Odysseus tried the Voice himself. He glanced at Telegonus, who with a barely discernible head shake indicated his impressed approval. Odysseus took the amphora and poured a small amount in the bowl, took it from Agni, and handed it to the sentry himself, using his other hand to steady the man's arm. All the Northmen close by leaned forward to get a look into the bowl. The sentry swirled it about and sniffed it, made a sound of pleasure, then tentatively tasted. His eyes widened.

"Marvelous. What is it?"

"Made from the fermented juice of grapes, a fruit of the south, where we purchase it. It has the ability to cleanse the belly, lift the spirits, and ease troubled thoughts. Folk there call the making of it an art. The makers *take us to their*

leaders to get their approval before we may buy and sell it—
they permit only the traders most friendly with them to
share it, and then in small quantities. What you see here on
our sledge represents a year's bargaining and all we have."

"I can't make up my mind. May I taste again?"

"Of course you may, sir," Odysseus answered, "but you
will want your *king's approval,* and he will appreciate the
man who has brought the wine more than the man who has
drunk it."

" 'King's approval'? I can get you nowhere near the king.
Why would you say *king* when the best a merchant can hope
for is steward?"

Odysseus feared he had misspoken; he had forgotten that
Ithaka was after all only a small island and he an unusual
king in the careful management of his own affairs. "You see
why I had my ambassador speak for me: I merely used the
wrong word. 'Steward,' you say, for the man who provisions
a lord's household with drink that may *calm the thoughts?*"

"Yes, 'steward,' though in this case I will take you to the
king's steward, since I believe you when you tell the drink's
virtues, and the king may well do business with the folk who
bring it, particularly an ally he has long sought. Make way,
then, to the stronghold," the sentry called to the men who
had crowded round. They immediately fell into file, leaving
a clear path directly toward the center of the enclosure,
where Odysseus spotted a tall wooden structure within an
additional wall. Surrounding the grounds stretched broadly: a greensward with lawns, pools, animal
pens, and training grounds for soldiers. "I shall take you
there myself," the sentry said confidently to Odysseus.

As they followed the sentry, Telegonus fell in next to
Odysseus and whispered in Gallic, "Will the son offend if
he call the father a fine student? You have learned the Voice

189

even better than the spear, and you have learned the spear well."

"Not at all," Odysseus answered in the same language. "Who mustn't learn more than he himself can teach, if he wishes to survive in the world?"

The enclosure felt even larger from within than it had appeared from without, and the parade of men took some minutes to reach and pass across the greensward through the internal wall. Once they entered, the sentry sought to relieve the travelers of the need to haul their own goods, calling servants to take the burden, but the Greeks insisted on carrying their own wares—such, Odysseus said, was Menapian custom. They stopped for a time at a watchman's hut appended to a much larger building, waiting for the sentry to retrieve someone from the king's household—a steward for such a place would be a busy man if he wished to keep his job and his head. The Greeks were just beginning to feel restless when the sentry returned with a stern, clean, but anxious-looking man who obviously held authority and understood it, yet knew it precarious.

"Menapians, eh? I don't believe that for a minute. And what have you brought, some drink from the south? We don't need that here."

The sentry tried to draw him aside to tell him about the wine, but the steward brushed him off. "And what about these other crates, the long cylinders and these heavy boxes? I don't suppose you have brought gifts from a people notoriously stingy with their goods. If you'd brought grain last fall we could have talked, but not now. We trade elsewhere and have got all we need for the summer, and we never trade in trinkets. Before you exit the gate, though, you will show me what you have in all its glory. You will not be permitted to travel in our regions with anything the spokesmen of the Aesir have not approved."

The use of "Aesir" caught everyone's attention, but Odysseus was already busy plotting how to deal with the officious steward.

"Steward, *you need not trouble over us.* Your lords will thank you for having acquired our wine. If you doubt its virtue, allow us to bring it to them ourselves. We will risk our own necks to attest to its quality. As your lords are Aesir, they will know wine and will not bless the man who turns merchants away. *Come along* and see for yourself," Odysseus said, praying to Apollo to bless the power of the Voice, "and you yourself may experience the power of the red liquor's flow."

"What's that you're saying?" asked the steward, agitated. "There's something odd in your voice that I don't like. Who are you merchants, anyway? I don't trust you." With a wave of his arm the steward called armed soldiers, who hurried quickly to his side. Telegonus caught Odysseus' eye and spoke.

"Good steward, allow me as ambassador to speak for my lord, who has earned respect for his deeds and who has traveled the wide world bringing kings from many lands the goods they have sought. He employs me for my gift with words; I follow him for his goodness and the quality of his blood. Your soldiers trouble themselves unnecessarily: *let them rest.* Please *bring us to your lords, so that we may share with them our gifts and our wares.* You will win no better deal by keeping them or us waiting. *Ease your mind, and gain our thanks for your help.*"

"You, too, speak oddly—I don't like it. I will have these soldiers . . ."

"You will *ask them to relax.* They should *not trouble their lords* unnecessarily. *They should sit down and rest and enjoy the beautiful day while you take us to your lords to parley.* They will want our wine, and you may present the wine for us. *Be calm; you have no need of trouble.* You are like us; you merely want to get ahead in the world. Let yourself *enjoy what we have to offer,* since life is short, my friend." Telegonus put all his effort into the magic of the voice. Hearing his voice, the Norse soldiers began to wobble where they stood, and some sat down with pleasant, empty, tired smiles on their faces, but the steward, though his eyes glazed, remained tough as an old tree stump, and Odysseus could tell that the magic had sapped Telegonus' strength as well. Then Odysseus heard the sound of soft singing.

> The lion, the lion,
> sleepy, sleepy lion,
> the lion, the lion,
> the sleepy, sleepy lion,
> Hey, wup! hi:
> Hush, my steward, my faithful steward,
> the wine is good tonight!
> Hear, my steward, my sleepy steward,
> the wine will please tonight, ho!
> Hey, wup! hi, Hey, wup! ho!

Orestes, coming from behind the other men, was singing, the rhythm of his silly tune as moving as if he had by listening acquired the Voice and was using it for song. The soldiers already sitting on the ground began to move their heads and shoulders back and forth, swaying to the tune, while all those still standing either dropped beside their comrades or began a simple step-dance. Even the steward, despite his self-control, began to bob to Orestes' rhythm, and the Greeks, catching the spirit, began to dance: stepping, dipping, turning, humming along with Orestes' gibberish.

"Come, steward," Odysseus said, "you hear the music! *Let us bring wine to your king."* Odysseus grabbed Telegonus' arm to gird him, and all the Greeks and the remainder of the Northmen who could still stand fell in line as the steward spun about on his heel and, bobbing and swaying as he walked, led the singing Orestes and his strange dancers along a pathway, through an alley, across a courtyard, through another passage, and to an enormous door to the great hall of Asgard. As they passed Norsefolk busy with their duties, anyone absorbed in an activity had listened, shaken his head at the inexplicable sight, and moved on either laughing or incredulous. Any absent enough of thought to listen to the song had fallen into line behind the soldiers and joined the dancing line, until at the door the company had acquired sufficient numbers to trouble Odysseus' plans.

"I don't, don't, I don't like this, sleepy, sleepy lion, like this at all, hey-wup! sleepy lion wine, and I won't knock," chanted the beleaguered steward, who grasped the door knocker in his right hand, but tried to keep himself from moving it.

"Of course you want to knock!" Telegonus said, having regained his strength in the release of the dance. "You wouldn't burst in on your king without knocking."

"I don't even know if the lion, sleepy lion—I mean king—is inside the lion, faithful steward, wine tonight, tonight—if the lion—king!—is inside."

"Knock, and you may enter; seek, and you may find," Odysseus said, wanting to help Telegonus save his strength.

The steward could resist no longer, and knocked; then, without waiting for a reply, opened the door into a great dark hall and stumbled in.

The Greeks hurried through the door. Ori and Agni lifted huge amphorae of wine, while the other Greeks grabbed the boxes and cylinders. At the end of the line Philoctetes thrust the steward right back out the door into a large group of folk who looked terribly disappointed to find their dance at an end. "If I were you, I'd drink as much beer as my bladder would hold. It won't do you all that much good, but considering what may happen, you probably won't have it in you long enough to do much harm. Better to meet your fate with a dull head," he said and shut the door and threw the bolt, casting a quick smile at the steward's astonished face.

Inside the hall the heroes advanced quickly, doing their best to catch their bearings and harden their hearts. In the center of the hall they saw a fire burning. Many men and some women stood around a dais where several richly-clad figures sat as light poured from some high windows down upon them. A medium-tall man wearing a long, white robe rose as he spotted them. He had long, silvery hair and wore a green garland around his forehead. His dark skin shone olive in the light of the hall, and his eastern features, like those of his seated companions on the dais, set him apart from the light features of the Northmen who served him. Odysseus led the heroes toward the dais; the others fanned out behind him. With two quick hand movements, the man on the dais sent guards scrambling to outflank them and surround the room, while several stout men with axes at their belts took stances between him and the intruders. When Odysseus got just outside the range of an axe stroke from the guards, he stopped and addressed the king. Behind him stood Diomedes and Idomeneus, then Ori and Agni with their amphorae, then Gangleri and the other Greeks spreading themselves out as widely as they could without actually bumping any of the Northmen and without stepping too far from the containers they'd carried in.

From the dais rose a man with a wild shock of curly black hair tinged with grey, carrying a warning horn, which he placed to his lips, about to blow.

"Too late for that," Odysseus said in the northern tongue.

Odysseus cast a quick glance about, hoping beyond hope for a look at the blond-haired girl. Failing, he addressed the king.

"Leader of the *Aesir*, we have traveled long to meet you, and we have brought something especially for you." Without turning his back to the king, Odysseus motioned with one hand toward the amphorae.

"Leader of the *Vanir*, what have you brought me?" the king asked in a deep, resonant voice shadowed in irony.

"Pardon, but you mistake us, lord: we are Menapian traders who carry a great boon. Perhaps you have heard of it: wine, red wine, from the lands of the far south, such as few men of the north ever taste."

"Be sure, I do not mistake you. But why should you bring me this boon?"

"Maybe you have something we want in return."

"What do you want from us, or should I say from me and my family, Othysseus of the Vanir?"

"What *does* that word mean?"

"Ha! It means 'expected ones,' Othysseus One-Eye, for we have long expected you, though we knew not when." The king had answered Odysseus in Greek with an eastern accent.

"And how have you come to expect us, and what do you expect of us, Trorash of the Anchae?" Odysseus noticed out of the corner of his eye soldiers jockeying for position around the periphery of the hall.

"The people here know me as *Thor*. Did you not have an encounter with our goddesses, our Norns, off the coast of Latium? You might have paid Aeneas a friendly visit as you passed, though they'd have told us of that, too. I'm sure he would have felt glad to see you again—and you him. Ha! Well, and not only Achaians have their sibyls, you know. We have ours, and ours has spoken, though your movements have been dark to her since the autumn. She, I believe, will be glad to see one of your men, though she probably won't see him for long. Come forward, *volva*."

From the rear of the dais a thin, pale, wispy girl with long blond hair and great dark eyes advanced slowly to the edge of the dais. She was breathing rapidly and shallowly, and her eyes moved rapidly and uncertainly among the crowd, which had fallen to utter silence.

"Orestes!"

The girl's thin voice rose like the chirp of a sparrow, circled the hall, and found its landing place. From the back of the hall, from somewhere amidst a group of northern soldiers, came an abrupt, sharp, pained answer:

"Ah!"

"Ha, ha, ha," the king laughed, "you see, Othysseus? We know you, but you have no wooden horse to hide you, and I have the best-trained soldiers of the north to aid me, for, you see, *I am their god, and if I had been yours, you had survived this day, though I made a slave of you.*"

The king too had the Voice—Telegonus sucked in his breath, but Odysseus didn't wait for him to speak.

"Will you not taste the wine we've brought you?"

"We will taste it, but after we have tasted your blood."

"You may not have that chance."

"How will you stop me? Athena and Apollo have no sway here, and neither have you."

"The gods hold sway everywhere, and so yet may I here."

Telegonus had been gathering his strength, and from him rumbled a sound that nearly sent Odysseus, with all his veteran's strength, sprawling.

"SLEEP."

Odysseus shook his head rapidly to clear his thoughts, and as he gained control of his senses—he took little more than a second—he could hear the sound of men tumbling to the floor all about him. The warriors before the dais looked stunned and wobbly, but held their ground, and the king himself stood with his jaw agape and his eyes dazed. The poor little sibyl let out a shriek, but even that couldn't have waked the soldiers who had fallen into a deep slumber.

"*Wake, my soldiers,* and protect your hall against the godless thieves who burnt Troy."

Some of the Northmen tried desperately to scramble to their feet, but Odysseus called out to his comrades, "Now!" and, dazed but ready for the adventure that had brought them from the world they knew to the wild cold of the north, they burst open their boxes to grab swords and shields or their cylinders for long spears. They dashed over sleeping bodies to positions in the corners of the room from which they could both defend themselves and prepare their attack.

The party on the dais rose almost casually to take up weapons, as though they had fought as many battles within their hall as without. A man with long arms, a long grey beard, and skin dark as if burnt by the fire of a forge handed Thor a huge-headed war hammer. "What do you hope to gain, Othysseus of Ithaka, by fighting the gods of the people of the north?" Everyone looked about for a position of advantage.

Diomedes, gladdened to hear spoken Greek, chimed in for

himself. "We have come, Tror-Trorash, not to assault the gods, whom we honor, but to kill Trojans, whom we despise."

"And you must be Diomedes? Who else! Then you have come to the wrong place, for you will find no Trojans here. We did not contend with you at Troy, or you would not have outlived the war, and you will offer us little challenge now. Why would you kill a few men and offend Zeus' law of hospitality only to die in minutes yourselves? You have no chance against our strength and numbers far from your own land: we have you locked within our stronghold!"

"Or," said Idomeneus, "we have you locked within your stronghold. We haven't come for hospitality, so we offend no god; we have come to fight, and fight we will, with the same gods at our sides who stood by us at Troy."

"Don't be too sure of that, hmm—you must be Philoctetes? No, no, he is known as a spearsman, and you carry a sword, which must make you: Idomeneus! You know, you should have parlayed with us; we would as happily have taken your wine as your blood." As they continued carefully to assess their positions, Odysseus noticed leaping from the dais not only armed men, but women warriors as well, two of them older, but armed with long, light bronze swords and moving nimbly on their feet. He had fought Amazons before and had not liked it, but one must take enemies as one finds them.

Odysseus sought to circle the dais to determine as well as he could the full size of the hall and the full numbers of the enemy. "Tell me, Tror, Thor if you prefer, how you have got these folk to deify you?"

"Othysseus, you wish to be a god yourself? Is that the real reason you've come? Ha! Then all you need do is drop your weapons, bow down before me and my Aesir, and we will name you minor deities who have come from the ancient south to serve us. If that doesn't appeal to you, you may take the job of my steward, who has clearly failed me. I should dearly love to have someone who can procure good wine for me, and who knows what else. Here, if you want to become gods, you must do it by deeds: prove yourselves better than the old ones. You have but a moment to decide: I have sent for reinforcements, and your chance of getting out alive, never good, has now diminished to nearly nothing. Let my smith show what's in store for you."

A shower of vermillion sparks, bursting over the top of the room in a puff of smoke that smelled of bronze and sulfur, fell upon the soldiers like a shower, sizzling and rousing muffled shouts of pain as embers fell on exposed arms and necks.

"Your last chance to surrender, One-Eye, or at least to pray," Tror called as Odysseus continued to circle the dais.

"You can't scare Achaians with false magic or false gods; we have magic and gods of our own, and may Athena, Apollo, Poseidon, Ares, and Zeus himself bless our arms. Spears, lads! Let's see if these Trojans can fight as well as they preach."

Over the heads of several Northmen Achilles tossed Odysseus a spear, and, working together as powerfully as spokes of a wheel, Telegonus, Achilles, Odysseus and Philoctetes began whirling in a coordinated attack. Following their lead Diomedes, Idomeneus, Dictys, and Gangleri, beginning with their backs to the walls, hacked their way toward the center of the hall. Ori and Agni jammed the front door and pulled short bows to fire into groups of Northmen knit too tightly. Orestes had wrapped the end of his whip around a rafter, and with a rising wail flew across the dais, sending the Aesir diving out of the way, and landed near the rear door to guard it against reinforcements; and as he swung his whip with one hand and cat-o-nine-tails with the other, he looked about the crowd for sign of the delicate young sibyl who had pierced his heart, but couldn't see her, and so he began to sing:

> Gods save Diomedes, gods save Odysseus,
> Father One, Father Two;
> Make them victorious, liberally glorious,
> sing out stentorious,
> sibyl and Orestes, too.

The Northmen, grim as ice, found no humor in Orestes' song, for the battle over Asgard had begun. The percussion of wood on wood, the hiss of metal on metal, and the sough of warriors' rushed breathing filled the hall like the sounds of a storm venting through a mountain pass, as the soldiers, spinning, slashing, pounding, engaged in a controlled frenzy of violent power such as even Troy, with its man-to-man duels and one-sided attacks had never seen. The Northmen advanced like demons, unyielding, with no intent of sparing their own lives or others'; the Greek heroes unleashed a focused, horrifying pleasure in battle as they unleashed months of pent-up planning in a fury of cuts, parries, and thrusts.

With a flick of his whip Orestes pulled from the hands of a huge Northman an enormous sword which he stuck in the doorlatch to bolt the entryway. Ori and Agni, having plugged the front with amphorae, crates, and benches from the hall, fired missiles over the heads of groups of enemy soldiers to keep their heads low and their attacks weak. The wheels of Greek spearsmen and swordsmen spun and sawed their way through troops who had never seen such choreographed battle maneuvers.

Odysseus felt once again the youthful joy of battle in his heart, but this time the weight of age slowed his limbs. He conserved energy, fought with rhythmic grace rather than confident abandon, realizing he would not have the strength to carry on indefinitely. His thoughts, even as he swung his spear in great airy circles, then punctured them with two-handed blocks or pointed thrusts, drifted to the dead Antilochus and the grieving Thrasymedes, brothers for all ages, to the shrine where Thrasymedes, he hoped, offered prayers not only for his own brother, but also for Odysseus' many fathers, to Telemachos on Ithaka who had known a father's love, but little of his heart, to Penelope who had waited beyond the greatest boundaries of human patience, only to keep company with shades, and finally to the blond-haired northern maiden of whom he had an hour before caught a glimpse on the greensward, and his thought of her blood left his arms and filled his manhood, so that an observer so inclined might have thought that the great Odysseus derived sexual pleasure not from women, but from battle. As his arms weakened and his thoughts strayed, Odysseus relied more on technique than resolve, and as, pushing one Northman from him with a two-fisted blow of his spear, he turned around, he had just time to see an enormous, beautiful, regal young man, his face and eyes olive-dark, but his hair golden and falling about his shoulders, raise a sword high above his head to deal the death stroke to the leader of the invaders.

As the blow began to fall, time seemed to Odysseus to have slowed intolerably, as a thought, faster than a diving bird of prey, entered his mind, asking if in such a way as this one all people experienced death, with a terrified but resolute assurance that darkness waited an instant away.

Then Odysseus observed that time must indeed have

stopped, for the hall, having rung with the wild dance of spears and swords, had fallen to near exact silence, pierced only by a sound that reminded Odysseus of the suffering, pent winds blowing their escape form Aeolus' bag. The sound ended with a tight *thwipp,* and the young man stood with the sword still raised over his head and an astonished look flashing from his eyes. Blood spurted onto Odysseus' face, and his attacker's eyes glazed. With a lurch forward, he fell backward like a great oak tree tumbling to clear land for the business of men.

The entire room seemed to have watched the soldier's fall, and a gasp seemed to rise from them as though from a single person, and that person a parent. Light dulled in the hall, as though a cloud had passed over the sun. The arrow that had killed the young man snapped as he fell backward onto it, pushing the point forward through his chest.

Not far from him Odysseus heard a high-pitched screech, and a woman of at least middle age, dressed in studded-leather armor and wielding a staff, came at him with a ferocity and speed he wouldn't have thought possible. He had just time to duck as she struck him on the left shoulder, then she swung again and caught him behind the knee. His feet flew from under him, and he landed on his head with a thud, bringing blood as though in a huge clot to his nose. Though short on breath, he threw himself to his feet and with a deft, wide circling of his spear caught the woman's feet from under her and sent her sprawling into the pool of blood that collected beneath the fallen young man.

As he rose to his feet, another lithe and supple figure followed from behind the woman who attacked: a round, youthful, glowing face, glowing like a healthy peach, with wide, round eyes the color of the sky and rosy lips just parted to show teeth white as wave caps. Her smooth, slim fingers held a light staff defensively, but aggressively, before her.

"*Stop!*" yelled Tror, who had bounded onto the platform, and he brought down his war hammer with a thunderous blow that split its slats and resounded in the hall like thunder. "Stop, I command, I beg you!" As the first imperative had issued from his lungs with defiant insistence, the second followed with heart-wrenching pleading.

Every other combatant stood still as Tror in three bounds reached the side of the fallen woman, who raised her head and opened her dazed eyes. Odysseus noticed that her face bore the wrinkles of motherly joys and sorrow, and iron-grey hairs strayed from their binding and whisked her temples. Seeing her alive, Tror snapped his fingers, and an older man, with no interference from the Greeks, fell to her side and cradled her head.

Tror took in his hands the face of the fallen giant, but he was too late: life had left the body upon the instance of the arrow's entry, and its shade had already turned for Hades.

Tror's tears dotted the pale face like raindrops.

Then with a roaring growl he rose and turned his wrath on Odysseus, his voice rising as from underground. "Until now I felt no anger, but I will be avenged for this deed."

Then the battle might have climaxed, with Tror and Odysseus grappling each other and wrestling until one had squeezed the life out of the other, but a pained, youthful voice sprang up from behind the crowd that had grown around the fallen body.

"Father! Wait! You may not avenge him, for the shot was not theirs, but mine."

Tror had raised his arms to attack Odysseus, to try to throttle the breath from him, but when he heard the voice, he spun around. The crowd had parted to admit the figure of a boy, a younger, smaller copy of the youth who had fallen.

"Hod, what have you done?"

"Father, we do right to defend ourselves against these heathen, but you must not blame them for Peldeg's death. I took aim at their leader, had him in my sights, until Peldeg rose before him and I could not call back my shot. Forgive me, Father, for I have killed your son, my brother."

"Then I must kill you."

Hod dropped his bow and arrows and stood still, facing his father's wrath. Tror took from the limp hand of one of the northern warriors a short sword of gleaming bronze, and took a step toward his son.

"No!" screeched the fallen woman, regaining her senses if not her feet. "Husband, I have already lost one son."

"The law speaks more loudly than a king," Tror muttered, and again he raised his sword, preparing to strike. Hod, his eyes still fixed on his father's face, bent his head.

Tror's arm, about to fall toward its tender target, was restrained from behind. He turned his eyes angrily.

"From one father to another, I tell you, you must not. The gods' laws stand higher than men's."

"Who are you to stop me?"

"I am you. I stand in for you, father for father, when your wit has gone, following one beloved son to Hades. Let it not follow another as well, one lost by your own anger and your own hand."

"Why should you care? You are about to die anyway. And he shouldn't even have been here."

"We will all die. But in this time, in this place, you may choose not to kill, and for whatever life remains to us, we will both be glad if you spare this blow."

"Why should you feel glad, one who has come from the other end of the world to kill us?"

"A just question and one hard to answer for a man who spent good years of his life fulfilling a vow by killing Trojans and who would risk his waning years to finish a job long ago begun. But as a man who has lost his wife and gained back his sons, I tell you—no, ask you, Tror of the Aesir—to hear the law of your blood." Odysseus noticed Orestes had dropped from the rafters via his whip right behind Hod and had placed his hand on the boy's shoulder. "See, Lord Tror, the face of a boy who avenged family blood with family blood—for that the gods have given him gifts, including madness. Turn your wrath on me, as you should, and bless your son's courage, though you curse his luck."

Tror let his weapon fall to the floor. "If only you had been simple wine merchants, I might have let you live."

"For a time I have been a wine merchant, though never, praise Athena, simple." Odysseus turned and walked to the front of the hall, where he recovered one of the amphora. He returned with it to the center of the hall where, taking an axe, he swiped off its top, sending clay and droplets flying. Swiping away the clay shards floating atop the red liquid, he offered the remains of the jug to Tror. "Drink with me," he said, "to the shade of your son gone, to the spirit of your son living, and to the comrades, to the woman your wife, whom I regret to have harmed, and to the golden-haired maiden who I fear is your daughter, brave as her parents and brothers."

"You fear?"

"Will you drink with me?"

Tror bent his eyes deep into those of Odysseus as he balanced anger and sorrow and resignation and admiration.

He took the broken jug from Odysseus' hands and tipped it, drinking a long draught, swallow after swallow, until the red liquor joined the tears running down his chin—then he turned the jug over to Odysseus. "I have left you some."

Odysseus nodded, received the jug, and tipped it, drinking beyond his fill, until he could drink no more. A small quantity remained in the bottom of the jug. "You have defeated me, king, in this skill." He raised the remains of the jug, and smashed it on the floor, spilling the remaining wine like blood.

"You have more?" Tror asked.

"We have more."

"I will grant your soldiers quarter to drink with us, then we must fight again. If you had joined me rather than fought me, we could have assembled an army to rule the world from South to North and East to West."

"With whom as king?"

"Do you want to be king?"

Odysseus thought for a moment then sighed. "Not I, but I have sons."

"Do they want to be kings?"

Odysseus had to stop himself from turning to Telegonus.

"You have a son here? Ah—then we must fight until I have avenged my son with a son. But first, as I promised, we drink."

Ori and Agni, with the help of some Northmen, rolled the remaining amphora to the center of the hall, and Tror ordered bowls and drinking horns, and there the soldiers drank together, occasionally uttering a few words among themselves about the quality of the wine, about the make of their weapons, about their families, about the weather that spring. The warrior woman, Tror's wife Sif, rose to her feet, and, with the help of Tror's counselor, Hothines, and the golden-haired girl, she departed the hall, Orestes opening the rear door for their exit. As they left, the girl turned her head to receive Odysseus' longing glance, her face a mixture of confusing sentiments.

"Latch the doors," called Tror, emptying the last of the wine into Diomedes' bowl, "and admit no one else. You will permit, Othysseus, my young son to leave, since I have lost one too many already? Thank you. We here will battle for Asgard and the rule of the north." Hod and two servants carried the body of the hapless Peldeg from the hall, and Orestes blocked the door behind them.

Unsteadily the men rose and took up their weapons. With a spear thrust, a man from behind Odysseus caught the hero unawares and nearly pierced him, the wine-daunted blow just drifting wide of its course. Odysseus, already nursing a painfully disabled shoulder, bled from a cut on the left arm, but Diomedes repaid the man's blow by killing him with one swipe of his sword, and the battle began anew.

Darkness fell, and the men fought on in shadows. Clouds had passed, and moonlight shone in the windows, the only light by which the soldiers fought, their having no opportunity to light torches. Waves of battle rose and fell, the advantage tossing to one side, then the other, skilled fighters slowed by weariness and wine defending more intently than they attacked. The night passed slowly in pain and blood, and when dawn cast her fingertips feelingly through the windows, the red of her eyes matched the red that mottled the hall, the sacrifice of sword strokes.

The battle continued into the morning, long after Apollo's light had pushed Eos' from the hall. Finally, once again Odysseus and Tror met, spear versus war hammer, in the middle of the hall at the foot of the dais, ready to conclude their fight. Both men panted, sick with weariness and loss of blood, sick of each other, sick of fighting.

"We must end this sometime," Tror said. "How about now?"

"I have enjoyed it," Odysseus said. "It has quite fulfilled my expectations."

"Do you still insist on my death?" Tror asked.

Odysseus tried to lean on his spear, missed, and slipping to the floor, sat there with his legs crossed. "We must ask my comrades, of course, but I'm no longer certain that I do."

"I must insist, of course, on the death of your son. Yes, you gave him away to me with your eyes. That is fair: a son for a son."

"Then we must fight on."

"To death, if necessary, yours or mine or both."

"And our sons—if you and I die, who will stop this business? Telegonus, do you want this man's kingdom?" Odysseus called.

"No, Father, I do not. I have long ago got what I came for."

"Diomedes, do you insist on having this man's head on a pike, or that of any of his family?"

"Ody, I am growing old, but I have fought with the young men, fought my Trojans and survived. Soon I will insist on sleep and not much else."

"Tror, I can't compensate you for your son—no one can; I will not give up my own. Can we come to some other bargain that will satisfy us both?"

"Othy—I hope you don't mind, since I heard your soldiers call you that—I am willing to try."

"Gangleri, have you found what you sought?"

Gangleri was slow to reply. Odysseus spotted him seated

with two men, one dead, one living. "I have found my father and my brother," he said.

A mustachioed man looked up from the fallen body, turning his glance toward Odysseus. He looked a slightly older version of Gangleri. His eyes, like Gangleri's, were filled with tears.

12

PRIZE AND COST

Gangleri painfully rose to his feet, bracing himself on his brother's shoulder, and spoke. "Othy, please greet my brother, Grettir. The man lying here, his spirit gone to the Hall of his Fathers, was Gromr, our father." He lifted a longsword from a fallen Norseman and stumbled toward Tror, who hadn't strength enough left to regain his feet. "Now, in the sight of the men here, friends and enemies alike, I will avenge myself for what you have taken from my family." He raised the sword and brought it down toward Tror's neck.

Odysseus reached for Tror's enormous hammer and swung it in a sweeping arc. It intercepted Gangleri's sword with a clang, breaking the blade, and Gangleri lost his balance and fell beside the two kings.

"I must have my vengeance, Othy. You may get what you came for or not, but you must not deny me my own quest."

"You have had your quest, and you have had your vengeance. Look about you. And didn't you tell me that one who has friends is blessed? Now you still have your friends, and you have got back your brother. What exactly will you gain by killing King Tror, except certain death for all of us?"

Bodies lay dead or bleeding across the long floor of the

hall, and all the men yet alive and conscious listened carefully, fingering their swords, trying to muster strength for another stand, should they need it.

Odysseus continued. "He has lost a son. You have lost a father. Who has suffered the greater sorrow?"

"And you, Othy, what have you lost?" Gangleri asked.

Odysseus scanned the hall: he saw the eyes of Telegonus and Achilles, of Diomedes and Idomeneus, of Philoctetes and Dictys. Orestes, standing not far away, was humming and twirling a sword on its point like a top, trying to keep it spinning without falling. But before the entrance of the door lay two young bodies, silent and unmoving.

"They were not my sons, but for the kinsmen of Calydoneus I bear the responsibility."

"They were not of your blood."

"If you understand my responsibility, they might as well have been. Ori and Agni: when I accepted their service, I didn't even know their names. I could have sent them back with Thrasymedes, but I have sent them to Hades instead."

"They chose to fight. They accepted their fate."

"They chose what we showed them. They followed what we taught them. They valued what they saw us value. Did they accept fate or follow bad leaders?"

"So goes the world, Othy," Tror said. "Had they not followed you, they might have fallen to pirates or another army or accident or disease. Even kings, even the gods, can't change fate."

"If you believe those words, lord king, you must absolve me and my men of the death of your son, and you must absolve me as well for that of my wards. Do you have that power? If you do, I accept absolution for neither. Even if the gods appoint our fates, you and I lead men to them. We don't control what the gods choose, but we control how we lead and where we lead, and we could as well choose to lead men to peace as to war. That responsibility remains with us. Where the young cannot choose without us—we give them their models and their blood—we choose often without them, so the responsibility falls to us until they have lived enough years to outstrip us and become their own models and make their own choices."

"You didn't lead me, Ody: I'd have come here without you, though I must admit I'm glad I brought you along. Wouldn't have had as much fun without you," Diomedes said.

"At least we're not dead yet. Who would have believed that a palmful of old men and untested boys could have got this far—fftha!" He spat red droplets. "That's blood. Philo, are you well enough to look to me? Tror: I propose that we rest and tend to our people, and then we must either fight on or parlay."

"I should urge a negotiation. But I warn you: you have wielded the hammer of the gods—no, I don't mean myself. Here and now I drop all such pretenses. No, my smith Wela made it, inspired by the gods, and I have known no one to touch it without incurring its curse. This morning I caught Hod hefting it. The old sibyl, not this young one, told me years ago when Wela handed it to me that with it I should lose and gain what I love most. I don't know what that means, but I didn't like it then, and I don't like it now. No weapon has ever stood up better in battle, yet the son who held it has killed his brother, my heir. Ah—too much talking: if you allow me to walk out that door, I will do you no treachery. I will disperse the soldiers who await word from me, and I will clear a hall where your men may sleep in peace. Tonight we will eat and tend our wounds. Without any more wine, you will drink my mead, a honey liquor, and I think you will like it. Tomorrow we will meet on the greensward and choose our course, as much as fate will allow us." Tror tried again to rise, but couldn't. "You, north-Greek," he said to Gangleri, "you have heard your leader speak. Will you help me up?"

Gangleri glared down at Tror, turned when a hand touched his shoulder to face his brother.

"Brother, before you kill this king, know that Father and I, though he took us from you unwillingly, have served on these years because we chose so. This court has won great glory, and we have shared it. I can't even tell you whose blow killed our father—it might have been mine or yours for all I know—but I can assure you that in the great Hall beyond this world, he now awaits us gladly and proudly: he died as he wished to, with sword in hand. King, if I may, I will broker peace between you and my brother."

"Willingly."

Reluctantly Gangleri reached a hand down to Tror, and Grettir grasped the other shoulder, and together they pulled the tall king to his feet. Philoctetes and Telegonus each grasped an elbow of Odysseus' and raised him as well.

Odysseus looked about him and said, "Whatever conclusion we reach tomorrow, brothers, we owe this Trojan king a debt: we have attacked him, and he grants us respite. Let us look to our dead."

"I wish you would stop calling me 'Trojan.' I am not one now and have never been."

"We came to fight Trojans," Diomedes said, "so lacking any better, we'll have to make do with you or keep looking."

"Now that's a thought," Tror answered, stumbling toward the door as several of his soldiers came to take him from Gangleri and Grettir. "See that they have a proper hall, Counselor, and that no one molests them."

Nodding, the king's counselor approached Odysseus, who also aimed to steady himself on his feet. "We bear the same name, you know, O king of the south. I hear them call you 'Hothy'? I am Hothines—it has but the Eastern ending. I heard about your exploits at Troy, though I never went there myself. The only one of us to have done so is Keimtales, who served as ambassador to urge them to return the beautiful Helen to Menelaos."

"Don't say that name, that of the woman, if you please," Diomedes growled.

"No offense intended. You know, if you wished to fight Trojans, we have heard that Aeneas has founded a new empire in the south—how could he not dwell nearer you than we do?"

"Best not to say that name either," Diomedes added.

"Friend Diomedes, you don't leave me much to say. You should know that Trorash has always greatly admired the Achaian peoples."

"If you would, Counselor, you may, as your lord asked, lead us to a place where we can rest and clean our wounds," Odysseus said. "You have an excellent reputation as a military strategist; I'm pleased to learn we may count on you for hospitality as well."

"Gladly. I will see also to the bodies of your comrades."

As Hothines led them to the door, the other Northmen warily parted to make room for their exit. Outside in the cool northern light they found what looked to be hundreds of soldiers ushered back from the hall by Tror's nobles. They glared at the Greeks as they passed, but Hothines led them only to a smaller hall nearby, where he had servants quickly start fires, boil water, and bring herbs and bandages, and there he left them to tend their wounds. Only

Orestes had remained entirely free of outward injury, but his face looked pale and anxious—Odysseus could not get Orestes to say why, but he guessed.

After checking everyone's wounds and allowing Philoctetes and the young men time to treat them, Odysseus asked Philoctetes, tired though he was, to make him another eye patch, larger and of more beautiful material than the old. Then he sought out Telegonus.

"Son, do you have in your pouch any more spear tips—just the very end?"

"Yes, father."

"I need one, preferably one unbroken and that you haven't tipped with poison."

"Here: I have just one left. Why do you need it? They can serve well in surgery in a pinch."

"I hope I won't need to show you, but trust me that I think my need more than frivolous."

Later, while the others dozed or absorbed themselves in their own business, Odysseus sat in a corner where only a single ray of light fell by which he could work. There he sewed into the back of the new eye patch Philoctetes had made him the slightly blunted tip of Telegonus' spear. He replaced the patch gingerly to make sure that he didn't cut himself. The scar tissue around the old eye felt tough and grainy, yet Odysseus took care with his operation.

In the evening Hothines entered the Greeks' hall. He offered them the choice of dining alone there or joining Tror's party in another hall. After much discussion they agreed to join their enemies turned hosts. Led in by Hothines, who insisted they carry no weapons to dinner, they found their path free of obstruction, and, by the light of an enormous fire, they met Tror's people around a great oblong table where one-by-one they introduced themselves.

"Quite the fancy eye patch you have there, Lord Othin," Hothines offered, inspecting it more carefully than Odysseus wished he would.

"Something to serve a little better for dinner with your king and his nobles, Lord Hothines."

There they met in all their splendor the Norse gods, the men and women who had traveled from the east of Troy into the north, winning lands, treasures, and allegiances and building such a reputation for ferocity and wisdom that folk there believed them divine.

"Here," said Tror, rising to his feet to greet his guests, "the Aesir meet the Vanir, the people of Asia meet those we have long expected. I must ask you only to assure me that you have brought with you no weapons, as we have none. Tonight we share this table in peace. Tomorrow we will learn what shall become of some of us or the lot of us. Grekkir, meet my family, those who have ventured with me to take these vast, cold lands as our own and to raise a culture as far-reaching, wise, and powerful as that of the south. Join us here and meet the noble council of the north. Beside me stands my wife, Sif, whom, Othysseus, you have already met in battle. I am glad you have spared her for me, for no truer wife or warrior ever lived, and perhaps she has spared you to be my friend. Beside her you see an empty seat: there sat Peldeg, my son and heir, whose absence I attribute to the true gods, whoever they may be, rather than to any man here or elsewhere. May the Great Hall at the end of the world receive and warm his spirit. You have met my strategist Hothines; beside him stands Keimtales, our ambassador and herald. Surtir, my greatest swordsman you see, taller than all the rest of us, and by him Wela, sword and metalsmith, nearly a god of his craft, and so noble. Next: Para and Preya, brother and sister, teach the people the arts of growing and nurturing foods and of fighting together in battle: they have taught me much, but from what I have seen today, even they may have something to learn from your young ones. Beyond them you see Skef, my ally from the west: he did not fight with us today. Having learned from his own sibyl of the battle to come, he came here by ship and has just arrived. I value him as if he were my own son. He would call all his forces against any enemy if I asked, for he embodies loyalty, faith, and indefatigability. Next, Dares, our court scop, not only fights as well as any mortal, but sings the songs of our people for all to learn and remember. Finally you will see my sons, two sets of twins: Loresh and Lokesh, born in the east, and Modi and Magi, born here in the north. Beside them I have left two chairs for your lost youths.

"You see, men of the south, that we sit upon no dais, but arrange ourselves around this oval table together as equals. Like us you have come to these lands to fight and conquer, but also to join and teach. Would you do us the courtesy, Othysseus, of teaching us the names of your comrades? Then we will sit together to eat and drink and tell our adventures."

Odysseus saluted his host in the northern fashion by holding out his palms high before him. "King Tror, I accept your hospitality as more than men of war, however hardy and adventurous, can ever expect from their intended targets. I present you Diomedes Tydeides, the greatest living soldier of the Trojan War. Idomeneus, once king of Crete, who fought there, too, with the courage of a hundred lions, knows, as you do, king, the unavengeable loss of a son. Philoctetes, our best spearsman and physician, has carried more than his share of ill fortune, which I hope this day has passed from him. Dictys, our poet, a man of many tongues

217

and yet great courage—such traits seldom fall together to one man—I trust he may sit next to your Dares, so that those two men may share stories that we all may learn from them. You may not believe when I tell you that the next young man bears the name Achilles. I hear your incredulity: his grandfather, the greatest soldier of any age, killed Hektor in one-on-one combat before the walls of the great city, and he has his forefathers' heart and lungs, if not their years. Next him I acknowledge my own son by the sorceress Circe; her beauty and magic surpass that of other nymphs as her son's skills and desire to find and join his father surpass my worth.

"Last of us you will find Orestes, son to every man here, and if you don't know his pitiable story, I will tell it first. And I believe we must pity him even more if he may not win the love of your sibyl, whose voice I think has pierced his heart—I ask your pardon if by saying so I offend your custom, which if so I do only out of ignorance, not intention.

"Two men we have lost in our journey here: Antilochus, son of the wise and ancient Nestor of Pylos, died in battle, to the honor of his fathers. Thrasymedes, his brother, left us to honor his dead right hand, for no two men born of the same father have ever lived lives more tightly woven together. Though they, too, could they have done so, would have come here as your enemies, I ask you that our first drink honor them: they were noble men and would have praised your hospitality no less sincerely than do we, who accept the gifts of your table with gratitude and hearts free of enmity."

When Odysseus had spoken, the Aesir raised their palms toward their guests in the ritual gesture, and all sat together to feast and drink. Odysseus found his eye inexplicably drawn among the servants, who appeared not as the slaves common in Achaian households, but as well-dressed and well-groomed young nobles, their light, calm features and unhurried gestures adding dignity to their service.

Something familiar hovered near the corner of his glance, appearing and disappearing among the limbs and shadows of the servers. He conversed with Tror, ignoring the cold glances of Sif, his wife, but only halfheartedly, his thoughts troubled.

"Here, king of the south, try this drink, the mead I told of: you will find it sweet, but warm and powerful, golden as a ray of sun." Tror himself filled a large horn from a wooden jug and passed it to Odysseus.

From the middle of several of the young servers, bearing a large pot of drink, emerged something out of a dream, out of a vision that had drawn him north, Odysseus of Ithaka, who had come a long journey not to fight Trojans, but to learn if he had seen not a mirage, but a truth as beautiful as a goddess.

The golden hair, the slim, supple figure, the round, rosy cheeks, the eyes blue as day-sky: as she ducked the plate of a young man passing by, the smile lit her face like a torch that pierces absolute darkness.

For an instant Odysseus felt himself transported to a world made only of sound. The vision passed from his eyes, and a voice plucked his spirit like the deep string of a lyre.

—As I promised, you have found her.

"Athena?"

—You thought I'd left you, but I never have. You had much to do—you yet have much to do—but you have found what you sought. Though your gods will ask more of you, your own quest ends here, fulfilled. Does her face please you?

"Ah! Less only than your own."

—Always the flatterer and occasionally a liar, though only, I admit, at need. The gods do not love lies, but we do admire wit, and sometimes we reward the one who uses it well. You may need your stratagem to win the girl—yes, oh yes, I see what you have in mind.

"You approve?"

—I see that you do not intend to break Zeus' law of *xenia,* and I am pleased that you don't, since you may trust that your hosts don't, either. Odysseus, you have uncommon luck as well as your gods' blessings—few men living have had better fortune. You have known true love and immortal passion; you have returned from the brink of satiation and despair; you have enjoyed the faith of the best of companions; sons who may have hated you love you loyally; a journey at which a madman, let alone a sane one, would have laughed, you have accomplished; you have learned as much about your world as any person who has ever lived; even as you age, you will know again the excruciating joy of young love; your wit has grown when that of most men begins to fade. If I felt generous I might say that you have earned your blessings, but you must certainly love your gods for what they have given you.

"I hope you believe me, beloved Athena, that I do: above what all other men do, I love you and all the gods."

—More than does Aeneas, he whom the ages will call "pious one"?

"Yes, my goddess, even more than does Aeneas, though he be a goddess' son. For this once I don't disparage him, but even as I praise him, I must believe I love you more—to say less would dishonor us both. I love Antiklea, my mother. I have built a shrine to my fathers and to you, my spiritual mother, and I have tried to honor your gifts with deeds even more than words. This last deed troubles my thoughts: I would not choose to kill again, other than at need, and need recedes for a man old in adventures, even as it rises for younger men."

—Odysseus, you have never had trouble rising.

"And I hope I may not now!"

—Have you failed to trust me?

"Never!"

—More than once, I think, but you are mortal, so I forgive you. You have as much faith as any mortal may have, and so the gods love you as you love them. Even Poseidon, who has tormented you, has grown to love you: you see that at last you may use his penance to save yourself and your fellows and complete your quest and win your beloved. But the crisis comes! Prepare yourself, for I have kept you too long.

"Athena . . ."

Tror had been watching Odysseus, and hearing him speak aloud, interrupted his thoughts. "Othysseus, why do you call aloud to someone who isn't here? I hope you have sustained no injury to the head that sends your thoughts wandering. Such a man had better die, at least such a man as you, than lose his wits. Here, you have barely touched your mead."

"Apologies, Lord Tror: I merely let my mind stray to my home and my gods. I didn't realize that I had spoken, but if I did, I should have thanked you for the drink."

"A wise man thanks his gods and remembers his home, in good times or bad. You like the mead, then?"

Odysseus drank again, this time making the effort to taste, and fought off a wince: the thick golden liquor felt heavy and sweet in his mouth, unappealing to a man who drinks the dark and leathery wine of the south. "Excellent,

Lord King. You must forgive my tastes, uneducated in such delicacies, if I commend it too faintly."

"You live up to all the stories, my friend: I can tell that you don't like it, and yet you seek not to offend your host. I regret that what I offer can't suit your preference as the wine you brought suits mine; well, perhaps we may sail south together and get more from the Menapians, eh?"

"I should like that, indeed." Odysseus' eye had again strayed among those serving, seeking the girl who, born in his visions, had materialized in the flesh, and who moved gracefully from person to person, pouring mead, dodging her companions busy in their own service, smiling, as someone complimented or thanked her. Drawn to her like the eye to light or the warbird to prey, however he wished to keep his thoughts on the necessary diplomacy, his heart and loins swelled with her closeness, and warmth filled him until his face burned and he had to lock his manhood tightly between his thighs.

Odysseus drained his horn, thinking that less disagreeable than sipping its contents. He choked down the cool, thick honey-beverage and felt its warmth spread through his throat and belly. The warmth rose again to his face as he noticed the blond girl approaching to fill his horn. She moved behind him and bent over his shoulder, dipping her jug to pour him mead. Several strands of her hair, fallen from where she had tied them behind her head, fell and tickled his cheek and neck. Her hair smelled warm, like grain and summer breezes heated by the sun. He turned his head to meet her eyes, only to find them already focusing on her next task, Diomedes' cup. Before his heart could sink, her eyes turned momentarily to his, their cerulean blue filled with a mixture of recognition, expectation, and caution.

"Thank you, young woman."

"You're welcome, Lord Othysseus."

Her voice, not youthful, blended the mellifluousness of the mead with the steadiness of adult confidence. Odysseus noticed that her skin hadn't the smooth perfection of an unripe fruit; beneath her eyes a hint of wrinkles proved her no girl, but a woman grown. As she turned toward Diomedes, he noticed a firm, curving roundness of forearm and the blue lines of veins that showed strength and activity, and he noticed that she moved not with the quick, clumsy heedlessness of youth, but with the control and confidence that come from comfort with one's own body. A sense of love grew in him until he almost cried out—he squelched a cry with a long drink of the awful golden liquor. Allowing his glance to shift back to the woman, he saw that she had already passed quickly by Diomedes to Idomeneus. Diomedes' eyes followed her hawkishly, and Idomeneus looked up at her almost in awe. As she moved on, Diomedes turned to Odysseus, his eyes glowing, winked, then raised his eyebrows twice, motioning with his head toward the woman. Odysseus realized that he had to win her not only from her father, but also from all the other heroes, Greek and Norse alike, and in that moment he felt old and tired. But as he allowed the memory of the eyes to drift before his sight, he understood what he'd seen in them, that he had an advantage over all of them, no matter how young and strong. He had seen in them recognition, and in the few words she'd spoken he'd heard understanding.

Her name: he didn't know hers, but she knew his. He wanted to call her back, but he had first to empty the drinking horn again or find some other excuse. Tartaros take the horn, he thought. Her eyes floated again before him, communicating something else, something he could hardly identify, something he had seldom seen or even known.

Then it struck him: honesty.

Penelope had had it. One might have said Aias had, too, but Odysseus wouldn't have called Aias honest so much as stupidly guileless. Diomedes? He had faith and loyalty equaled by few men, but he had once seduced and abandoned the Trojan Cressida, and he had the character to do such a thing again. Telemachos had it, but had learned from his father the value of the ability to deceive. Odysseus wondered then if anyone would have looked in his own eyes, no eye, and perceived it—hardly any longer, after all his years of adventures, of, dare he call it by name, deceit, even treachery? Lacking it, why did he find himself at that instant valuing it so much? Seeing her, he knew he wanted it back.

At that point, knowing what twists might lie before him, he could hardly afford honesty.

Odysseus noticed then that all the while his thoughts had wandered, Tror had been chattering on to him about affairs in the north: shipping, trading, harrying, managing large numbers of settlements.

"I say, man, don't you listen? For all the information I have given you, you can spare me something about Menapian trading practices in the West Isles."

"Certainly, I will tell you all that I know, but I must ask you one thing: what is the name of the young woman?"

"What young woman? Oh, that one, yes, my daughter."

"Her name."

"No."

"No?"

"You don't need to know. I will marry her off to some Northern prince when I'm ready and she's willing. She has proven diffident about marrying in the past—no one good enough for her, I suppose, but I will find an ally powerful enough for me and handsome enough for her, and she's no longer a fledgling."

"I ask only her name."

"And I won't tell you."

"I believe you have no intention of giving her up."

"That's no concern of yours now, is it? Don't push me, Lord Othysseus, King of the South: you have attacked me in my own home, and yet I feast you and your soldiers. You must not try my patience."

"I try neither patience nor friendship; I merely ask a question that one father may ask another."

Their talk had grown heated, and as anger entered their voices, conversations around the table and in the wings quieted.

"And I have said I won't answer. I see now what you want: you intend to match my daughter with one of your sons. Don't believe it: that won't happen. If you have come to win my kingdom for your southern sons, you will depart disappointed if you depart alive at all. Wait—I see the truth, you gristle-nosed boar: you want her, my daughter, not for your sons, but for yourself! I should kill you here and now."

"Pris."

The voice came from behind Tror, who, as he tried to rise from his chair, found his daughter's hands on his shoulders pressing him back down.

"My name is Pris. Lord Othysseus can do no harm by knowing my name."

"You don't know that. Names have power, and knowing one's enemy's name gives access to magic."

"Not if one asks of a friend rather than an enemy."

"No friend would want what that man wants."

"But any man might," interjected Diomedes, at which all the Northmen rose from their chairs, considering what weapons they might find near at hand, followed by the Greeks, who did the same.

"Father, wait before you act rashly. Do you believe that no man will want me?"

"I have always seen that you have wanted no man. Most women your age have married and borne children. You can't mean to tell me that you have any interest in this old deceiver?"

"I am younger than you," Odysseus said quietly.

"Not by much, and even that doesn't matter. You have come here to make war."

"He has come here to find me."

"How do you know that?"

"He has seen me in visions from the Lady Goddess of the South. She has shown him to me as well; I have known that he would come long before the Norns and the sibyl told you so."

"Don't tell me you would have him."

Pris looked at Odysseus. He saw in her face the smile that had haunted his visions, and, experienced man that he was, he nearly fainted. Idomeneus placed a supportive arm around his back and whispered, "Here's what you've been waiting for, Ody."

"Yes, Father, I would have him, I will marry Othy."

Tror rose to his full height, turned to Pris, and placed his hands on her shoulders. "Let me tell you this once: no. Let me tell you again: no. If he asks, I will say 'no,' and if you try to agree, I will say 'no.' You may ask until doomsday and I will say 'no.' Can I possibly make myself any clearer than that, to say with all my will and all my strength: 'no'?"

As Tror spoke, Odysseus had taken the patch from his eye and extracted from it Telegonus' spear tip, then he quickly replaced the patch, hoping that Pris, not Tror, had not seen the empty socket. He eased over to the king, placed one arm above Tror's elbow, and with his other hand, as Tror was absorbed with his daughter, brought the point to the skin along the line of the king's carotid artery.

Tror, still remonstrating with his daughter, drew in silence with a hasty breath as he felt the tip against his skin.

"Treachery, as I expected," Tror said.

"Not necessarily," Odysseus answered. "I have simply placed you where I stand myself, on the brink of that greatest abyss. If I send you, your nobles will send me after you, and I will gladly go."

"You need not do that," Pris said sternly. "Put it down."

"You aren't my wife yet, beautiful lady, so you may not command me, but because I would do nothing to harm you, I will do better than you ask. King Tror, what I hold against your neck is the poisoned barb of Telegonus' spear, honed and tipped by the great witch Circe of the Middle-Earth Sea. A scratch could kill you, and depriving your daughter of you, and thus me of your daughter, it would kill me as well, regardless of what your soldiers would choose to do with me. I brought you to this point not to force your choice, but to persuade you. I make you here this gift, which you may take or give to your daughter." Odysseus stepped back, took Tror's hand, and placed the spear tip gently and safely in his palm, then he turned his naked neck toward Tror and his eyes toward Pris. "Barely met but beloved lady, Pris, warrior woman and girl brighter than the southern light of Apollo's chariot, I give to your father this dowry, which he may take or bestow on you: my life, all that I have won, all that I have learned, all that I may yet accomplish in the world but what I render to the gods who have blessed me with the sight of you in this last good eye. If I read your look correctly, you have chosen as you spoke. We need now only await your father's choice."

Tror stood amazed, his mouth agape, somewhere amidst disbelief, anger, and wonder. He grasped the barb between thumb and forefinger, measured with his eyes the distance to Odysseus' neck, looked from Odysseus to his daughter and back again.

"Father!"

After a soundless moment, Tror spoke. "What man can ever guess a woman's taste, even if that woman shares his own blood? I would at least have picked you someone young and vigorous and handsome. I couldn't have found a wiser or braver man than this old grandpa, and his gods must love him dearly to bring him all the way here to have you, my dearest daughter, but you have spoken, and having put his life at my disposal, I must now accept him as my— ugh—son. Does that make anyone else here happy? It makes me feel bloody awful."

The smile that had for so long stirred Odysseus' longings and illuminated his dreams melted away as Pris glided toward him and, with her eyes and lips just parted, kissed him gently and lovingly on the mouth.

"You will make an old husband, but a true one, Othy," she said, "so the sibyl has told me, and I believe it in my deep heart." She smiled again, and Odysseus felt her presence so powerfully that, hero that he was, he lost himself in her touch, her scent, her eyes. He turned to Tror.

"King of the North and father-to-be, I can't speak for my comrades, but for myself, having won more than I dared admit I sought, I commit myself here to your service. I am no youth, and I have learned and practiced all the wiles of

the world, but I vow that I will, in what number of years the gods allot me, remain the truest of husbands and the best of friends. I seek to rule nothing, only to please my wife, find my pleasure in her, and help secure what I can of the north to your power and allegiance."

"Father?" Pris inquired of Tror.

"Don't worry, Friggy, I see the value of the man. No, my friend—I can't bring myself to call a geezer like you 'son'— Othin, if you will, I can read the truth in my daughter's eyes as well as in yours, and while I know you make those vows sincerely, I will not accept them other than with this amendment: you and I will rule the north together as brothers. The Aesir and the Vanir will make one family, our feud done, our blood mingled, and north and south will share equal nobility. We will share our wealth and our skills and build such an empire as will stretch from sunrise to sunset.

"Someone bring beer. My new son-in-law doesn't like mead, and we will at least drink to this wedding with something that we both like. Someone take this infernal dart before I kill myself with it."

Telegonus took the barb from Tror, looked at Odysseus, and moved away.

"Well, I've lost this girl, but I'll find another, no doubt," Diomedes mumbled to Idomeneus.

"I have another I can't wash from my thoughts," Idomeneus replied, "or I'd offer to find us a pair of sisters. These northern women with their strong arms and legs and golden hair appeal to me, I must say, but once your heart is full, you can't easily empty it again."

Surtir the swordsman approached Diomedes and Idomeneus as they talked, and he said, mixing nearly incomprehensibly the Norse speech with a few Greek words, "Diomedes, I have heard what you said, and rather than insult, I take your words as my duty to fulfill: I will find you a woman who will have you, though your grisly southern features would scare a witch. I will teach you my art of the sword and learn from you your Greek arts of battle and building, and we shall be friends and do battle together. What say you?"

Diomedes looked the tall northerner up and down. "As long as the woman doesn't look like either me or you, and as long as you prove you have art worth learning, I declare myself your friend, pupil, and, where I can, teacher. And Ido here will study with us, though I know his heart lies irreversibly in the south, with a violet-eyed widow there—am I not correct, old friend?"

"Correct, as usual, on all counts."

When he could tear Odysseus from Pris for a moment, Telegonus pulled his father aside and whispered to him. "You dulled the barb, and it bears no poison. Why? You feared that the hidden tip would scratch you?"

"Not me."

"Him, then."

"I didn't trust my hand to keep still."

"You risked your own skin, but not his, even after you risked all our lives to get here? His folk might have killed you, even if the barb couldn't."

"She could have loved me dead, but she would not have had me as a husband if I had killed her father. You have loved me as your father both because I am your father and because I welcomed you as an equal to share my risks. Knowing what I know now, with all I have seen of the world, I would not wish to live on without her love any more than without yours."

"That's what has motivated you all these months, all those years, love?"

"Sometimes duty, sometimes the will to live, sometimes adventure and learning, sometimes restlessness, sometimes friendship, sometimes necessity, sometimes love of my island, sometimes desire for another, sometimes the need to do something worthy of my fathers, sometimes love—now love."

"How can you call it love, when you barely know her? Isn't it just longing for her body? She is, I admit, beautiful, and quick and lithe as a ferret. But how, when you say *love*, do you *know?*"

Idomeneus had sidled up to the whispering men, and he answered Telegonus' question. "You know, young man, by the feeling, not by the thought. You can teach yourself to court and marry for practical purpose, but you can't teach your heart to feel what it won't feel on its own. Once Aphrodite has fixed your love, you may enjoy another's body, or even love another, but the one you loved and love will never leave your thoughts or senses. She, even the thought of her—not merely her body, but herself—will burn, stir, raise, please you achingly until you die. Or you will pine for want of her, though you be the best of men."

"Pretty funny."

"Wait and see for yourself."

And through that night and all the next day and the next, too, the Greeks and Norsefolk drank, sang, told stories, dozed when they could fight sleep no longer, and began to shape the oddest but most strongly bonded family that history or legend remembers, persisting for more than two thousand years and exploring the four corners of the world.

After the feast, having mourned their losses and celebrated their peace, the heroes, northern and southern, held a funeral and burnt their dead. In the Greek style they held games, such as both sides could agree suited their tastes and skills, and shared prizes among the victors: swords, armor, heirlooms. Odysseus and Tror took pains that no game should get out of hand, but that each participant should honor the other, at least for that occasion, above victory. The young people competed for prizes; the old watched, envying their youth.

In a week, with dawn pouring rose petals over the horizon, Odysseus married Pris Trorsdaughter, and all those who ever knew or met them said that marriage was happy. The Norse sibyl did not object to the ceremony, and those on hand took that as evidence that the gods blessed the union. It lasted the duration of Odysseus' life. Tror withheld his concern, while Sif, his wife, remained angry at her son-in-law, eager for another chance to get at him with a spear, and learned more of the art in which Telegonus reluctantly instructed her.

After the wedding Orestes stood hand-in-hand with his new beloved, her wide, expressionless eyes ablaze, his face lit with a silly grin. As they celebrated, he hummed strange, soft tenor tunes, and she made soprano harmony lighter than the flight of finches. In time her pale countenance gradually adopted a healthy glow, and his songs lost their wild incomprehensibility for a pleasingly syncopated and variable harmony. Dictys, the Greek poet, and Dares, the northern poet come from the southeast, held contest to find who could sing the better wedding song—Tror and Odysseus awarded them both prizes.

The wedding festivities lasted for days, and then they folded easily into daily life, and Odysseus became, as joint leader of the north, Tror's other self, devoted in his service—the most restless of kings found peace and pleasure with the golden-haired girl who had haunted his dreams. In a year's time Pris bore a son, whom they named Vithar, a joy to his family and his people. The Norse folk and their Asian leaders came to accept their battle with the Greeks as one among many, past and done.

Northern traditions explain that an old warrior, feasting among his folk and his one-time enemies, will sidle up to a young man, explain to him how another soldier bears the sword that he should carry, an heirloom of his father's, of his kinsman killed, treacherously, in battle. The youth, inflamed by the story, will stew in its fires until, finding an opportunity, he will strike a blow against the swordsman, figuring to regain his father's weapon and his family's honor. Tror knew such stories; partly he feared them, partly he desired to have them told—at least for a time, until he felt firmly in his heart the devotion of his new family. Odysseus hadn't heard such stories—nor did he need to, since he knew the depths of the human heart better than any man living. He had fought in the greatest and strangest war of vengeance that the world has known. So when he could, he eased doubts, assuaged fears, made amends, won loyalties. Time does not heal all wounds, nor does goodness—not to say that Odysseus was what one would readily call a "good" man—but the lucky one may use goodness and time—and resourceful wit—to build unity and make peace.

And in time the other Greeks who had shared Odysseus' adventure began to ponder the course of their future, the quests that lay ahead of them, guessing that this world offers little more glory than they had already achieved.

Gangleri, having found what he sought and reunited with his brother, wished to stay no longer in the company of the Aesir, but to return home to his own people. With some reluctance he left his southern friends, and they served Tror by keeping good terms with their erstwhile companion.

Gangleri and Grettir came later to rule their folk, and though that people hadn't great power, they had many skills sufficient to make them formidable enemies. Odysseus mediated with Gangleri to forgo vengeance, and later generations kept peace, though a cool distance, between themselves and the Aesir.

The people formed by the joining of Aesir and Vanir spread their influence far over the world, through all of the north and even into the south. They gained great fame, and some of them infamy, as sailors, soldiers, explorers, settlers, and models of heroism. Their name became synonymous with courage, stout-heartedness, and piracy.

Their greatest strength began not with a war, but with a peace.

And so Odysseus, with the help of luck, the worthiest companions, and, some say, the gods, achieved his northern adventure, that man of many turns whose restive energy wouldn't leave him safe at home in Ithaka. So restlessness often drives people, until they find rest where everyone finds it at last.

EPILOGUE

IN DUE COURSE

"Telly, I've never quite learned that fancy spin and twirl move," Odysseus said one morning as he and Telegonus practiced with the spear, which they did nearly every day.

"Better, then, not to use it at all, since it's more flash than function anyway—dangerous, in fact, if one doesn't do it right."

"I've learned it well enough, old man, why can't you?" Sif taunted—she practiced with them regularly as well, at first to Odysseus' consternation, but later to his amusement, as he found himself impressed with her skill and vigor. "Even my daughter manages the spear as well as you," she said, whistling the spear-tip over his head.

Tror would occasionally watch them, but had no desire to practice: he wielded only one weapon, his war hammer, and that seldom, only in the battles that arose but occasionally in those later times. The hammer served more as a symbol of his strength than as a tool for his arm, and he had learned years before to prefer it so. Once he had enjoyed battle; then he enjoyed peace and his family.

The world followed its course, as it tends to do even now.

Achilles, having reached Telegonus' skill with the weapon and having used it so successfully in the Battle of Asgard, as the great encounter between north and south

235

had become known, lost his taste for battle and had given up its practice. Having in his youth desired the rush that comes with skilled fighting, and having experienced the veteran's conflict in victory, in full adulthood he had taken instead to consulting with those sibyls, priests, and wise or holy folk he could find across the north. From them he sought no other skill than wisdom. Philoctetes often accompanied him on his journeys, having devoted himself to the study of medicine, to see what he could discover from consulting those learned and mystical ascetics who could tolerate the cold of the utter reaches of the globe. From extremes one learns the sense of everyday wisdom.

Diomedes and Idomeneus traveled with Surtir and his best swordsmen to the Isles of the West to try their skills, and they established a formidable army who brought peace where they wished or battle where they pleased—the fierceness and the desire for challenge had not yet left them. Dictys and his northern colleague and competitor Dares traveled with them, sometimes to fight and sometimes to remember and sing the heroic deeds they witnessed.

Orestes married his sibyl, and they had a daughter. As she grew, she seemed to draw from her parents more and more of their wild and unpredictable abilities, and in later times she gained fame as a musician and prophet, while as they aged they acquired health and steadiness that seemed to come from their mutual closeness. They retired to a quiet life, serving the gods, occasionally welcoming their friends, but most often finding solace, even bliss, through trust in their untroubled lives together.

With Hothines' help, Odysseus learned the ways of the north and became to Tror the most helpful counselor a king ever had. Though Tror offered him a share of the kingship, Odysseus desired no rule, but only to retain what he might of his youth for as long as he could: the wily one found contentment in loving his wife, whose beauty outshone the sun and the stars for him. Telegonus had become to him more like a brother than a son, and along with Pris and young Vithar and Tror and his retinue, they traveled the northlands teaching, learning, and deepening alliances, so that finally Tror found himself in family and friends the wealthiest man who had ever lived.

Though he had turned his attention to promoting the peace, Odysseus retained his famous energy, expending it however in homier pursuits, desiring never to stray too far from the body of his young bride. Instigated by the urgings of Tror's son Lokesh, Odysseus also rekindled a youthful passion for hunting; skills he had acquired at home he learned to apply in icy winter as well as cool and pleasant summer.

And so their lives continued for more than five years, some people would say without incident, those who find noteworthy incidence only in battles and world-shaking deeds, rather than in the day-to-day prospects of loving and living. Then one day in early Autumn, Lokesh, ever eager for games and tricks and jokes and adventures and learning of all sorts, convinced the family to ride north into the far forest for a hunt. He had heard of enormous beasts ravaging the few outposts there, and he thought it not only his father's duty but also their mutual fun to see for themselves and rid the marchlands of trouble.

"Othysseus, famous soldier and traveler, you must hunt with me, teach a young man your tricks. Perhaps I can teach you something, too, of hunting in the north," Lokesh offered.

"Young Loki, in these lands I'm sure you have more to teach me than I you, so if my wife can spare me, these old bones will join you."

Tror had not gone so far north for some years, so he agreed to accompany them also, wishing to offer assurances to those brave folk who secured a dangerous part of his territories. Odysseus, too, felt eager for the chance to stretch his influence to lands beyond those he had ever visited, to see wonders he perhaps had never seen, to leave his footprints in soils or snows beyond even his imaginings, in the ultimate *Thoule*.

And so the Aesir and Vanir, long one family, provisioned themselves to test the northernmost borders of their world. For many days they traveled, Odysseus and his household and Tror and his together, guided by the wild, unpredictable Lokesh, riding slowly, visiting the sparse settlements, consulting about their needs, providing advice and assistance where they could, mediating the few disputes that spring up as the number of persons dwindles, and assuring folk of the king's support. As they reached the last outposts, they found first damage and later devastation, and from survivors they heard stories of giants and night-beasts, ghouls and werewolves who attacked them, shredded their livestock, and burnt their enclosures. Prepared for battle, Tror's folk urged their horses as far north as they could, but eventually had to rely on their own legs to carry them to the edge of the ravines, misty wastelands, and ice-sheets that blocked the frosty way to the pole. There they found no sign of prey and did well to preserve their extremities from the hungry gods of ice and frigid winds, who obscured their passage long before they could touch the top of the earth.

Returning from that snow-blind world to the habitable regions, they found themselves again enmeshed deep in the last forested land, which quietly engulfed them in mazy green. Having found no direction for headway, Lokesh announced that they had lost their path. They camped there as best they could, making progress by slow sorties, but soon enough they found their nights haunted by whistles, shrieks, and glaring eyes that seemed to glow red, peering from among the trees. At last the battle they sought came to them: a tribe of monstrous, frost-burned men who howled like wolves and fought like bears. What might on firmer ground have amounted to no more than a skirmish became on uncertain terrain a pitched battle, and Tror's folk fought with grim commitment to save their lives, wielding their favorite weapons together for the last time.

The wildmen seemed to come from everywhere, emerging from snowdrifts, mounds, and the trunks and tops of trees. Tror, swinging his hammer less surely than in his younger years, struck Odysseus a glancing blow on his shoulder as he tried to defend his back against a bear-shirted heathen who had dropped behind him, axe in hand, from the trees above. Injured, Odysseus still plied his spear, and with Telegonus, Sif, and Pris formed a four-cornered defense that kept the frost-men at bay, driving them toward those skilled in the use of Wela's bronze swords who, working slowly but methodically in the bad footing, gradually mowed them down, strewing them like pelts over the snow.

When a man in wolfskin, howling like the north wind, surprised Pris by rising up out of a pile of branches beside her, grasping her feet and dropping her to the ground, Odysseus slid forward, executed the spin and twirl move he had practiced for so long, and cut the man's throat from ear to esophagus. The force of the move on slick terrain caused him to lose his footing. As he returned the spear to defensive posture and scrambled to recover, he broke the spear in the belly of the next wolf-man who threw himself upon him. Keeping his eye toward the enemy for the next attacker,

Odysseus reached behind him for one of Telegonus' spears. As he grasped, he slid, and the razor tip cut him deeply on the arm. Pris, calling out for help, rose quickly and covered for him as he bound the wound with a leather thong, but the press of battle left no time to tend it more than simply to stanch the bleeding. Odysseus re-engaged the enemy with the spear whose first taste—but not its last—had been his own blood.

In half a day they had obliterated their enemy, driving a stray survivor or two into the icy ravines from which they could hardly hope to return. As soon as he could, Telegonus tended his father's injury, but the spear tip had borne poison, which had passed through the surface wound into the blood. Odysseus didn't blame Lokesh for the mis-adventure, but some of the Greek folk never forgave the prince for his ill counsel, which brought about the mishap. Among the northern men of Asgard, some found in the twist of events apt irony and even a hint of justice: Odysseus received a mortal wound defending the folk he had come to destroy.

"I fear, son," said Tror, "that your hunt has wrought what our best fighting men couldn't do, and that too late to do anyone any good."

"Death comes too soon for every man," Lokesh replied, "but I will try to make up for it by getting the rest of us home safe."

Eventually Lokesh found a path out of the forest that led to a familiar clearing. The party rode home as quickly as they could, with Pris tending her husband as his fever grew. By the time they reached Asgard, advance messengers had found and alerted Philoctetes, who ministered with all the medicines within his sphere of knowledge. He and Telegonus, along with the devoted Pris, cared for their leader as the longest, coldest winter in memory settled in. Achilles stayed at his side, offering meditative prayers, and Tror sent far and wide for medical or metaphysical aid among the Northmen, all to little avail. Young Vithar sat by his father's bed through the winter, and Odysseus, when he could thrust away the ravings of the poison and sustain his strength and wits, found his love for his family growing and his desire to live unflagging. Few men who have strayed so far live long enough to enjoy such familial devotion. Odysseus, looking in the face of Vithar, saw little of Telemachos there, and he wondered if this son of his age would grow into a man like the son of his youth.

When spring came, beyond all hope Odysseus lived, and his suffering eased with the rising warmth. He began to walk, and then to ride, and then to practice with spear, but he could feel, creeping from the incompletely healed wound through his limbs and into his breast a cold numbness—the effects of the poison they couldn't wash from his veins. Even Odysseus' endurance was nearing its limits.

Through the summer he improved, even joining Lokesh for a hunt, but when winter returned, the numbness extended its grip deeper into his bones. The world seemed to recede from his eyes, and first his dreams and then his days lost coherence. The warmth he drew from Pris brought him solace, and the rapt attention of his little son eased his heart—anyone who has watched children knows that they fix their minds only on those people or things they most love or fear or that they find most fascinating.

One night a dream took clear shape as it had seldom done for Odysseus in his years in the north and as it had never done since the poisoned wound. He found himself at the edge of a chasm, staring into it, unable to focus his gaze. Athena appeared and gently warned him that he must soon teach what he had yet to teach, express what he had yet to express. Then he felt himself falling into an abyss. He caught the thick limb of a knotty tree that grew from the brink of the chasm, and he hung on. The numbness in his arms hindered him, but with his last strength he pulled himself across the limb and up the trunk into a light that shone upon the top of the tree. There, in the last branch, incised in gold letters, he found his name, as Athena had counseled him to draw it. Across from him, on the largest limb of the tree, a hart munched at the deep green leaves, growing fatter as Odysseus watched, and the entire tree seemed to sag toward the chasm, until he felt himself slipping. The dream faded with his waking, and his waking faded into uneasy doze.

The following day, as Odysseus sat in a stingy ray of sun, trying to warm the chill, Telegonus, Achilles, and Dictys came to see him. "One thing, Father, we have long wished to learn from you," Telegonus said. "Idomeneus told us how, at the tomb of Antilochus, you carved symbols into the stone representing the names of your fathers. We should like to know those symbols."

Recalling Athena in his dream, Odysseus replied, "Yes, I must teach you. Call Loki, too, if you wish, in case he would learn as well." For that task Odysseus summoned his will to clear his mind.

Through the winter, guiding their practice on metal, stone, wood, and cloth, Odysseus taught them a systematic method for drawing symbols for sounds. "I learned it many years ago. Scribes in the east have symbols rather different than these, but Athena taught me a simpler method. Other men have used it, I have adjusted it, and now you may perfect it."

They learned, the Greeks passing that wisdom to their folk, and Lokesh, "Loki" to Odysseus, passing it to his, after his own fashion.

"And this last thing I'd teach you," Odysseus added. "Bless the gods for your family and friends and for the pleasures of the day. Anyone who has done what I've done and seen what I've seen and who may yet know the love that touches both body and heart and who has at last found a peaceful life at the end of the world has received more than anyone may hope, though no more than everyone may seek. Use these signs to record your love and your stories as well as your business. And while we're speaking and I have the energy for it, this one thing I must ask you to do: my bones, what's left of them that I can still feel, yearn for the warmth of the south. In the spring let them be taken there with or without what the gods have left me of breath."

Odysseus survived into the spring, but on a cool, rainy day, having told Pris for the thousandth time that he loved her, his weakened body could sustain that powerful spirit no longer, and the Odysseus the world knew passed quietly among the shades. Where it went, the wise and less wise have debated, but as for the body, his family, in honor of the resourceful adventurer who had learned to love, and those of Tror's folk who could journey, took it to the shore, placed it on a ship, and carried it south, along the coast of the Great Western Water. When they reached the northern tip of the land of the Menapians, they turned east and sailed up the Rhine river, all the way to Ascerbergium.

There, by the shrine that he had built for his fathers, they burned the body of Odysseus, once king of Ithaka, later a lord of the north, and buried the ashes beneath a mound not far from those of Antilochus and Thrasymedes. The devoted brother had died defending the Bructenians against pirates.

Together Telegonus and Achilles inscribed two names, as Odysseus had taught them, alongside that of their comrade

Antilochus, on the wall of the shrine. Dictys and others sang funeral songs, but all agreed that neither the south nor the north had ever seen such a hero for courage and wisdom and stratagems, nor would the world soon see such another.

This poem Dictys spoke as the troop departed Ascerbergium:

> No man's greatness spares him
> joining the dust that bore him.
> Perhaps the world has known
> men better than this one;
> I have known none.
> In his loss alone
> I have sown the seed of my own.

Pris answered with this verse of her own devising:
A young woman seldom finds fortune in an old husband. I did, despite what we are told.
I will miss him in summer's heat, winter's cold.

Pris, princess of the north, known to some of the peoples of her region as Frigg, mourned her husband, but she praised the gods for the time she'd had with him and for the son he'd left her, who already looked as though he should grow into the renewed image of his father. Stories differ on whether or not Pris married again. Many men knew of her beauty and strength and goodness, but they also knew of her devotion to the old soldier from the south. No one doubts that, whatever subsequent choices she made, the memory of Odysseus never left her heart or her lips, for stories of his exploits extended from his family to all the peoples of the north, so that his name, as she rendered it, entered the realm of myth.

That is the last the old stories tell us of Odysseus, though they do say that Vithar honored his father and mother with many brave deeds, that he cleared the last of the monstrous wild men from the northern settlements all the way to the sea in every direction, and he kept during all his life the strength of arm and will his parents and grandparents had given him. He too in later generations grew into a figure larger than life, as heroic as his father and longer-lived, though fewer tales remain of his deeds.

We do learn something of the fates of Odysseus' comrades. King Tror outlived his guest, fellow, and son-in-law only by a year. In the following summer he traveled east, wielding his war hammer for the last time, to battle a great, destructive beast that some legends call a dragon, but for that identification no proof exists. He and his valiant soldiers killed the beast, but local folk, who had worshiped the beast as a god, ostensibly welcomed them, then treacherously attacked, giving Tror his death wound before his followers subdued them. Legends say that the poison of their betrayal killed him, and that when he died, his breast opened up and his spirit flew to the heavens like smoke from a raging fire. Afterwards Northfolk led by Para and Preya resettled that land and spread the arts of agriculture eastward. Tror's wife, Sif, governed her people for some time after her husband's death, and then Modi and Magi shared rule, until Vithar came of age. All agreed that, bearing the blood of both kings of the north and the south, he should rule, and legends tell that he brought a time of peace and prosperity to the north, supported by his brothers, who despite his youth loved, honored, and followed him.

As for the Achaian heroes, after the funeral of Odysseus few had any desire to return north from Ascerbergium, their southern blood yearning instead for lands of sun and plenty. Only Orestes, his mind never quite cleared of the sufferings of his parents' deaths, felt ease in the distance that the north provided, and he returned with his wife to frosty woods and dales of Sveria. Some people think that the prophets and seeresses of the north descend from them, while others believe that their peaceful union quenched the troubles of the past, and their descendents differed little from normal folk, save an unusual penchant for song and poetry.

Of the remaining members of the fellowship Idomeneus departed first, being nearest his goal. He returned overland to north Gallia, hoping to find the violet-eyed woman he loved. He did, and he lived with her for many happy years, until in an accident following a hunting dispute, her younger son, flailing a spear without thinking, struck Idomeneus in the breast and killed him. Family and friends mourned him, burning the body and burying the ashes far from his ancient homeland, but honoring his beloved memory for generations.

Achilles, grandson of history's greatest warrior, never lost his speed of hand and foot, but after Odysseus' death he never again raised a weapon against another man. He sailed to the West Isles, where he continued to search for spiritual practices to satisfy a soul once so eager for and later so troubled by battle. He lived there for many years as a hermit, practicing the worshipful appreciation of Nature, until he met others willing to learn what knowledge he had acquired of flora and fauna. One story says that he eventually traveled across the world to the far east, where he found peace in the practices of meditation, active prayer, and physical discipline.

Dictys, having learned all he could of the poetry of the

north and traded verses with his friend and rival Dares, returned to the land of king Menapus to serve as his bard. There he communicated the use of drawn signs to record language, and he taught those youth who would learn them the poems of Troy, of Odysseus' travels, and of the north. His name survived, one of the great makers of his time, and through him the learning of the north-Greeks passed to the wide world.

Diomedes and Surtir had become devoted friends and battle comrades; Philoctetes accompanied them south to warmer climes, where the three hoped to share further adventures. Eventually Philoctetes continued on to Corsica to teach the medicine he had acquired to the learned if rustic physicians there—like so many of the companions, he became a teacher at last. Diomedes and Surtir followed several adventures, ending up in the north of those lands controlled by the Latins, where each became in time overlord of a small region adjacent to the growing Latin empire. Surtir fought many battles in those lands, defending them from marauders from the west and north. Norse legends say that some day Surtir, who never gained the comfort that Diomedes found in the south, will return to the north bearing a flaming sword, some say bringing respite, but most say destruction and doom.

Diomedes "of the great war-cry," as the epic poets called him, finally fully cleansed of the will to make war, settled down to become a wise and generous leader, if not an especially powerful one—that no longer mattered to him. One story says that in his last years, he actually saw Aeneas inspecting the reaches of his Latin lands, though after such a long interval that king, who had himself experienced so many trying adventures, no longer recognized him. The legend suggests that, spotting his old adversary, Diomedes did not feel nearly so disgusted as he had always believed he would. He gained the balance that defined the later generations of Greek wisdom, even if he found it in a far land. Fathering a child in his late years, Diomedes contributed to the Latin world a strain of Greek heroic blood that in the course of time strengthened Aeneas' legacy.

Telegonus, after Wela's death, served the north as master-craftsman of weapons. Eventually, in search of greater skill, he traveled as far away as the deserts of Libya and Arabia to learn more of metals and smithing. In Carthage he met a princess and feel deeply in love with her, but unwilling to believe the stories of his descent—he seemed to her no more than a lonely weapons-master—she spurned him. He had many affairs, searching for a woman like her—history does not record her name—but never found anyone who could so wound his heart. Eventually he tired of weaponry and returned to his mother's island, where Circe with her magic cleansed his thoughts of the girl. He married a sea-nymph, fathered a daughter, and paid several friendly visits to Telemachos, his half-brother, who ruled Ithaka well, but always with anxiety for the father who never again returned to him. Telegonus then passed out of all stories; perhaps his wife and mother transported him from this life to the service of the gods on Olympos.

As Dictys did in the west, Dares told versions of these stories in the north, but neither recorded anything beyond what this tale tells, and I know no more of it.

GLOSSARY OF NAMES

Achaians, Homer's name for the Greeks

Achilles, the elder character was the greatest of the Greek soldiers at Troy; his grandson, by the same name, becomes one of Odysseus' companions in this story

Aegisthus, helped Klytemnestra kill Agamemnon when he returned from Troy

Aeneas, a soldier of Troy who founds the nation that will become Rome

Aeolus, god of winds

Aesir, the "people of Asia" who, led by Tror, went north to settle after the Trojan War

Agamemnon, king of Argos, leader of the Greek army at Troy

Agni, one of the Greeks' rowers

Aias, one of the great Greek soldiers at Troy

Alkinoös, king of Phaecia

Antiklea, Odysseus' mother

Antilochus, son of Nestor, brother of Thrasymedes, one of Odysseus' companions

Aphrodite, goddess of love and beauty

Apollo, god of the sun

Ares, god of war

Ascerbergium, settlement on the Rhine

Asgard, the hall of the Aesir

Artemis, chaste goddess of the hunt
Athena, goddess of wisdom
Brucca, spokesman of the Bructeri
Bructeri, a Rhinish tribe
Calydon, city on the Greek mainland
Calydoneus, king of Calydon
Cicones, a people of Thrace
Circe, sorceress, mother of Telegonus
Cressida, a woman of Troy
Cumae, location of an Italian sibyl
Daunus, a king in Apulia
Demos, Nikaean coast guard
Dictys, Idomeneus' poet, companion of Odysseus
Diomedes, a Greek hero at Troy and one of Odysseus' companions
Djulo, lieutenant to Iolu of the Menapians
Elysium, fields of bliss in the Greek afterlife
Eos, goddess of the dawn
Eumaeus, shepherd who serves Odysseus
Galli, a tribe of what is now southwestern Europe
Gangleri/Gylfi, a northern hero who joins the Greek companions
Gartheow, a northern soldier, among those who attack the Greek companions
Grettir, Gangleri's brother
Gromr, Gangleri's father
Hades, god of the underworld
Hans, smith of one of the Rhinish villages
Hektor, prince of Troy, killed by Achilles
Helen, wife of Menelaos, kidnapped by Paris to start the Trojan War
Hephaestos, god of smithing
Hermes, messenger god

Herodotus, governor of Nikaea
Hesiod, Herodotus' scribe
Hod, a son of Tror
Horsa, trader with whom the Greeks sail north from Menapia
Hothines, Tror's military counselor
Idomeneus, once king of Crete, one of Odysseus' companions
Iolu, a chief of the Menapians
Ithaka, Odysseus' island kingdom
Kassandra, Trojan prophet, daughter of Priam
Kalypso, sea-nymph who loved Odysseus
Keimtales, Tror's herald and messenger
Klytemnestra, wife of Agamemnon
Laertes, Odysseus' father, once king of Ithaka
Latinus, king of the Latins in Italy
Lokesh, a son of Tror
Lorelei, goddess of the Rhine
Loricus, Thracian king
Magni, a son of Tror
Menapians, a tribe from south of the Rhinemouth
Menapus, king of the Menapians
Menelaos, king of Mycenae, husband of the famous Helen
Modi, a son of Tror
Nausikaa, Phaecian princess
Neoptolemos, son of the elder Achilles, father of the younger
Nestor, king of Pylos, father of Antilochus and Thrasymedes
Nikaea, Greek colony in what is now southern France
Norns, the Norse Fates, in this story similar also to the Furies
Odysseus, King of Ithaka and a hero of the Trojan War
Olympos, mountain home of the gods
Orestes, son of Agamemnon who avenged his death, companion of Odysseus

251

Ori, one of the Greek rowers

Orpheus, ancient musician who tried to bring back his wife from the dead

Para, Thracian warrior maiden, companion of Tror

Patroklos, friend of Achilles, killed at Troy

Peldeg, a son of Tror

Penelope, wife of Odysseus

Phaecia, land where Odysseus stopped for rest after the Trojan War

Philoctetes, Thessalian warrior, companion of Odysseus

Pirithous, Odysseus' and Penelope's second son

Polyphemos, a Cyclops, son of Poseidon

Poseidon, god of the sea

Preya, Thracian warrior, companion of Tror

Priam, king of Troy

Pris/Frigg, daughter of Tror and Sif

Pylos, city of southwest Greece

Rud, a fisherman whom the Greeks meet on the Rhine

Scylla and Charybdis, monster and whirlpool that guard the coast between Sicily and mainland Italy

Sif, Tror's wife, queen of the Aesir

Siracusa, settlement on the Sicilian coast

Sisyphus, human son of Aeolus

Skef, a king of the northwest

Surtir, Tror's finest soldier

Sveria, a land of the north (Sweden)

Tartaros, pit of punishment in the Greek afterlife

Telegonus, son of Odysseus and Circe

Telemachos, Odysseus' and Penelope's first son

Tencteri, a Rhinish tribe

Tencto, and elder of the Tencteri

Thrasymedes, son of Nestor, brother of Antilochus, one of Odysseus' companions

Tror/Trorash, king of the Aesir
Vanir, a name the Aesir have for the Greek heroes
Vithar, son of Odysseus and Pris
Wela, Tror's metalsmith
Zeus, king of the gods

ABOUT THE AUTHOR

EDWARD S. LOUIS lives in Wisconsin where he teaches and does scholarly work on early literatures. He and his wife, a painter, enjoy travel in Europe and practice Mediterranean cooking and amateur archeology.